As Simple As That

As Simple As That

Published by Inkblot Books
Dayton, Ohio
www.inkblotbooks.com

ISBN 1-932461-02-7

Printed in the United States of America

In memory of Moe
Who always said she was
Half Full, Half M.T.
But she was never half of anything
She was always full of everything

And for my mom
For childhood memories of things that were
Like Snickers bars and Dr. Pepper
Comic books from the PX
And homemade pizza
A life of love

Also by K.A. Thompson

Charybdis
Finding Father Rabbit (August 2003)

As Simple As That

K.A. Thompson

ONE

1994

Doug

They were supposed to ride off into the sunset and live out the cliché of happily ever after. They were supposed to have two-point-five kids, buy a minivan, carve out a slice of suburbia, and stay healthy and young and beautiful forever. They weren't supposed to make mistakes, have tempers or fights or bad days. They weren't supposed to split up.

Of course, it was easy for the rest of us to sit back and become a collective of consummate armchair quarterbacks; from where we sat we could read the audibles, and we could scream like madmen when our team fell out of synch and did nothing we wanted. We watched, not so quietly, hoping for some fourth quarter miracle that would win the game for them in the last seconds.

Terry fumbled the ball too close to the end zone without a single time out left to reposition her players. She didn't look ahead; she failed to give her star running back a good chance to be there when he needed to be to catch the ball.

When she dropped the ball Chip began to shuffle off the

field. He didn't look at the clock, never bothered to see how much time they had left, didn't question whether or not there was another down to play. He never thought he was good enough for her to begin with, and he didn't listen for the final whistle.

Nick

I thought my parents had the perfect marriage. Even after sixteen years it didn't take much more than a lingering look across the dinner table or an unexpected brush of fingers to set the lights in my father's eyes dancing or for my mom to laugh. It wasn't unusual to catch them out by the pool late at night, making out like a couple of teenagers, so much at ease with their affections that it was as normal to our lives as breathing. Just Something Parents Do. I don't think it ever occurred to any of us that the electricity that shot between them was rare, especially after so many years.

They loved each other and weren't afraid to show it. Their kids took it for granted; I probably heard "Just turn around and go the other way, sport, I'll talk to you later," more than a hundred times. I'd wander into the kitchen and they'd be tangled around each other, and my dad would simply tell me to go someplace else for a while. Nothing mattered to him more than she did. He made it clear that she came first, above everything else.

They were also great believers in honesty; if we had a question, no matter how far out there or uncomfortable it was, we got an answer. If it hit a little too close to home, or was so personal that we had no business asking in the first place, they'd say so, but always with respect to our budding curiosities.

Never once did I hear "It's none of your business." It

was always somewhere along the line of "Sorry, sport, but that's between your Mom and me. And God, if He's peeking."

He was pretty sure that was the case.

My dad made his way back to his religion when I was five years old; he was a lapsed Catholic, too bitter with life to allow God into it and too terrified of himself to admit he needed God. I'm still not sure what drove him back to his faith, but he admits it was one final kick in the teeth that did it, something overwhelming that he won't talk about but credits with opening his eyes.

He went jogging one afternoon and found himself standing at the steps of Holy Spirit Catholic Church, and then spent the next three hours coughing up thirteen years of confession to a young priest who was so intrigued by what he was hearing that he had to step out and meet the anguished soul on the other side of the confessional.

Whatever he confessed, that too was between him and Mom, and God.

I walked into a church for the first time at five years old, clinging to Aunt Kris's hand, Paul holding her other hand, with Uncle Doug carting Kevin on one hip and Eileen on the other. I had no idea what was about to happen, but I remember a feeling of calm in the room, and an elation I couldn't have described if I'd been old enough to have the vocabulary. After six years of marriage they were reaffirming their vows; Dad wanted to stake his claim to Mom in front of a priest, and especially in front of God.

"Our marriage," he told me, "is a sacrament. I don't think I really understood that at first."

Before the Mass began I'd been warned to expect a few tears from my grandmother, and possibly from Aunt Kris. I never expected to see my father cry.

He stood at the altar with tears in his eyes, and for years I wondered why. At his happiest and his saddest he never allowed his kids to see him cry, but he stood up there that day watching his bride of six years slowly coming towards him on her father's arm, tear tracks visible on his cheeks.

I wish I had been able to understand how much that ceremony meant to them. I was just too young to understand the significance of my parents professing their love for each other in front of God, their friends, and half the parish. I wish I could remember why they did it.

Maybe then I could have reminded them later, when they needed to hear it the most.

Chip

"Nick, she was just an old friend. I took her out to dinner and that's it."

My oldest son regarded me with suspicion beyond his seventeen years; the fact that he had seen a woman step out of his father's car late at night was reason enough to pry, in his opinion.

The question was pointed enough.

"Are you sleeping with her?"

Not that it was any of his business; I answered anyway, reasoning that my honesty gave me the right to pose the same question to him at some future point. I had no doubt that Nicky was, however discreetly, sleeping with his girlfriend, and I was fairly sure he'd be honest about it.

It was none of my business, either. That didn't mean I'd avoid prying.

"She's not bad looking," he observed, planting himself firmly on my couch, arms crossed at his chest.

"Nope, not bad looking at all, if you like that type."

"What type do you like?"

Nick was hoping for the perfect description: blonde hair, blue eyes, about five foot six, smooth, easy going demeanor, a smile that would light up the night sky, hands as soft and gentle as newborn baby skin, and a voice like laughter on the wind.

He wanted me to describe his mother.

And I wanted to give him that description, God knows I did. Even after two years the woman haunted me; I'd wake up nights soaked in sweat and desire, and found myself reaching out to hold her in my sleep. I still wanted to know what she was thinking, if she'd approve of what I was doing or if she'd roll her eyes with a grin, trying to sway me away from my own impulses.

Instead of answering my son, all I could do was turn away and toss my shoes into the closet.

I'd have hoped that after that much time the pain would have subsided a little, or at least be bearable.

It was worse than ever.

From experience I knew that one of my children would pose the question sometime during the week: if you're not sleeping with Mom, then who are you sleeping with?

My boys especially can't see how a grown man used to having sex practically on demand can survive without it. They don't understand – and probably don't believe – my answer.

"No one. I'm still a married man, for Christ's sake. I don't sleep around and I won't."

What hurts is that I'm not sure Terry shares my convictions. On more than one occasion my youngest two, Kevin and Eileen, have let it slip that she goes out to dinner with her boss at least once a week.

"Brad's a bust," Nick told me. "There's nothing there. I swear, he's a hiccup away from floating out of his loafers."

"He pees sitting down," Paul added with twisted giggles.

Peals of adolescent laughter is almost always decent medicine for what ails me, but I had to put a stop to the verbal attacks, regardless of how much I wanted to hear their opinions. If Terry was indeed seeing Brad Colt, if she was really happy with him, I didn't want to be the one to turn the kids against him.

I wanted Terry to be happy.

And it occurred to me, when I was really down and scared to death she might be falling in love with this creep, that I had yet to hear anything from a lawyer, and I knew she hadn't petitioned the church for an annulment.

That counted for something. I didn't have to face the prospect of my wife walking down the aisle with someone else until she had a divorce decree in her hot little hands.

For whatever comfort it gave me, I kept a picture of her by my bed, a photograph taken on a trip to the beach, her smile broken wide with laughter and her eyes looking right into the camera lens. Kevin smuggled it out of the house, apologetic in his own way, that he couldn't find one with the two of us.

I spent a dozen or more nights talking to that picture, yelling at it, screaming at it, trying to figure out what went wrong. I couldn't fathom the despair of being locked out of my own home by the woman who had been crawling all over me just two weeks before, whispering her love in the dark, lips touching nearly every square inch of my body.

I told her I wouldn't be gone long enough for her to even miss me; I'd be gone two or three weeks at the most. She balked furiously at the idea that I was letting myself be drawn back into the agency, but I thought I had convinced her it was just a matter of greasing the bureaucratic wheels of the Secretary General's office. I'd be back before she could miss me.

She was angry, I realized that.

I had no idea how angry.

I came home to find Doug waiting to drive me away from my family, my clothes were in the backseat of my car, which she had left in the parking lot of the Charybdis. I hadn't seen her since then, and had only spoken to her a few tense times on the phone.

Whatever truly sparked her anger, she never said, but I was effectively cut out of my family, lowered to seeing my children once or twice a week, sometimes more when Doug let me know they were at his house. I didn't see my wife.

As Nick sat on my couch fishing for personal information, I couldn't help but again wonder why.

I carried the memory of her smile, the touch and taste of her body with me the entire time.

I had to. It was all I had left.

I knew it was difficult for Doug and Kris, maintaining their friendships with both of us, trying to keep us separate and keep straight what might have been said and to whom, biting back the gossip that might not be welcome and dishing out something that might be.

From Day One I was intensely curious about anything involving Terry; that didn't necessarily mean I welcomed their opinions about our marriage.

"You never know," Doug said, sitting in the thick heat of the club's steam room, his towel pressed to his face. I was used to the muffled conversations, listening to him lecture through folds of terrycloth and sweat. After eighteen months of separation my pain was as raw as it had been when I realized I was no longer welcome in my own home, and he was still trying to give me hope. "Footballs bounce funny."

"All right. I'll bite."

"She was going to pass but there was no one there to catch the ball and take it into the end zone. It made her nervous, so she fumbled. The questions are, which way is the ball bouncing, who's going to recover it… and is the game over yet?"

"Game called on account of rain."

"If the game has been called then why are all the fans still in the bleachers?"

"Stupid fans, I guess."

It's not to say that I didn't still carry the spark of hope that one morning I'd wake up and find myself flat on my back in the waterbed with Terry tangled all around me. That hope was what kept me from diving off the deep end into an empty pool.

I wondered if they hounded her to see me as much as they hounded me to see her.

That I doubted. Doug wouldn't want to be the one to make her cry, and unless she'd changed a lot, Terry cried at the drop of a hat. She would cry if she laughed too hard, she'd cry if I said the right thing at the right time, she'd cry if one of the kids was sick and miserable and there was nothing she could do about it. She'd cry when I'd refuse to fight with her. The dam could give way anytime, day or night.

The only thing I cried over was Terry, but I wasn't about to admit that.

"I think she misses you," Doug said through his towel.

Maybe I needed to hear that, but I didn't believe it. "She

knows where I am."

"You know where she is, too."

Of course I knew where she was. That didn't negate the fact that she obviously didn't want to see me. I'm not the one who had all the locks in the house changed. I'm not the one who dumped closet full of clothes into the back seat of a brand new convertible and then parked it next to the restaurant's dumpster.

If she missed me, she sure as hell knew where to find me.

"Quit the agency."

Doug's words of wisdom, spoken firmly while my face was stuck under the spray of a hot shower, water beating in fine needles into my abused body. I'd been telling myself for nearly twenty years that enough was enough, I could do without the pain and the sweat that were part of the gym experience. Life would not come to an abrupt end if I let the six pack grow into a keg.

It was total vanity. At least I knew that much.

"I'm not active," I reminded him. "Not so that you'd notice me there, anyway."

"Given up the spy trade?"

"Phfft."

He slapped his shower off and shook the water from his hair. "So you weren't a spy. I bet Terry doesn't see it that way. She doesn't really know *what* you were up to."

Doug had no clue what I'd been up to.

Terry at least had an inkling.

I don't even remember what we'd done that night; it could have been as simple as a movie and a pizza afterwards. What I mostly remember is coming home, closing the front door slowly, deliberately locking it, and rechecking the locks, and the long walk up the stairs, my heart pounding and gut churning because I had no choice but to tell her I was leaving in a few hours. I debated as my feet touched every stair: tell her now and get it over with, start the fight right off the bat and hope it ended well, or get her into bed and tell her later, hoping she'd be too tired to balk much.

I'm an idiot.

I got her into bed first.

"All right, Irish," she whispered later, her head on my shoulder and fingers feathering over the scar across my chest. "You're about a million miles away when you should be right here telling me how incredible I am."

"You are incredible. And you already know it."

"Of course I do." She pressed a kiss into my neck and laughed. "Spill it, mister. A quiet funk is not the way I want to end a perfectly good night with you."

Making her cry was not the way I wanted to end it, either.

Neither was making her so angry she'd storm out of bed and stomp into the guest room.

"I have to go somewhere tomorrow," I said, whispering into her hair. "You're not going to like it."

"Meeting your mistress at some ritzy hotel in the Bahamas?"

"Something like that."

She sat up, tilting her head and looking at me like I was a toddler trying to tell his first joke. "Okay, I'm listening. Where are you going and when are you coming home?"

"I can't tell you where I'll be."

She pulled her pillow onto her lap and clutched it to her stomach.

"I got a call from the agency today."

"Oh, crap."

"I met with the Assistant Secretary General," I went on. "Alex Barstow is missing, and they want me to go after him."

"Who?"

"Alex Barstow, the Secretary General. He left a month ago on a vacation and vanished. He missed his check-in and there's no trace of him in the places he said he'd be."

"And they want you to go find him?"

"They want me to bring him home, yes."

"Chip, they have a million other people who could do this. Why you?"

I didn't tell her that three people had already tried, and each of them turned up with necks broken and various body parts missing. I also didn't tell her that from the little intelligence they did have that it was suspected he was being held somewhere in South America. I didn't tell her that I had no choice; the agency still owned my contract and it was a choice between going after Barstow or finding myself on the wrong end of an agency misunderstanding.

I didn't tell her any of the things she had a right to know.

"They want me because they know I can find him and get him out alive," I said.

"Bullshit."

"It's a straightforward case, Terry. Someone else is doing the leg work, all I have to do is show up, get their info, and go get him. I'll be gone for two or three weeks tops."

"Three weeks is straightforward?"

"In this case, yes."

"Turn them down."

"I can't."

"Yes, you can! You just pick up the phone and tell whomever it is you have to that you're not going and you're not doing anything for them again, ever."

"It's not like – "

"It's not like what, Chip? It's not like you're just wandering off to some place I can't know about, chasing someone I don't give a damn about? It's not like you're giving *me* any choice in the matter? Just 'oh, by the way, I'm running off to play with my agency buddies and, hmmm, I might *die* while I'm at it.'"

"I'm not going to die."

"You can't promise me that, can you?"

"I'm good at what I do, Terry."

She shook her head. "At what you *did*, Chip. How the hell do you know if you're any good at it now?"

She asked me that once years ago. *How do you know you're still any good?* Nick was missing and I promised to find him, and I did. I hoped she remembered that.

"Have you been working with them all along?" she asked suddenly.

I didn't answer quick enough. Just a half of a second hesitation and she was off the bed, reaching for her robe. "I don't work for them."

"Obviously you do!"

"Just this once."

"Until the next time they ask? Chip, don't go. If you give them this time, there will be other times, and it will never end."

"They didn't ask anything for the last fifteen years. Why would they ask after this?"

"The last time they asked you were gone for five months. I spent five months not knowing where you were or if you were even alive, and we both know how *that* turned out."

"I won't be gone that long. And everything else that

happened…"

She jerked the belt on her robe and reached for her pillow. "Are you going?"

"Yes."

She stuffed the pillow under her arm, turned around and walked out of the room, leaving the door open. I heard her footsteps fade down the hall, the door to the guest room click shut, and then nothing else.

That was the last time I saw her.

"Yep," Doug said one last time before leaving me sitting in the locker room alone, "footballs bounce funny."

Nick

I think turning forty was a major shock to my dad. It was something he knew was lurking around the corner yet somehow expected to avoid. Under other circumstances he probably would have enjoyed his birthday, but being stuck in a cramped apartment with four teenagers had to be the last thing he wanted. He could have been out with friends, having dinner with Uncle Doug and Aunt Kris, or even pestering Ted at the restaurant, but instead he fumbled around the apartment like he was looking for something he'd lost.

There was no question where we'd be; Mom expected it, and would have boiled into a rare explosion if any of us had tried to beg off for other plans. She made it understood that I would pick up Paul, Kevin, and Eileen from school and take them over to his apartment. No excuses. Your father only turns forty once and you'd damn well better be there to try to lift his spirits.

He seemed surprised to see us; when we got there he was sitting out on the balcony, watching Red and the throngs of kids she babysat play in the pool below. He had a Diet

Coke in one hand and a pretzel stick in the other, one end mushy and wet from where he'd been sucking on it to stave off cigarette cravings.

He had quit smoking four years before and still had a hard time with it.

"It's a bad habit I picked up in a place I never should have been," he groaned once. "You try it on for looks and a week later you're hooked. Then you stink like crap and there's not a female within a mile who wants to lock lips with you."

Father-speak for, "Don't smoke, because if you do and I find out, your ass is mine."

Paul leaned over the balcony rail and peered at the people in the pool. "If it were me," he said, "I'd be gawking at the girls. You're watching all the little kids, aren't you?"

"Hello to you, too." He got out of the chair and kissed Paul on the cheek, grabbing Kevin by the arm before he could get away to avoid being hugged. "To what do I owe the honor of having all of you here at once?"

"We decided you'd take us all out to dinner," Paul said, dropping onto the couch.

"Something expensive," Kevin agreed. "Steak and lobster."

"Well, thank you, I think…"

Eileen rolled her eyes and reached out to hug him. "They're idiots. Happy birthday, Dad."

"Ah, that time of year again? You didn't get me another cat, did you?"

She poked him in the stomach. "You love your kitty and you know it. But I'll change the litter box for you today."

"Best birthday present I've gotten so far."

"You expect more?" Kevin asked.

"You're such an obnoxious prick," Eileen fumed. "You

could at least try to be nice today."

"I was *kidding,*" he yelled after her as she stomped off towards the bathroom. "I am just kidding, Dad."

"I know, son." He sighed and sat in the chair across from the couch, setting his feet on the coffee table. The living room was small enough that if I sat on the couch and put my feet up, our feet would not only touch, but overlap. The apartment was too small for five people, but I know he never intended to be there so long.

He looked tired, his eyes rimmed with dark circles and his face pale, and his posture that said he would tolerate us for the evening, but he really did want to be alone.

"Did you have other plans?" I asked. "We really should have checked with you first... I mean, we can do this some other night if you want."

"No other plans, Nicky. And even if I did, I'd rather spend my birthday with you nut cases."

"You don't lie very well," Paul said.

"Trust me, if I wanted to be somewhere else, I'd tell you."

He wouldn't, but I wasn't going to say anything.

"He looks like shit," Paul muttered when Dad wandered back into his bedroom to change clothes. "Maybe we should just order a pizza or something instead of dragging him out in public."

Even Kevin agreed.

Dad seemed relieved when I asked him if he'd rather stay in; Paul called in a pizza order and we sat around the living room, grilling Paul on his love life – "Damn right, I'm the stud of the year, they all want me" – and embarrassing Dad as much as possible, and left before it was completely dark out.

We'd intended to spend the night, but realized he wasn't up to having his kids hanging all over him. Even Kevin at his most obnoxious could see that. After we ate we gave Dad his birthday presents and a cake, then Paul herded Kevin and Eileen towards the car.

I still had something to give him.

"It's from Mom," I said, pressing the small box into his hand. I waited to give it to him because the last thing I wanted to see was my father fighting back tears and I had the feeling that he'd be close to it when he opened it.

She still loved him, in spite of the emotional distance and the time that had passed. It occurred to me then, when I was walking away from my dad, that it was all some stupid, stupid mistake that could be fixed if they would just start talking to each other; for whatever reasons she had tossed him out in the first place, she wanted him back.

He was still standing at the door when I got into my car. He looked pale, and for the first time, he looked old.

"He looks like shit, Mom. Maybe not forty, but pushing old, that's for sure. And white as a sheet. I didn't think it was a good idea for us to stay."

I was perched on the counter, staring down into the glass of milk she had pressed on me, not sure I wanted to look at her face. Her pain was just as bad as Dad's. I felt torn between them most of the time; sometimes I just wanted to grab her and shake the living daylights out of her, scream that she was killing him bit by bit.

I had enough sense to realize she wasn't terribly proud of what she'd done, and she didn't need me to point out the obvious.

"Are you sure it was a good idea to leave him alone?"

She had the same image of him that I did, slumped over the kitchen table slurping up whatever was left in his liquor cabinet. I swept the cobwebs of that picture away by reminding myself that he didn't drink alone, and in spite of how much he could drink at any given time, he wasn't an alcoholic.

He also wasn't stupid. I wasn't worried about him drinking himself into oblivion, but I also wasn't especially comfortable with having left him alone.

"It might not have been the greatest idea, but it was the best we could do. He really didn't need us there breathing down his neck."

She put the milk carton back into the refrigerator. "That's too bad. I hoped he would have a good time tonight."

"I'd bet good money he went over to the church tonight after we left. He's probably going to cheer himself up by harassing Father Parker in the confessional."

She let the start of a smile tug at the corners of her mouth. Dad liked to slip into the confessional when he knew Father Parker was there, and he made up the most outrageous sins he could think of – "and yes, I know I'm going to hell for it," – and related them in hushed, pious tones. It took Father Parker about five minutes to realize his leg was being royally yanked on, who was yanking on it, and told Dad he was to say the Lord's Prayer (*Our Father*, Dad insisted vigorously) five hundred times, on his knees in the gravel driveway behind the parochial school.

We both knew that without his children there, as soon as he opened her gift he would head straight for evening Mass. I would have liked to have seen the look on his face – sans tears – when he opened it; I caught a brief glimpse of the gold crucifix when she wrapped it.

It was definitely not a cheap one.

"Do you think he'll like it?"

"Come on, you knew that before you bought it."

That garnered a sad nod. She knew damn well what the gift would mean to him; they had exchanged crucifixes just a day after they reaffirmed their vows. Dad's sunk to the bottom of the pool one night and got caught in the drain, and was pretty mangled by the time he pulled it loose. Jesus dangled by his toes.

I didn't think Mom was aware of what she was whispering to him with that gift. And as dumb as Dad could be where she was concerned, he probably didn't hear it.

"It was my fault his old one was ruined," she said, looking past me out the kitchen window. "Too much horsing around..."

"He didn't see it that way. He said that only you could leave Jesus hanging by his toes and make him enjoy it."

If I had been raised by anyone else, I'm not sure I could reconcile my religion and sex, but my parents seemed to be able to put the two together with ease. If they were in the same room, they were touching. They watched TV together on the couch, dad's arms wrapped around her and her head on his shoulder. The night dad put a pool table in the study Paul caught them making out on it. I always knew that if I heard music drifting up the stairs late at night that they were probably contorted around each other in the living room, dancing. The guilt of married sex just wasn't something we were raised with.

There were times the current that shot between them was palpable. When I was thirteen and just barely aware of girls as something other than nuisances, I stumbled into the dining room and saw them out in the back yard, standing at the end of the diving board, not touching, staring hypnotically into each others' eyes. It didn't seem as if they were breathing or could stand to look away for even a moment.

I was close to throwing the back door open and yelling something stupid – "Push her in, Dad!" – when she leaned forward and placed a gentle kiss against the crucifix he had hanging around his neck.

That picture still stays in my mind as one of the most erotic things I've ever seen.

I'm sure they managed to combine piety and sex without much difficulty.

So even if she missed the not so subtle message behind her birthday present, I didn't.

Dad might.

I was just about ready to pour out the milk and head to bed when she let go with a deep, contemplative sigh. Not done with me yet. That sigh was a signal to stay put.

So I stayed, trying to decide if I wanted the damn milk or not. What I wanted was an ice cold beer but there wasn't a chance in hell I could get one.

"Is he smoking again, Nick?"

Cigarettes. One of the few points of contention between them and her main threat to make him live in the guest room. "I don't think so. At least he doesn't around me and I don't remember seeing any ash trays around."

"You'd smell it on him."

"Dad smells like Listerine and cologne, but I couldn't tell you which he slaps on his face and which he uses as a mouthwash."

"Honestly, I bet there are mornings he couldn't say, either."

I poured the milk out. "So, did you go out with Brad tonight?"

Not a fair question by a long shot, but I wanted her off the subject of Dad and I wanted her to let me go to bed.

"Don't look at me like that."

"Like what?"

"Like I'm the scum of the earth for having a social life. No, I didn't go out with him tonight, but you know damn well he's just a friend."

"I never said he wasn't. Just asking about your evening, that's all."

She sighed again. I was free to go.

Free to go, maybe, but I didn't move. I wanted to scramble off the counter and sprint up the stairs to my room, but I kept my butt glued to the Formica. She needed company, and she needed a change of subject.

"Hey, have you seen Spider lately? He's got this *huge* hickey on his neck. Aunt Kris nearly wet her pants when she saw it."

"Good lord. And I'll bet Doug hasn't stopped teasing him about it."

"Dunno. He really seems to like this girl, though. She knows sign language and doesn't take any crap from him. She even slapped him a couple weeks ago… he tried to avoid an argument by closing his eyes and she let him have it right by the burrito line in the cafeteria."

"He didn't."

"He did. Dumb sucker never stopped to think she'd pop him one."

Spider shut out his parents by closing his eyes, too. They could scream all they wanted, but he only had to close his eyes to shut off the noise.

He tried that with Dad, but only once. Spider was around twelve, it was freezing cold out, and the pool heater had been turned off for a couple weeks. Dad picked Spider up, took him outside and held him over the water by his feet, and then dunked him in, just to his eyebrows, with the warning that the next time he tried crap like that he was going all the way in.

Godson or not, Spider didn't get away with any more crap than we did.

"What about you, Nick? Is Katie treating you well these days?"

"You know it." I hoped she wasn't fishing for anything more than that; while I figured my dad knew just how deeply I was involved with Katie Forrester, I doubted my mom had figured it out.

"Discretion is the better part of valor where your mother is concerned," Dad said. She might be perfectly open to talking about sex, had no problems with birth control, and honestly believed that sex education belongs in the home, but deep down she didn't want to be confronted with the knowledge that her two oldest sons were screwing around.

I didn't want to embarrass her, either.

Paul, dense shit that he could be, was bound to sooner or later. I half expected him to get caught shagging Monica Russell out by the pool.

I hoped to hell Mom didn't die right on the spot.

"I ran into her mom a few days ago. Honestly, Nick, she has you two married with kids already."

"You never know," I chuckled.

"You already think she's the one?"

I shrugged. "Could be. We've been going together for like four years, you know. But she might realize what I jerk I can be and drop me like a hot rock."

"You're not a jerk."

"You have to say that. You're my mother."

"No, I don't have to say that. I've told Kevin more than once he's being a jerk."

"He's fourteen, he'll outgrow it."

"We can only hope. I'm sure Katie knows she struck gold when she latched on to you."

"More like when she sunk her claws into me? She likes to fight too much."

"And you don't. Another gift from your father. I couldn't get him to fight, either."

I missed an opportunity. At that point I could have told her it was worth another try, that by now he was open to a good fight, but I didn't. I opted to be as dense as Kevin and ignored it.

"Go to bed, Nicky. I've picked your brain enough for one night."

No choice in the matter. Where I was free to go before, now I was dismissed. Mom was taking his birthday as hard as he was.

I didn't race up the stairs after all. I trudged up slowly, wishing to hell there was something I could do.

Two stubborn, stupid people.

I got Mom's message loud and clear.

Dammit, I just knew Dad wouldn't.

Terry

I was never able to explain to any of my children why I locked their father out of the house with absolutely no warning. I couldn't expect them to understand, not after having seen me locked in his arms just the day before, obviously enjoying the attention, with no hint of the storm that was about to roll in and consume us all.

We never created any illusions about our marriage; if our children thought their parents were overly affectionate and deeply in love, they were right. Chip was more than I ever thought I would need and it meant the world to me that no matter how long we were together he never seemed to need or want anything more than I could give him.

He knew when to draw back and leave me alone, and he knew when to break down the barriers. He had an eerie instinct that told him when I needed simple affection, his arms around me in a tight, healing hug, with no expectations of anything more. And as a father he was overwhelming; he played and romped with the kids as often as he could to the oldest age they would permit. He catered to their reasonable demands and drew the line when he should. And with the exception of Kevin on a bad day, they adored him.

But what they don't see is the person outside of who their father is, they don't see the core that sparks him to life. He would say "it's whatever makes me me," and it alternately attracted and distracted me.

It angered the hell out of me, too.

I sent Nick off to his room on his father's birthday and felt like I had betrayed the entire human race. I was married to the man most women would give their eye teeth for. He was handsome, witty, charming, playful, generous, and after years of insistence, accepting of my affections.

He was always good at showing his affection. Accepting it in return frightened him. He never understood how anyone could love him as much as I did.

And for everything Chip Davis was, he never grew up. Things tended to be done on impulse. Most of the time his urges were harmless enough and I'd go along with it; sometimes I put my foot down, and he'd listen.

I learned to draw the line as well.

So how was I supposed to go about telling my kids that I locked their father out of house and home in a drunken fit of anger, that his impulses had stepped over the line and I was furious?

I couldn't, not without exposing them to a part of their father he insisted they never know about. And I couldn't explain to them without giving them the background that I wanted desperately to forget, the five long months when he was gone and I was so angry at not knowing if he was even alive that I got drunk and did the worst thing I possible. I couldn't tell them without destroying the foundation we'd made for them.

I didn't think he'd really leave. When I got up the next morning and found his suitcase gone and car still parked in the garage, my heart broke. I'd drawn the line and he jumped over it. After the kids were asleep that night I took every piece of clothing of his that I could find, tossed them in a huge pile into the back seat of his car, drove it to his restaurant, and took a cab home. I resolved that in the morning I would call about having the locks changed.

I let the two weeks go by without softening my stand; when I thought he might be coming home, I packed up the kids and took them to the mountains for a week and left Doug with the message that Chip needed to find someplace else to live, and he damn well knew why.

The anger unaccountably lasted for three months, made worse by the realization that he never tried to reason with me.

By then it was too late.

I wouldn't have known how to begin to ask him to come home. After enough time had passed, I assumed he didn't want to have anything to do with me. My children scrupulously avoided mentioning him for the first year, never completely sure where my stand on their father was. I knew they never understood.

Wacky, spaced out Mom kicked Dad out on his ass for no good reason.

I thought I had a good reason then.

Nick knew, I think, in the kitchen on Chip's birthday, that I had every regret in the world. He spent those two years trying to mold himself into a young man sensitive enough to shoulder his family's agony, too much too soon for someone his age. He saw both sides of it, and with the little information he had, tried to balance it all.

He saw that I should have been with Chip that night, that I had taken another chance and thrown it away. I would never know if Chip wanted me back if I didn't take the chance.

Which is why, and I could never tell my son, I stayed behind.

Losing him again would suck the wind out of my soul.

Nick

"Someone should go check up on Dad tomorrow."

I had no sooner gotten into my room and stripped down to my underwear when Eileen drifted through the door. Quiet as a mouse, there's no other way to describe how she moves around. No one ever hears her sneaking up.

"How come?"

She folded her arms in front of herself and looked at me like I was biggest dork on the planet. "He looked horrible, Nick. I just think you should go over there and make sure he's okay, that's all. Something is wrong."

An Eileen Proclamation.

"His life is all wrong, Eileen. He didn't count on spending his fortieth birthday with us, that's for sure."

"Take that up with Mom. All I care about is that he looked awful."

"I know. And I already told Mom that."

My baby sister was hardly a baby anymore and it was getting to the point where I felt like I was about to step into some serious big-brother shoes. At fourteen she was a magnet for the guys my age, but she didn't seem to notice them around her. Where Kevin was still scrawny and falling all over himself, Eileen was shaping up into one hell of a beautiful young woman. They no longer looked like twins; Kevin looked and acted his age, Eileen could have passed for eighteen.

That bothered me. And Dad wasn't around to talk to her, to arm her with all the information she needed to be safe and smart and still enjoy her own life. Paul and I both benefited from long, private talks with him, we had his promises of understanding and not judging as long as we were smart enough to protect ourselves. Eileen would need it and Kevin wouldn't know who to ask.

"Promise me, Nicky." Her green eyes were beginning to mist over.

"I swear. I'll go over there before he leaves for work. Maybe he'll be in the mood to let me take him out to lunch or something."

"I hope so. I feel like he got cheated out of a birthday today."

"So do I."

"Does Mom even care?"

I nodded. "She cares like crazy, that's what makes it so sad. She wanted to be with him, too. Hell, she had me give him a birthday present tonight. She spent a small fortune on a new crucifix for him and you don't do that if you don't care."

The tears welled up and spilled over. "Nicky, I miss Dad living here and I want him to come back home."

"So do I."

"She wants him, he wants to come home, we all want him to come home." She was crying hard; I slipped into sweatpants and then went over to hug her. "Why can't he come home?"

"I don't know," I whispered.

Chip

"Christ, who died?"

A wonderful way to be greeted by your priest. Will Parker met me in the back of the church after Mass, frowning. If he was sizing me up for the attack, his defenses weren't needed. I was in no mood to give him a hard time. Any sins I confessed that night were honest to God screwups. Any absolution I sought was genuine.

"Seriously, Chip. You don't look so hot."

We headed out the door and settled on the front steps of the church. It was a nice enough night, I noticed at least that much through the fog wrapped around my brain. "Headache."

"Hangover?"

"No such luck." My head was pounding, too, ten drummers drumming to a different beat and a room full of preschoolers given pots and pans to bang together to their tiny hearts content, all within the confines of my skull. "Teenagers."

"A visit from your kids. Any special reason?"

My kids didn't need a reason. Nor did they feel like they

were obligated to give me advanced notice when they were coming over. Had I chosen to view this separation as a license to fool around, I might have provided them with one hell of an education. As it was, I usually welcomed their frequent intrusions, it made me think that if nothing else, my kids still wanted to spend time with me when they weren't forced to.

"They wanted to watch their old man take another step towards their inheritance."

He nodded as if he understood.

I'd been pestering Will with my marital woes for fifteen years. When we met he was a brand new priest with aspirations of saving the world; I just wanted him to save my marriage. He always felt his decision to become a priest was a good one, and he planned on sticking with it; he just hadn't counted on it being as difficult as it was.

"I'm too horny for my own good," he confided once. "I thought I'd be immune."

He learned to balance his desires for every unattached female of the parish with his desires to be an effective priest. He had some close calls along the way, and once came perilously close to leaving for a raven haired wonder he fell head over heels in love with. She put an end to the idea, terrified at the idea of taking him away from God.

A hell of a lot of people counted on him.

He baptized all four of our kids and presided over our canonical wedding. He absolved me countless times for sins he claimed to be venial but I swore were mortal. He might not have been my best friend, but he was a damned reliable one.

If it's sex he wanted, I wasn't too prudish to think it would bother me much to learn he was fooling around; hell,

I was guilty of encouraging him on several occasions.

"Find yourself a good, horny woman and screw your brains out, Padre. It'll do wonders for your thought process."

I didn't know what to think when he finally did.

"What's this?"

His fingers brushed against the gold chain around my neck. I sighed and pulled the crucifix out from under my shirt and showed it to him. "Birthday present."

"Nice. The kids must have saved for a long time to be able to afford this."

I couldn't look at him just then; I turned and stared out at the street. "My kids gave me CDs and t-shirts, both of which they knew I wanted and needed. This was from Terry."

No comment from the peanut gallery.

"And no, I didn't see her. She sent it with Nick."

"Too bad."

I agreed.

It was easy to tell myself that if she had walked through that door with the kids I wouldn't have let her leave. Tie her down, sit on her, do whatever it takes. But to be honest, I felt as bad as Will thought I looked, operating at half speed at best. I couldn't have made Terry do a damn thing. Listening to my children babble was hard enough – though educational in the things I learned – but my head was already pounding when they got there and their adolescent conversations only made it worse.

Paul had a serious girlfriend, and he was "taking care of it." I learned that much by keeping my mouth shut and listening. Kevin was being railroaded into taking classes he didn't think he was ready for, much in the same way Nick had been his freshman year. Eileen was able to command their attention without the snotty comments that had been too familiar just a year before, and they were all listening to her. Nick loved being in college, even as young as he was; he was not the only academic prodigy prowling the campus, and older students were going out of their way to make him feel comfortable and included.

They talked animatedly and I soaked it in.

They avoided mentioning their mother. I noticed that most of all, and selfishly hoped she wasn't out somewhere with Brad Colt. Selfishly hoped he was as gay as Nick seemed to think. She was still my wife, after all. I might have had no rights to her body but then neither did anyone else.

"Would it be some kind of violation for you to tell me if you see much of my kids around here, Will?"

"Generally I see them all, except for one of the boys. Nick's here more than the others, but he's helping out in the sign language classes."

I didn't need to ask to know which son was copping out. "Give me a week or two. Paul will be back."

"It's got to mean something, Chip. Forcing him will get him here but it won't make it mean anything to him."

"It doesn't have to mean anything right now. It will later, when he's old enough to understand how important this is."

"Let him rebel a little," Will warned. "He lives in a state of utter confusion as it is. Don't make it worse."

By that point the drummers and toddlers in my head had been joined by tubas, electric guitars, and a heavy metal singer with no sense of rhythm. My head was ready to split wide open.

I struggled to my feet. Part of me wanted to get drunk, but a greater part didn't relish the idea of puking until dawn. There was no sense wasting good liquor that would only wind up floating down Fairfield's sewer system.

I went home instead, stripped down to nothing, and decided to put on the flimsy nylon jogging shorts Terry used to like so much, and crawled into a desperately cold bed.

I should have gotten drunk anyway.

I heaved all night long.

Nick

I waited until after breakfast to head over to Dad's apartment. Mom had to run into work and was gone before I'd have to give any explanation where I'd be going; if she came home she'd assume I went to Katie's, and I wouldn't have to lie. I planned on heading over to her house after I made sure he was all right and could honestly tell Eileen I'd checked up on him.

Mom was on her way out the door and I was headed upstairs to get my keys when she turned around, the days mail in hand.

"Nick…"

I stopped and turned around.

"I still haven't gotten the bill for your tuition."

"Ah… I know."

She closed her eyes briefly and sighed. "Did he pay for your books, too?"

"He paid for everything, Mom. I figured you knew."

She didn't say anything, just dropped the mail onto the stand at the end of the stairs and left, closing the door with a bang.

For a while they argued about money over the phone. She was determined to make it on her salary and he was determined to give her a thick and comfortable cushion. When she discovered he had deposited huge amounts of money into her checking account, she wrote him a check for everything, swearing loudly when he sent it back, torn in half with a terse note reminding her that he was still our father and he was damn well going to support us.

That was when she called him, at the height of her anger. I was in the other room and could clearly hear her side of the conversation.

"Keep your goddamned money, Chip. I don't need it."

Short, tense silence.

"I swear to God, I'll just have the money transferred back into your own account."

I imagined I could hear him on the other end, shrugging at the prospect. So, go ahead, it'll wind up back where I put it and you'll just get tired of trying to keep up with me. I'll win and you know it.

"Son of a bitch."

Dad claimed it was child support, but I doubted it took Mom tens of thousands of dollars to keep all four of us clothed and fed. She didn't bother trying to reason with him when she realized she wasn't getting credit card statements or utility bills.

He only called her once that I know of; a few weeks after she kicked him out he called to give her his address and phone number, and to let her know he wanted to spent time with us on a regular basis. As pissed off as she was, she never once raised the possibility that we wouldn't see him.

Paul and I both grumbled about being pulled between two homes until we saw his apartment and how the balcony overlooked the pool. Our first summer we spent almost every afternoon there, either in the pool or sitting on his balcony, ogling everything female over the age of fifteen. Red moved in that summer, and Dad started spending his afternoons on the balcony, too.

"I'm allowed to look," he reasoned.

He looked often; he watched her grow through a pregnancy and discovered the baby's father had died, and went out of his way to befriend her. The times she needed a few hours to herself he jumped at the chance to baby-sit. He looked, all right, but I don't think he ever touched. I don't thin it even occurred to him.

Red was at the pool with her little boy and her niece when I got there; they looked up and waved as I climbed the stairs. I waved back, thinking if it came down to it, Dad could do worse.

I found him passed out in the hallway that separated the living room from the bedrooms. He was curled on his side, knees drawn up to his stomach, skin flushed and hot to the touch. The cat was pacing by his head, crying and rubbing his face into Dad's hair, peeking to see if Dad's eyes would open.

I brushed Max aside and kneeled next to Dad, trying to roll him onto his back. He groaned but didn't open his eyes.

"Come on, Dad." I shook him by his shoulder. "Wake up."

Max climbed onto his chest and butted his head into Dad's chin.

"Okay, furball, how long has he been out?" I asked as if I expected an answer. Max looked up and cocked his head to one side, waiting. "Are you worried about him or are you out of food? I bet you're out of food."

I stretched to look into the kitchen; both of his dishes were full.

"Okay, you're a good kitty. I'll take care of him." I rubbed the top of his head and then lifted him off Dad's chest. I shook him again, hoping he'd at least open his eyes.

At that point, if I'd been thinking logically, I would have called an ambulance or at least would have called Uncle Doug. I opted instead to think like a kid.

I got Red to come up from the pool to help me carry him out, got him into my car, and took him home.

Eileen helped me wrestle him up the stairs and once we had him in bed and under blankets she pulled me out of the room.

"Call Uncle Doug, Nicky."

I nodded numbly and headed back downstairs. Every bit of first aid I'd ever learned was effectively erased from my memory. Dad had one hell of a fever and any other time I'd have known what to do.

It was almost noon on Saturday, the offices of Douglas V. Stone and Associates were closed, and his home line was busy. I was pissed off.

"Any other bright ideas?" I called up the stairs.

She poked her head over the banister. "Keep trying. Call his answering service."

I nearly froze when Mom bounded through the door and headed straight for the stairs. She was halfway up before I found my voice.

"Mom, wait…"

"Not now, Nick. Brad will be here in about ten minutes."

"Mom…"

"Not now!"

"Goddammit, woman, stop already!"

First point: one never, ever, swears at my mom in anger. She accepts the fact that my use of the language is often sprinkled with a few vulgarities, but I've never yelled at her.

Second point: only Dad can get away with calling her

"woman." From him it's affectionate; from anyone else it's sexist.

I managed to get my head together before she could get all the way down the stairs and wrap her hand around my throat.

"Dad's upstairs. He's sick."

She looked up to her bedroom door. "How sick?"

"Sick enough that if I can't get hold of Uncle Doug in the next five minutes, I'm calling an ambulance."

I expected to be yelled at; why hadn't that been my first thought? Why did I bring him here, and especially why did I put him in her bed?

Mom surprised me.

She ran up the stairs, two at a time, without saying another word to me.

Terry

Two years is not enough time to erase the memory of your deepest love from your mind. Without a photograph in front of me, I could close my eyes and see Chip there, and I had his children as a constant reminder of his smile and his eyes, his easy going manner and his terrible temper. If Kevin survived his adolescence he would be Chip's mirror image by the time he was sixteen. Paul carried Chip's darker moods and quick wit, and Eileen was a subtle mixture of everything gentle and kind that Chip could be.

I should have been prepared for the sight of my husband laying miserably in our bed. It shouldn't have been a shock.

I took one step into the room and felt my soul crack wide open.

Tossing my purse aside and easing onto the edge of the bed, it was difficult to remember why I had been so angry in the first place. Chip could be a charming, slightly wayward little boy sometimes, but he never meant any harm. He did what he thought was right, even if it was a badly timed impulse. I had no right to eject him from his own family.

The thin scar that ran straight from nipple to nipple seemed ghostly white against his flushed skin. I knew before I touched him that his skin would be hot. When I set my hand on his chest he didn't even stir, and barely sighed.

The tattoo just above his left nipple turned from green to almost black in the heat of his fever.

I touched a finger to the small Shamrock, a flood of memories misting my eyes. The tattoo had been a drunken impulse, his birthday gift to me the year Kevin and Eileen were born. It capped the end of months of hell, what had been, until I kicked him out, the worst year of our marriage.

He should have left me then. What I did was far worse than anything he could have done to me simply by taking a two week job with the agency.

Nicky appeared behind me sometime while I was exploring the memories of my marriage; I wasn't sure how long I had been sitting there with my hand on Chip's chest. Nick touched my shoulder, forcing me back into reality.

"Uncle Doug is on his way, Mom. He said we need to take Dad's temperature, and then get him into a tub of tepid water if we can."

Fine, you do what the good doctor tells you to. I swear to God I felt like I was trying to cut my way through a blanket of fog. It took forever to walk the few steps into the bathroom and then make my way back to the bed.

I stood there, looking at Nick uncertainly. "All right, did Doug say *how* to take his temperature?"

Nick took the thermometer and held it under Chip's arm.

"One hundred three," he said after a few minutes. "That's not good, is it?"

"I don't know. How did he get here in the first place, Nicky? A cab?"

"Don't get mad." He took a tentative step away from me. "Eileen asked me to go check on him since he looked so bad last night, and when I got there he was out cold on the floor… so I brought him here."

What do you do when your son has taken what could be the biggest chance of his life? I stood there looking at a young man who for all his life had never directly questioned my decisions, invariably had done what he'd been told to do, and had been as devoted as a kid can be and still maintain his own dignity.

I hugged the hell out of him.

"You go run the water for me," I whispered when I finally let him go. I pulled the blankets off Chip, wondering how I could possible get him from the bed into the bathtub.

Tight flimsy nylon jogging shorts. If he wasn't sick and we'd been on speaking terms, I would have accused him of planning a seduction.

With a deep sigh, I invaded his modesty and stripped the shorts off. I expected Nick would have to drag his father into the bathroom; nine inches shorter than Chip and at least sixty pounds lighter, I couldn't drag him anywhere if he wasn't coherent enough to cooperate.

He solved the dilemma by struggling to sit up, then stumbling into the bathroom, where he threw up violently. Nick managed to distract him from heading back for the bed and eased him into the water, sliding a rolled up towel under his head for a pillow.

"Well, we may never get him out, but he's in now."

I reached for a washcloth and began dripping water over Chip's neck and shoulders. "Nick, you did the right thing by bringing him home. Your dad doesn't get sick often, but when he does he goes all out, and he has this thing about hospitals…"

"You're not mad, then?"

"Nicky, sit down."

He sat on the edge of the tub next to me; he took another wash cloth and followed my lead in dribbling water over his father. "Have you ever heard me say that I don't love him anymore?"

"No."

"And you realize how good a marriage we had before, don't you? He was my life."

He nodded.

"I never gave any of you the slightest idea why I let this happen, did I? Seems like one day he was here and the next he was gone."

"I'm sure you had your reasons."

"Not really."

He dropped the wash cloth into the water. "I don't get it."

"At first I thought I did, but honestly, Nick, the longer he was gone the bigger an idiot I knew I'd been. I was just so mad I wouldn't let myself see that he was only off doing what he thought he had to do."

"What was he doing?"

Chip turned his head and moaned. I folded the wash cloth and set it across his forehead. "I'm not sure I can tell you."

Nick was reaching for the other cloth. "Mom…" He looked down and Chip and then back at me. "Look, you're right, none of us have a clue what happened or why, but I think we all figured that whatever it was it would blow over and you guys would be back together already. Hell, you don't even *talk*. If he did something that started it, yeah, I want to know. I think I have a right to know."

He had a right to know why his family had imploded but I wasn't sure he had a right to the details Chip wanted kept private.

"Do you remember when you were about three years old and he was gone for such a long time?"

"Sort of. I remember telling some department store Santa Claus that I wanted my dad home for Christmas, and when I got up Christmas morning there he was, sitting next to the tree waiting for me. He was gone for a long time, wasn't he?"

"Five months. He was doing then pretty much the same thing he was doing two years ago when I wouldn't let him come home."

My son wanted the truth and I wasn't sure I was up to giving it to him. He waited patiently, silent in his demand to finally know what had gone wrong.

"Before I met him," I said, trying to choose my words carefully, "he worked for the government. His job was to hunt down missing people or go God knows where after weapons or airplanes or anything else someone had that they wanted. When you were three years old he and Kris accepted an assignment to locate a missing CIA agent in Europe. Kris came home after four months without him... God, I thought I would die."

"They're spies?"

"No, not exactly. But when she came home and said they'd gotten separated and no one could find a trace of him, I was sure he was dead. He popped up out of nowhere that Christmas Eve."

"Santa," Nick grinned.

"I begged him to never give the agency another shot at him. I couldn't take that feeling again, wondering where he was and if he was even alive. The day before he left this last time he told me they'd asked him to look for someone else, and I just exploded. He left and I made sure he couldn't come back."

"Christ, Mom, it's not like he had an affair."

"I could have handled that better. Honestly, if it had been another woman I could have fought back, and I would have won. I can't fight the entire agency, Nicky. I didn't stop long enough to realize that he can't, either. Now it's too late."

"It's never too late."

"We have different lives now. And I doubt he could forgive me for what I did to him."

"How will you know if you don't ask?"

I shook my head sadly.

"The man doesn't even have a social life, you know. He's had one date in two years, and that was just dinner with some woman he'd known in high school. He sleeps with a damned cat and he swears he'll stick by his marriage vows until the day he dies. He dreads the day you sic a lawyer on him."

"That won't happen."

"Fine, then what about Brad? You can't just string him along, either. Be fair, Mom. I don't believe the crap about you being just friends and as much as Paul and I would like to think, I don't believe Brad is gay, either. Don't let him fall in love with you if you have no intention of making yourself available. It's not fair to you, it's not fair to Brad, and it's especially not fair to Dad."

Until then I had forgotten about Brad, who was probably cooling his heels in the living room. I had no doubt that Kevin had shown him in, promised to get me, and then disappeared into his bedroom.

I wasn't going anywhere now.

"I'm not playing any games with Brad," I told Nick. "He knows where I stand."

"Does he love you?"

"I don't think you really care about that, do you? It's between Brad and I, but I'll tell you if it will make you feel better. I'm not in love with Brad, I'm not sleeping with him, and though I know he has feelings for me, this is as far as it goes. He might be gay, but I think it's safer to say he's bisexual. He dates a lot of other people, too, not just me."

"So, you go out with him because he's what? Safe?"

"Not exactly."

"It's none of my business, Mom, I just think you're discounting your own husband too much."

"As long as he's sick, I'll take care of him, Nick. Don't get your hopes up."

Chip moaned and struggled to get out of the tub, nearly slipping on the wet tile before Nick caught him.

How, I wondered when he was back in bed and asleep, can I tell my son not to get his hopes up?

Mine were sky high.

Nick

I faded into the background when Uncle Doug showed up, proverbial little black bag in hand. Brad had already been shown the front door, and much to my displeasure, he went quietly and graciously. The flicker of disappointment in his eyes when I told him she was upstairs taking care of my sick father was unmistakable; given any encouragement he would have sprinted up the stairs to see for himself. It was fine with him if she wanted to play nursemaid, he just didn't care for who her patient was.

Mom had no idea. The switch-hitter had taken his stance and was aiming for a home run.

"Just the flu," Doug told Mom. She was pacing the bedroom like an expectant father, and I was lingering at the door, watching my dad flinch from Doug's touch.

"What do I do for him?"

"Do you want me to put him in the hospital, Terry? If his fever were any higher I'd insist on it, but I'll leave it up to you."

"He'd hate that and you know it. Just tell me what to do for him."

Doug Stone as a doctor and Doug Stone as a friend are two different people. Somewhere along the line he learned to separate the two when it came to treating our family for their various aches and pains. Sitting there next to my dad, though, I saw the two cross and touch, at least for a moment, the smile tugging at the corners of his mouth.

He saw the same things in Mom that I did.

"The first point of order is to bring the fever down. Start with liquid Tylenol. If that doesn't do it, try an alcohol rub down. And if all else fails, stick ice packs under his arms and at his groin."

I groaned at that, but he was serious.

"Try to get him to take liquids, as much as he'll tolerate. Don't force any solid food on him because he'll just heave it right back at you. Your best bets right now are Jello water and flat soda."

He reached into his bag and pulled out a big bottle of green liquid and handed it to my mom. "Tylenol. Two tablespoons every four hours as long as his temp is up."

"Even if he's asleep?"

"Right now it's more important to get the fever under control, Terry. He'll sleep a lot regardless." He snapped the bag shut and eased off the bed. When he stood up, the doctor was gone and dad's best friend was standing there. "Are you sure about this? He's lousy when he's sick."

"He's like a little boy when he's sick. If you put him in the hospital it'll take him twice as long to recover."

"Do you want a private nurse, then?"

"I can do it, Doug. If it gets to be too much I'll scream for help. Besides, I know him, he'll sleep like the living dead until he feels better. It's how he handles it."

That was true. Dad would go to bed with a head cold and sleep straight through for three days. He'd get up to use the bathroom or blow his nose, but he was never especially coherent. He'd wake up, be groggy for a day or two, and then be fine. Every time.

"Um…" They looked at me; I know they had forgotten I was there. "Do we let him wet the bed, or what?"

"He's asleep, Nicky, not in a coma," Mom said. "As long as he has a clear path to the bathroom he'll be fine."

Downstairs, Doug stopped at the door and said, "You let me know if it gets to be too much, Nick. I'm not thrilled about this."

"I don't think it's the highlight of her week, either, Uncle Doug, but she's right. If you stick him in the hospital he'll hate it and he'll take it out on some young nurse who's only trying to do her job. What other option is there?"

I could think of a few: hire someone to watch him in his own apartment, take him home with you – I just didn't want him to think of anything.

"I couldn't talk your mom out of this now, anyway. Just keep an eye on her."

"It's a start."

"Don't. Your folks have a lot of problems and a lot of anger built up between them. If you start playing matchmaker now the entire family could get hurt."

I doubted I'd have to play anything.

If Mom could work up the nerve to just apologize, the whole mess would be over.

Doug

"What do you think?"

I rolled over onto my back and folded my arms underneath my head. The question had nothing to do with what I thought about what she'd just done to me; no, my wife was backtracking at least an hour or so.

What did I think of Terry nursing her estranged husband?

"I think that it could blow up in her face."

"How so?"

"Chip sick is a lot like Chip drunk, and a couple of weeks ago I listened to a drunk Chip say some pretty mean things about her. If he spouts off now he'll hurt her so deeply they might not recover. Damn, you should have seen her, Kris. She's torn between being afraid of him being there and wanting to staple his ass to the mattress."

"Might be their only chance, you know."

I did know. That's why it bothered me so much.

"Spider's not home yet," I said glumly. "He missed curfew again."

"He's a big boy, Doug. And he's not that late, only twenty minutes or so."

Assaulted by kisses in the dark. Anything to distract me from our son. It annoyed her that in the afterglow of even spectacular sex I could worry about him.

I worried about him constantly.

"Who is this Janet person I've been hearing so much about and why haven't I met her?"

"Janet Torres," she sighed. "I haven't met her yet, either, but I hear from a reliable source that she's probably the most normal girl he's dated so far."

"I didn't think he liked normal," I grunted. I wished I'd have half the courage at his age when it came to girls. My sixteen year old son turned up nearly every week with a different girlfriend, and the fact that there was an obvious language barrier never seemed to bother him.

It bothered me.

"They communicate nicely," Kris mumbled against my neck. "Nick says they even talk."

"I'll bet."

She gave up on my neck and looked at me. "Don't you dare tease him, Doug. Janet's the first girl he's ever gone out with that he *can* talk to. She can sign, and Nick thinks she's probably more fluent in ASL than we are."

"So it's not just sex then?"

"At this point I doubt it's sex at all. Damn, can't you have a little more faith in your son?"

"I have faith in him, Kris."

She dropped back onto her own pillow, a message that she was fairly exasperated with me. I never proclaimed to be the world's greatest father; most of the time my son seemed more like an alien than my own flesh and blood, he did more what he pleased rather than what he was supposed to. I didn't pretend to understand him.

Spider didn't play any games at trying to make me think he understood me any more than that, either. Most of the time he regarded me merely as the other body in his mother's bed. We never had the time to build a real relationship. It was always been office hours and hospital call shifts, sign language classes or just bad timing. We just never connected.

But that didn't mean I lacked faith in my son. I saw the wonders he was capable of. He coped with frustration and disappointment better than anyone I've ever known. He existed in a world designed for people who could hear, and made it his own.

"I didn't mean that the way it sounded, Doug."

"I know what you meant. Let the boy be a teenager while he can. Maybe I just don't want to let him grow up yet."

"He'll do that whether we're ready or not. We may as well enjoy watching him grow now instead of kicking ourselves later for missing it."

"I don't know how Chip does it." She rolled back onto her side and resumed pressing kisses right where she'd left off. "He sees his kids ninety per cent less than I see Spider but he still has a good relationship with them all. He's tuned into them. I can't figure out how."

"Just talk to him, Doug. About anything. He's no different than Nick or Paul."

Except for the obvious.

As I was about to turn the table on Kris and return those kisses, the door creaked open and the light switched on. Never quite certain how loud he knocked or whether or not we heard it, Spider preferred to just reach in and turn on a light.

"Sorry," he signed.

I blinked away the spots in my eyes. "This had better be damned good."

"I had to take a cab home and I don't have enough cash to pay the driver."

Grumbling choice words, I climbed out of bed, reaching for my sweatpants and wallet. "How much?"

"Ten."

I gave him the money and waited in the living room while he paid the cab driver.

"You're late," I said before he could close the door all the way.

"I had to wait for the cab."

"Where's your car?"

He hesitated. "I left it in the school parking lot. Driving would have been a bad idea."

"Christ, are you drunk?"

He nodded.

"Paul?"

He nodded again, dropping onto the sofa. I tried to calm my anger by reminding myself he'd used some common sense, after all. "What about your girlfriend?"

"I took her home first. I'm sorry."

I thought he might be, or at least would be in the morning. "And just what was the point of getting drunk in the school parking lot?"

He shrugged. "Paul had a bottle and wanted to share."

"Paul *does* understand the word 'no.' You're not obligated to be his drinking buddy."

"He had a fight with his girlfriend, Dad. We had a couple drinks in sympathy. Just a couple."

"Spider, if you drink every time that boy has a fight with someone you'll be an alcoholic by the end of the school year."

By the time I climbed back into bed I was less worried about my son and extremely concerned about how Terry would handle Paul, who, by Spider's account, refused the cab and drove himself home.

"She'll handle it," Kris assured me.

I just hoped she noticed he came home, period.

Nick

Mom was waiting at the foot of the stairs for Paul, pissed off that he was over an hour late and beginning to creep over that invisible line from "he's grounded" to "if he's not home in two minutes he must be lying dead in the street somewhere and I don't know where to look or how to find him, and what will I do if something really did happen to him, because, oh shit, I can't take this right now…"

He made it inside the front door about fifteen seconds before she hit her two minute tolerance level.

He was home, obviously safe and in one piece; she was pissed again.

"You'd better have one damned good explanation, Paul."

"For what?"

"You're over an hour late."

"So?" He shrugged. "I'm late. I'm home. What difference does it make?"

"You could have called."

"I could have."

She caught a whiff of him about the same time I did. "You've been *drinking*?"

"Don't worry about it. I made it home."

"You drove? Goddammit, what were you thinking? You could have gotten yourself killed!"

"Yeah, well, I didn't."

She held her hand out. "Your car keys. Now."

"No way."

"Cut out the crap and hand them over *now*."

"Get off my back!" he shouted. "You want to crawl all over someone then go find your little faggot friend and maul him instead. I don't need this shit right now and I'm not giving you my fucking car keys."

If I hadn't been as stunned as Mom was at that point I suppose I'd have heard the door upstairs open.

"If I ever," Dad grumbled, "hear you speak to your mother like that again I'll kick the crap out of you. Hand over your keys in the next five seconds, mister, or I'll take the car away and have it scrapped for parts."

Paul went ghostly white and dropped the keys into mom's hand.

"A month. You can count on having an entire month to think this one over. And the next time you get behind the wheel with so much as a whiff of alcohol will be the last time you ever drive. Do you understand?"

Paul managed a slight nod.

Dad turned around and shuffled back into the bedroom, leaving the door open. We didn't hear another word from him for a week.

Paul came to breakfast the next morning dressed in a blue suit, his eyes bloodshot and rimmed with dark circles; I could only imagine the hell pounding in his head. Mom glanced up from the newspaper and tried to hide her amusement, biting back the comments she could make about getting his just rewards.

Kevin was nowhere to be seen; I know he would have had a few choice comments about Paul's hangover.

Eileen was playing the piano in the living room, quietly so that she wouldn't bother anyone, but loud enough that we could hear it at the table. She wasn't quite a prodigy, but she had a gift for music I envied. I could plunk out the notes; Eileen managed to find the magic behind the music.

We had breakfast to Beethoven and Barry Manilow. Dad's favorites.

Paul cleared his throat. "Mom?"

She glanced up.

"Is it all right if I go to church with Nick this morning? I need to see Father Parker."

She nodded. Permission granted.

"What about you, Mom?" I asked.

"I'll have to miss it today. I'm not leaving your dad alone that long. Do you mind taking Kevin and Eileen, too?"

I did, but I didn't have much of a choice in the matter, not really.

Paul picked up his cereal bowl and headed for the kitchen, but stopped and turned back. "Look, Mom, I'm sorry about how I acted last night. What I was thinking and what I actually said were two different things. I really am sorry."

She closed the newspaper. "Is there something you need to talk about?"

"No. Something personal that I have to work out for myself."

"I'm here anytime, you know."

I think if Mom hadn't been so preoccupied she would have pushed for more. She just couldn't see that the red in Paul's eyes was fear and not fatigue, and that the family agnostic was willingly running straight to his confessor.

He had yet to ask why Dad was asleep in Mom's bed.

"Will you do me a favor, Nick?" she asked.

"Depends."

"After church drop by your dad's place and pick up some of his clothes, and then drive his car back here. I'm not comfortable with leaving it there without knowing how long he'll be here."

"What about the cat?"

"Oh, God, I forgot about his cat. I refuse to change a litter box, but as long as you kids will take care of him, you can bring him."

Famous last words. As soon as she set eyes on the PsychoKitty she'd be in love. And Max was not as dumb as we all proclaimed him to be; he'd milk every ounce of affection he could from Mom and show her that she honestly only existed to serve as his furniture, bed, bathtub, amusement center, and provider of room service. She had no clue that as soon as Max stepped into the house, her lap would never again be her own.

"Is Kevin even going to church this morning?" I asked. "I don't think he's out of bed."

"He's up and reading to your Dad from Song of Songs. He seems to think your dad will absorb it in his sleep and be inspired."

"Kevin probably doesn't understand what he's reading."

"I'm sure he does. Your little brother is not as dense as you seem to think."

That was debatable.

Eileen drifted into the dining room, barely looking at us as she went into the kitchen. "Kevin's going to be a priest."

"Did he tell you that?" Mom asked.

"He didn't have to."

I wondered from time to time what it was that made Eileen tick. She was Daddy's little girl, no doubt about that, and Mom seemed certain most of the time that Eileen considered her mostly a nuisance, but there was something puzzling about her that no one could figure out.

Like the Eileen Proclamations.

Kevin would, no doubt, announce his intent to become a priest sometime in the near future. He didn't have to confess that to Eileen in order for her to know it; she just knew.

"Going to church with me, squirt?"

She came to sit at the table, glass of orange juice in hand. "And watch you fawn all over Katie? No thanks. I'll ride with Paul."

"He's riding with me."

"And I'm staying home," Mom said. "Ride with Nick. You don't have to sit with him. And afterwards you can help him gather up some of your dad's things."

"Max?"

Mom nodded.

"You get to clean his litter box," I said.

"That's fine, I don't mind."

She didn't mind cleaning up cat poop but she minded going through Dad's underwear drawer. Eileen stood in the middle of his bedroom, arms folded defiantly, refusing to so much as peek in the drawer.

"It's underwear, Eileen," Paul said. "It doesn't bite."

"But it's his *underwear.*"

"You see me in my underwear all the time," I said. "So what?"

"But I don't touch it!"

She scooped up the cat and kept her hands on him; Paul and I grabbed jeans and t-shirts for Dad, remembering at the last minute to get his keys and wallet. "You're a little freak," I teased her as I locked the door. "They might have medication for undieaphobia, you know."

"Well, at least they can cure me. You're stuck being you for the rest of your life."

Kevin was still sitting with Dad when we came home, reading to him from Psalms. Eileen deposited Max on the bed and sat to listen, so I headed back downstairs. I decided she might be right about Kevin, it wasn't all that unusual to find him sitting on his own bed, reading his bible.

My brother the Father.

I was feeling pretty good about that until I heard Brad's voice rumbling from the living room. I inherited my father's lack of restraint, and it was all I could do to stay in the hall at the foot of the stairs and not barge in there to toss him out on his ass.

"Is he staying?" he asked.

"I'm not going to kick him out, Brad. He's sick."

"That's not what I mean and you know it. How long after that?"

"It's his house. He can stay as long as he wants."

Mentally I awarded her two points. The fact that it was Dad's house – he inherited it from his father – had never occurred to me. He could have ordered her out right from the beginning. She didn't just toss him out of the house, she tossed him out of *his* house.

"If he stays," Brad asked, "do you?"

"If you think for a minute I'd leave my kids, you're insane."

"Take them with you."

"I'm not going anywhere."

"Then what about us?"

Mom's irritated sigh. A good sign – for me, anyway. Not so good for Brad. "There is no *us*, Brad. We've gone over that before. Friends, that's it. I may not be able to live with the man, but he's still my husband and I still love him."

"You can change the fact that he's your husband, and

love fades if you let it… Terry, I want a chance with you."

"Brad…"

"I do. I can see us together. I can accept the fact that you won't sleep with anyone as long as you're married to him and I accept that you'll have feelings for him for a long, long time, but if it's over, then let it go."

"What if it's not over?"

Quiet. I could hear the sofa springs give and wondered who had sat down and what they had been doing before that. Pacing? Standing there holding hands? And was my mom practically sitting on his lap on the sofa now?

"It's not over," Brad grumbled. "You're dying for me to leave so you can go back upstairs to him."

"No."

He chuckled. "I don't know why you're so willing to take him back, but it's obviously want you want to do."

"Take him back? It's my fault he was gone. And it's not the first time I've screwed up so badly with him, you know that."

"He's not exactly in the position to judge you."

"Come on, Brad. Chip has never cheated on me. How do you think he felt coming home to find out his wife slept with his best friend? It almost killed him. But he stood by me and he fought with everything he had to make our marriage stronger."

"Then why," Brad said evenly, "did you throw him out? He couldn't have done anything worse."

"I plead temporary insanity."

My mom had an affair? With Dad's best friend?

Uncle Doug?

"All right, Terry. Your kids hate me and you still love your husband. I have no chance at all."

If she replied, I didn't hear it.

"If you want, I'll go buy handcuffs and chains and bolt him to the bed and withhold the key until he promises to stay."

She laughed.

"I want you to be happy. With me or not."

In less than five minutes my opinion of Brad Colt turned one hundred and eighty degrees. Faced with the same situation I didn't think I could be as gracious. And somehow I believed him, his sincerity didn't sound forced or exaggerated.

I should have slipped into the study or gone up the stairs so that he could make a quiet exit, but my feet refused to cooperate. I sat at the foot of the stairs, staring ahead.

"Nick? You look lost, man."

I managed to stand. "Not lost, not exactly." I offered my hand. "We don't hate you, Brad. You just terrified us."

He shook my hand and laughed. "Great. See you around."

It wasn't possible. I must have misheard.

Mom appeared quietly from the living room. "How long have you been there, Nicky?"

"Too long."

"Shocked?"

I nodded.

"By the fact that Brad wants a relationship or something else you might have heard?"

"It's none of my business."

She pulled me into the living room and sat down on the sofa, looking at me with tear filled eyes. I wanted to tell her she didn't owe me an explanation, that I didn't want to know. I didn't want it confirmed. I wanted to think I'd misunderstood.

"This isn't something you want to know, but since you do know, you need to hear the whole thing. It's not fair to leave you with the wrong idea."

"You had an affair with Uncle Doug?"

"Not my proudest moment," she admitted. "But it's not exactly what it sounds like, and I hope to God you understand."

She took a deep breath and blinked back the tears.

I hoped so, too.

TWO

1979

Terry

"It's a giant lipstick tube," Chip grumbled. We stood in the parking lot of the Travis Air Force Base Visitor's Center, sweating under the hot July sun, watching one of the giant C-5 Galaxy planes come in for a landing in the distance. "Someone please tell me we're not flying in one of those."

"We're not flying in one of those," Kris said. She leaned against the car, grabbing Doug's hand. "You get to fly in a tiny little prop plane. You know, a tree humper. Barf maker. Tummy churner."

"Shut up."

"And lucky you, you get me as a pilot."

"No goddamned way."

She smiled and nodded. "Just to Washington. After that, who knows? Maybe they'll give us a bi-plane and I can do acrobatics for you."

I slipped my arms around Chip's waist and hugged as hard as I could. "Now tell me again how badly you want to go do this."

"I did before I found out *she's* the pilot!"

"You're not afraid of flying, are you?"

"Not that he'll admit," Doug laughed.

"I threw up once. Just once. You'll never let me forget it."

"Nope, not a chance."

Chip hugged back, and kissed the top of my head. "She's a good pilot. It's just part of my job to give her a hard time."

"You can give me a hard time right up until we land in Washington," Kris said. "After that I'll be armed."

"Funny."

"How much longer until they come out here and get you?" I asked him. We were waiting at Doug's car for the Travis security police to escort Chip and Kris to the flight line, a concession to the discovery that neither Doug nor I would be allowed past the main gate. Our goodbyes would have to be very public, standing at the side of the busy road that lead Travis residents and workers from Fairfield and Vacaville onto the base.

"About thirty seconds," he said, nodding at the airman walking toward us.

"No chance that you'll change your mind?"

"I can't. You know I can't."

Kris had already kissed Doug and was walking away. My arms didn't want to unlock from Chip's waist, and he had to pull them away, holding my hands for a brief moment before letting go.

"I'll be back before you know it," he said, leaning over for a kiss. "Just keep it in your head that I'm damn good at this, and I'll be home come hell or high water."

"Don't promise."

"I can promise." One more kiss and he stepped away. "I

love you, don't forget that, either."

We watched them climb into the back of a police car. Chip turned and waved one last time as they drove through the gate and down the road. I stood where he had left me until I could no longer see the car, imagining that I could see its taillights disappear over the horizon.

The only horizon I had was where I knew the bowling alley on the base was, somewhere towards the end of the main road. They would turn just past the bowling alley and head toward the flight line, climb into a plane, and take off for God only knew where.

God and the Secretary General of the United States Defense Agency.

"How unhappy about this are you?" Doug asked once we were back in his car and headed down the parkway.

"I'm not sure. Should I be unhappy at all? They both acted like this was like a trip to Disneyland with a free five day pass."

He laughed. "Yeah, well for them it's just as good."

"Do you know what they're doing?"

"Not in Technicolor detail. But I can tell you it's fairly simple. They're going overseas to escort a CIA agent home."

"But does this CIA agent want to come home?"

He shrugged. "Now that I don't know, but I don't think they'll give him much choice."

"How dangerous is it?"

"On a scale of one to ten? I'd say it's about a six. Chip is good for anything under a nine point nine nine."

"What happens on a ten?"

He glanced over at me, grinning. "We'll let you know if it ever happens."

"You're not very good at being reassuring, Doug, you know that?"

He took the North Texas Street exit, turning off two miles too soon. "A detour," he said before I could ask. "I know I'm not the best at making women feel better. You'll just have to take my word that he hasn't been up against anything he couldn't handle."

"Fine. Where are we going?"

"To dinner. I'm starving."

"Well, then you're paying, too."

"Fine. It's two for one day at Taco Bell."

"Fine. Tacos give me gas."

"Well, fine!"

"You're laughing and I'm serious."

"Well, God knows we don't want you farting all night. How about grabbing some pizza at the mall and seeing a movie? The babysitter is expecting to keep the kids until late, anyway."

We went to the movie first, sitting in the back of a nearly empty theater, and when he tried to slide his arm behind me I elbowed him in the ribs and accused him of trying to get fresh on the first date. He threatened to kiss me just to embarrass me.

"I wouldn't be embarrassed. I'm a damn good kisser."

"So I've been told."

"Are you serious?" I grabbed the popcorn from him and held it out of his reach. "Just what the heck do you and Chip talk about?"

"Same things you and Kris talk about."

"You talk about shoe size?"

"Yeah, right," he laughed, grabbing for the popcorn.

"You have kinda small feet, don'tcha?"

"Oh, kiss my ass and give me the damned popcorn."

I stretched over and kissed him on the cheek.

"Bitch."

I handed him the popcorn. "Yes, but I'm a loveable bitch."

"I've been told that, too."

"I think I need to start giving Chip a list of topics I'll permit for discussion."

"If it makes you feel any better, he won't tell me where your birthmark is."

"If it makes you feel any worse, I *do* know where yours are."

"I have birthmarks?"

"Evidently you have at least one, in a place you can't readily see by yourself."

He handed the popcorn back.

"Do you want to borrow a compact so you can go to the men's room and check it out?"

"All right, you win. I'm never letting that woman see me nekkid again."

Two weeks later he had changed his mind. Kris could not only see him naked, but she could play connect the dots with every mole on his body if she wanted, and with indelible ink. We found ourselves at the zoo – Kris's favorite pastime – listening to Nick's running commentary on wildlife, trying to keep him from terrorizing Paul and Spider.

Doug warned me against taking them into the reptile house but I ignored him; we stood in front of an anaconda, its mouth wide open as it stretched toward the glass.

"We could stuff Paulie into that, Uncle Doug. Can I tell him that snakes eat little boys?"

"That would make him cry, Nicky."

Nick shrugged, the light dancing in his eyes suggesting that was the general idea. He looked at his brother, half asleep in the stroller with a thumb jammed into his mouth, and then went to the next tank.

"You know," I said to Doug, "just a couple years ago Kris and I were standing right here. She told me she was pregnant."

He glanced at Spider. "I didn't think she'd have him. I swear, I thought she would never tell me."

"She was just scared."

"I look at him and have a hard time believing she seriously considered not having him. We'd probably still be together, but..." He took a few steps to catch up to Nick. "I don't think we'd have ever gotten married."

"Eventually."

"Probably not. I wouldn't have pushed and she was always scared of making a commitment."

"Think you'll have another one?"

He shook his head. "She thinks she's too old."

"Do you want another one?"

"I do, but not so badly I'd push her into it. I can always borrow your kids when the urge to have a houseful strikes."

"That's one way to get rid of the feeling."

Nick turned back, hands on his hips, scowling at us. "You guys are fucking slow."

"Nick!"

Doug shrugged it off. "And then there's this other way..."

"Don't encourage him! Nicky, you apologize right now."

"But you're slow."

"Nick," Doug said sternly, "say you're sorry for the bad word."

"What bad word?"

"You know what word."

"Fucking?"

"Yes!" I wanted to reach out and shake him, but Doug was snickering and Nick looked so serious that I had a hard time keeping the smile off my own face. "I don't want to hear you say that word again. Do you understand?"

"Daddy says it."

"Daddy shouldn't say it, either."

"Okay."

"Don't you have something else to tell us?" Doug prompted.

"Yeah." He pointed at Paul. "He just squirted shit right out of his diaper."

I set my forehead on Doug's shoulder. "Tell me he's not just three. Tell me he's an alien changeling, and the mother ship is coming to pick him up tomorrow."

"Heh. Wait until he's fifteen."

"Military school," I grumbled.

"You should potty train him," Nick said.

"Why don't you do it?" Doug asked him.

Nick scowled. "Yuck."

"Well, if you don't want to do it, why should your mom?"

"She gets paid to do it."

"No, I don't," I told him.

He looked up at me as if the idea I would take care of them for free was brand new. "Daddy pays you."

"No, Daddy doesn't."

"Well, you pay me and I'll do it."

"You want money for teaching your little brother to use a potty?"

Nick nodded.

"How much?"

"Don't tell me you're serious," Doug chuckled.

"I want a hundred dimes," Nicky insisted.

"Maybe," I said to Doug. And to Nick, "That's an awful lot of dimes, mister."

"I know you have a hundred dimes."

"But where did I get the dimes? Daddy doesn't pay me and I don't have a job."

He stopped to consider it. "Uncle Doug has a job. He can pay you."

"Pay her for what, Nick?" Doug asked.

"What mommies do! She can do that for you."

Doug had to turn away and hide his smile from Nick, who still had his hands on his hips and was regarding us as the most dense creatures to ever walk dry land. "I don't think Daddy would want me to do that. Would you do it for, say, a new toy car?"

He thought for a moment. "You don't have the dimes. You need dimes to buy it."

"Oh my God." Doug bent over to get Spider from his stroller, coughing to hide the laughter.

My mind raced to get just a fraction of a step ahead of my three year old son. "All right. I can buy it with a check."

"Can I have any car I want?"

"Within reason."

He glanced at Paul and then back at me. "Okay. I'll teach him when we get home."

"It might take more than one day, Nicky."

My son was unimpressed with the idea that it might take weeks for Paul to get the right idea. He rolled his eyes and then asked, "Can we go see the tigers now?"

"Will you stop using bad words?"

"Yeah."

"Okay, we'll go see the tigers, and then we'll go get some lunch."

"Can we eat outside in the park?"

"Like a picnic?" Doug asked.

Nicky nodded.

"Sure, why not. Maybe the fresh air will knock all three of you out."

It took a warm bath and four bedtime stories to get Nick to agree to even try to fall asleep. He played quietly while I got Paul and Spider into bed – both were out before I could get a book to read to them – and then tried to convince me he would sleep better if I'd let him watch TV first.

We reached a compromise; I left him in his room with a picture book and a flashlight, and a promise that he'd stay in bed.

Doug was in the living room stretched out on the sofa. He had kicked off his shoes and was flipping through the photo album he had found on an end table.

"You two had one hell of a wedding."

I pushed his feet off the sofa and sat next to him. "It would have been perfect if it hadn't rained."

"I hated wearing that damned tux."

"But you looked good." I leaned over to look at the pictures; it felt strange to see Kris with Ron instead of Doug. "Chip hated his tux, too. He would have gotten married in jeans and a sweatshirt if he'd thought he could get away with it."

He turned the page; there was a photo of the four of us standing at the altar.

"Think it was an omen?" I asked.

"The best man hooking up with the matron of honor? Maybe it was. I know Ron was hurt when Chip asked me to be best man instead of him."

"I don't think he was. How many guys have their fathers stand as best man anyway?"

"I always thought Ron figured himself to be more than Chips' father."

"Maybe. I'm just glad he never found out that he wasn't Chip's father after all."

"He was a good man, Terry. I didn't agree with a lot of what he did and I'm damn glad he and Kris didn't stay married, but he really was a good person. She still misses him."

I took the album from him and closed it. "I don't think she knows you realize that, Doug."

"She should. Hell, I was there when they first got together. I remember how crazy they were about each other. It drove us nuts, they were trying to be so sly and not let the whole world know they had this thing going... I mean, they made the concentrated effort to not let so much as their fingers touch in front of anyone. The team leader finally blew his stack, and right there in front of everyone told them to just go get laid already so the rest of us could get back to work."

"Dan Martin? I never knew him very well, but Chip misses him, too."

"Another good man. First time I ever saw him loosen up was at Ron and Kris's wedding reception."

"You were there? Does Kris still have any pictures of that reception?"

"I'm sure she does, but it's not like we'd hang them on the wall."

"Chip and I realized once that we were both there and don't remember seeing each other. It's not like it was a huge party, either. We can't figure out why we didn't meet. Or you, for that matter. I don't remember you there."

"You were about thirteen then?"

I nodded.

"You were way too young to be so much as a blip on Chip's radar then. He didn't notice you because he was looking for someone at least his age."

"And someone who would put out," I added. "Don't mince words, I know Chip was a horny little thing when he was a teenager."

"Do you really have any idea?" Doug laughed. "That was right about the time Chip and I met. I was so socially backwards it wasn't funny and started hanging around him just to get his leftovers. Hell, I was pushing into my mid twenties and learned to come on to a woman from a sixteen year old. He set me up on my first real date, ever."

"In your mid twenties?"

"I was a late bloomer. One of the drawbacks to finishing high school at twelve, you know. No one in college wants to date the little freak."

"Are you serious? How old were you when you graduated?"

"Undergrad at fifteen. Medical school at twenty."

"I'd have never guessed."

"What?"

"That you're so smart."

"Oh, thank you. Just for that I'm gonna grab my kid and take him home."

"Some father you are. Spider's sound asleep, Doug. Just leave him where he is. You can always sleep in the guest room tonight."

He pretended to be hurt.

"I'll be nice, I promise."

"All right." He leaned back. "But I'm warning you, I sleep naked, and you better not peek."

~

We fell into a routine; on Doug's days off we grabbed the kids and took them to the park and to the playground, out for pizza or for ice cream. On the days Doug worked he picked up Spider afterwards and brought him over to play with Nicky and Paul, and I cooked dinner for everyone; Nick and Paul accepted it as normal that they would wander in and play with them before dinner, and then leave just before bedtime.

After two months, though, Nicky missed Chip to the point of emotional pain. He asked daily when his daddy was coming home and his outbursts of temper were becoming more frequent.

The kids needed a break from us as much as we needed a break from them. Doug dropped them off with Mrs. Cooper, an older woman two houses down from him who had been babysitting for Spider from the time he was just a few weeks old, and came to get me. The idea was an evening without talking about kids or spouses.

That was all we could seem to focus on.

"I can't even tell Nick where his father is," I complained.

"I know. They could be anywhere. Hell, they could be in Sacramento or San Francisco for all we know."

We were in the bar at the Charybdis; the manager had offered to bump us to the front of the dining room waiting list – one of the perks of being married to the owner – but we decided to wait our turn and have a drink instead.

"They wouldn't be that close and not call."

"Of course they wouldn't call us, Terry. They're not going to risk blowing their cover and give some nutcase a straight line home to their families."

"Don't do that."

"Do what?" he asked.

"Talk to me like I'm stupid. 'Of course they wouldn't call.' How the hell would I know that?"

"It just makes sense, that's all."

"It makes sense to *you*, Doug. I've never played one of these stupid little games and I don't have the benefit of knowing the rules. No one bothered to clue me in. I'm just supposed to sit back and accept it, no matter how long it takes."

"Meow."

"Doug!"

"I think I'd be getting defensive right about now, but it's not me you're ticked off at."

"I'm not ticked off!"

"If I put a Chip mask on right now you'd lunge across the table and gouge my eyes out."

"I'm not mad at him," I sighed.

"Sure you are. You're as angry with him as I am with Kris."

He'd never hinted that he was anything but understanding. I thought he supported their assignment, standing in the background like their little cheerleader.

"Are you kidding?" He slugged back the rest of his drink. "When Kris told me she was going I was so ticked I put my fist through the wall. She doesn't owe the agency anything. They fired her ass when she was an inconvenience and she chose to ignore that fact when they came begging for her talents. She didn't stop to think about how long she might be gone, or about Spider, or even about me. She just saw the chance to do something exciting again and grabbed it. So yeah, I am so fucking pissed off you wouldn't believe it."

I waved over to Ted at the bar, pointing at Doug's glass. He nodded and brought the bottle to the table, leaving it there. "What is it we're so angry about?"

"We're angry because they didn't give us a choice," he said, filling his glass. "We're angry because we're the ones left here to deal with the kids and with not knowing what's going on, and we're mad as hell because no matter what they told us, we know there's at least some element of danger and that one or both of them could get hurt."

"Or worse."

He looked away. "Or worse."

"Should they have been home by now?"

"Not necessarily. Sometimes you just wind up bouncing from one place to the next, trying to catch up to whomever you're chasing. And that presumes you have the right information in the first place."

"And if you don't?"

"You improvise. One time," he said, finally smiling, "they sent a team of two guys to pick up a retired agent. It was nothing big, he was just needed to testify in a federal case and had been out of touch with the agency for nearly a decade. These guys went to Spain, to Italy, to England, hell, they searched the entire European continent. They kept all these notes, detailed information about the intelligence they'd been given, disguises this poor sucker might be using to hide from former enemies… they came home about a month later empty handed. Never could find the guy. Ron took a look through their notes and half an hour later he and Kris were in the air. The guy had been living in Missouri for five years, working for Budweiser in Saint Louis. Right there in plain sight."

"Must have been an important case."

"Important enough for them to keep looking, yes. But it made us all realize that you have to look at the facts objectively, because if you misread even one clue, you could wind up at the Vatican when you need to be at the Arch."

Chip was good at reading the clues around him. If he needed to be near the Pope, then he'd be near the Pope. Knowing that didn't keep me from becoming more frustrated with every day that slid past without him coming home, and it didn't keep me from anger that erupted with growing regularity.

Doug was right; I was angry.

I only wish I had realized how angry before it was too late.

"Slop shots count, but you can't use one of my balls to get to your own unless you've already hit one of yours. And you have to call the shot on the eight ball." Doug handed me a cue. "Make sense?"

"You don't want me to hit your balls."

"Very funny. If you're solid, then you have to hit a solid ball, not a striped. Better?"

I held up the cue. "So I take the stick, hit the white ball into a solid colored ball, and try to get it to go into a pocket. And I get to keep going until I miss?"

"You got it, just don't go after the eight ball. You lose if you sink it. Want to try to break?"

"Sure, why not."

I lined up my shot as he set up the rack, and fired off the break before he could get the rack back onto its holder. "I'll call solids," I said when the first ball dropped. "Do I need to hit them in order?"

"No. That's nine ball. We're playing eight ball."

"So I can pick any solid colored ball I want and if I get it in, I keep going."

He nodded.

"Do you want to play for money or just personal satisfaction?"

"I'm not taking your money, Terry. Granted, I'd like to get back everything Chip's won off me over the years, but I don't want to take advantage."

"Always the gentleman."

Doug perched himself on a stool and reached for a bottle of beer while I looked at the table to find the right shot. He stayed there for the next five minutes and watched one ball after the other bank off side rails and drop into pockets. I ran the table until there was nothing left except for his striped balls and the eight ball, which was blocked from the side pocket by the nine ball.

"Side," I mumbled, then jammed the tip of the stick down hard, jumping the cue ball over the nine and into the eight. It hit dead center, and the eight rolled into the pocket. "I believe I win!"

"Why the hell didn't you just say you already knew how to play?"

"Because you're so cute when you're trying to explain things. Are you sure you don't want to play for money?"

"Not if Chip taught you to play."

"My dad taught me," I said, chalking the cue. "He's not half bad. At least, he can beat Chip."

"I think I'll just sit here and drink beer while you play."

"Chicken."

"Yep." He took a long sip from his beer. "I'd like to find just *one* thing I'm better at. Chip can out lift me at the gym, Kris can kick my ass if she really wants, and now you're the better pool player."

"Poor baby. Maybe it would be better if you just got drunk."

He grunted. "I don't even do that well. One more of these and I'll already be more than halfway in the bag. Frigging lightweight."

"Drink a couple more. We can have a peeing contest, see who can shoot the farthest. I bet you'd win that one."

He sighed and reached for the rack. "With my luck, probably not."

November brought with it the chill of an unpredictable California winter; days were cool enough that the kids needed sweatshirts, and evenings were damp and cold. We played outside with the kids as often as we could, knowing that we couldn't count on the next day being warm enough for them to be out for more than a few minutes, or even warm enough for them to want to go outside.

Doug brought Spider over after work and we sat in the backyard in sun-bleached wooden lawn chairs, watching the three of them dig in the sandbox. Nick had scooped up enough sand to build a two foot tall hill, and they were running toy cars and trucks over it. Both Paul and Spider's cheeks were red from the cool air, Nick's nose was running and he kept wiping it on the sleeve of his shirt.

"We'll have to give them ten more minutes and take them inside," I sighed. "It'll be dark, anyway."

"They're fine. A little cold won't kill them."

"All right, when my kids are coughing and hacking all night long you get to be the one to come over and stay up with them all night."

"They won't catch colds," he grunted, staring out at the kids. "Old wives tale. Cold air does not give you a cold, it just makes you feel cold. Colds are caused by viruses, not air temperature. If they get sick it's not because we let them play out after dark."

"Yes, doctor."

"Seriously."

"I believe you," I said, "but we still have to take them in because no one will be able to see out here. Unless you're going to install flood lights out here in the next ten minutes."

He shrugged. "You never know, I just might do that."

"Chip wants to put a pool out here. Dig up the whole back yard for a great big water filled hole."

"Sounds like a plan."

"You think so? I'm not sure I want one."

He looked over at me. "Why not? The kids would love it and when they get older they can have pool parties, let their friends hang out here. You can be the cool mom and have the house everyone wants to be at."

"But they're so little now. What if one of the kids got out of the house? They could be in the water and we wouldn't know until it was too late."

"Put a fence around it."

"Oh, I get it. You want the pool so you can come over here after dark and skinny dip."

He smiled for the first time that evening. "Damn right."

"I suppose it would be fun for everyone," I allowed. "And it would give him something to do. He wants to do it all himself, dig up the hole and lay the drainage system, the entire thing."

Doug was staring out at the kids again, and sighed hard.

"Okay, you don't want to hear me bitch about a pool that we don't even have yet. What's wrong?"

"I don't mind hearing about the pool," he said quietly. He yanked at his tie, loosening it. "I need to ask you something."

"Ask."

He nodded towards the kids. "How spoiled is my son? I mean, is he just generally spoiled or seriously spoiled, or what?"

"He's not spoiled at all. Why would you even wonder?"

He shrugged. "Something the babysitter said."

Mrs. Cooper doted on Spider, and had watched him off and on from the time he was born. Nicky and Paul loved her; every time she watched them she baked cookies, and she loved to get down onto the floor with them and play. Mrs. Cooper, Nick said, could build the best block house ever. And she knew all the words to every song he wanted to hear.

"She said," he went on without prompting from me, "that we don't push him enough. If he wants something, he points and we give it to him. She thinks we're holding him back by not making him ask for the things he wants. She says he's far too quiet for a two year old."

I followed his gaze. The boys were drilling their cars into the sides of the sand hill. "He is quiet," I agreed. "And you do give him what he wants when he grunts and points. But he's not spoiled."

"Then what?"

The tension in his face reminded me of someone trying to balance on the very edge of a curb on one foot; if you lean one way you risk falling into the street, where a car could zoom by and splatter you onto the pavement. Lean the other way and you just have to skip a step to stand upright. Doug knew what he was thinking but wanted to lean the other way, to be able to skip a step and land with relative safety without having to give the thought substance.

He was watching his son play in the sand, and he was seeing the same thing I had seen so many times but had never been able to connect to a thought.

"Take yourself out of the equation completely," I said. "If I came to you with a two year old as quiet as Spider is, and told you he had never so much as equated 'da-da' with his father, what would you do? As a doctor, what would you do?"

"Terry..."

"Doug, just stop and think about it. It's more than Spider getting what he wants without effort. Watch how he interacts with Nicky and Paul. When they play together even my kids stop talking – they have this very quiet, private little world they slip into so that Spider can play as an equal. They don't get into the loud, ear-splitting games they do with each other. They change completely. Nicky speaks for him, when they want a snack or to turn on the TV it's Nicky who asks. Sometimes Paul. But never Spider."

He swallowed hard against the lump in his throat. Eventually he said, "If it were someone else's son I'd do a physical, check for neurological problems, and barring that, I'd refer them to a pediatric audiologist."

"Then why not do the same for your own son? Doug, Paul is younger than Spider and he's speaking now. He can ask for the things that he wants. You have to look past the fact that it's your little boy and find out why he's so not talking yet."

"What if you're right, Terry? What if something is wrong with him?"

"Then you'll deal with it."

Nick pulled a car out of Spider's mouth and used his shirt to wipe the wet sand off his cousin's lips. "Kris should be here. This isn't something I should be facing without his mother, for God's sake. Son of a bitch, I shouldn't have to have every possibility tumbling through my head while she's off doing her thing not even knowing there might be something wrong with her little boy."

"There might not be anything wrong with her little boy, Doug."

"Oh come on. You know as well as I do that we've ignored the obvious for over a year. He's more than quiet, Terry. He doesn't react, either."

"What do you mean?"

He nodded in the kids' general direction. "Watch them." He clapped his hands together, hard. Nicky and Paul both jumped and look over, but Spider kept playing. "I dropped a pan in the kitchen a while back. He didn't budge, never turned towards the sound. Dammit, Terry, I know there's something wrong, I just don't want to deal with it."

"You have to."

"And then what?"

"Who knows? But first you have to deal with it."

He turned and looked at me. His eyes were moist and tinged with red. "What if my son is deaf?"

"Then he's deaf."

"Fuck…"

"Doug, he's still your little boy. He's still just as wonderful and perfect and beautiful as he was this morning. He just can't hear. It's not the end of the world."

"It's the end of the world as we know it."

I reached over and covered his hand with mine. "It's the start of something else, for sure. You'll find out what's wrong, if anything even is wrong, and you'll start doing whatever you have to do for him. Get him the help he needs, learn to communicate with him… Spider may have an awful lot to say and no way to say it. Finding out could be a good thing."

He took his hand away from mine and stood up. "With

all due respect, Terry, that's a damned simple way of looking at something extremely complicated. This isn't something that can be fixed by shrugging my shoulders and saying 'oh well.' This is fucking huge, it's what Kris was afraid of when she was pregnant with him. This is going to kill her."

"She's not that fragile, Doug."

He lifted Spider out of the sandbox, brushed him off, and then carried him back to the porch. "This is all so goddamned unfair," he said, heading for the door.

Of course it was unfair.

Most everything had been unfair since July.

Nicky had Paul by the hand and was dragging him out of the sandbox. "Where'd Uncle Doug go?" he asked.

"He was tired, Nicky. He had a long day at work and wanted to go home."

Nick brushed the sand off his own clothes while I cleaned Paul off. "He didn't eat with us yet."

"I know, sweetheart. He'll fix dinner for Spider when he gets home."

"No he won't," Nick insisted. "Uncle Doug is gonna go get tacos."

"You're probably right," I laughed. "But that's okay."

"Can we have mac'roni and cheese?" he asked, struggling to slide the back door open. "And hot dogs?"

"You mean," I asked him, pretending to be insulted, "you don't want me to make my very special meat loaf? I was going to make it just for you, with spinach and green beans."

"Yuck."

"I bet Paul would eat it."

"Paul would eat poop if you let him."

I agreed to Nick's menu change, got both boys washed up and dinner made before he could change his mind. Paul had adapted to the way Nick ate when he was younger; every piece of food had to be mashed between his fingers before he would put it in his mouth. He'd eat everything put in from of him, but it had to be mangled first.

"Why does he do that?" I asked Nick. "You used to do that, too."

"Cause eating's hard when you got no teeth."

"Even bananas?"

"No. That's just fun to squish."

He cleaned his plate and asked for seconds; Paul squirmed and wanted down so I put him in the playpen with a cup of juice and his toys. Nick watched him, pushing the food around on his plate.

"You don't have to finish that if you're not hungry," I said. "You ate enough. And you can still have a snack later."

Out of nowhere Nicky said, "I miss Daddy." He put his fork down and looked up at me, so serious. "When's he comin' home?"

"I don't know," I said truthfully. "There were lots of places Daddy had to go and I don't know when he'll be done going to all of them. I miss him too."

He picked up the fork and threw it across the table. "I want daddy to come home."

"I know." He held out my arms for him, ignoring the fork and the streaks of liquid cheese splattered onto the table and chair. "Come on, come sit in my lap for a little while." He buried his head against my chest. "It's okay to be mad, Nicky."

"My tummy hurts."

I wrapped my arms around him a little tighter. "I'm sorry. I'd make it feel better if I could."

He was quiet long enough to make me think he had

drifted off sitting there. His body began to relax and his breathing slowed down, and just about the time I thought I should carry him upstairs he sighed and said, "Mommy?"

"What, sweetheart?"

"I can't make Paulie use the potty."

"That's okay."

He leaned back and looked up at me. "I really tried."

"I know you did." I gave him a kiss on his forehead. "Paul's still too young, Nicky. He might have to stay in diapers for a while."

He glanced at Paul and then back at me, eyebrows furled.

"But you know what?" I added, realizing why it bothered him. "You did your best, and that's a very important thing. You still get to buy a new toy car."

"You promise?"

"I promise. I'll tell you what, I'll call Mrs. Cooper and see if she can watch Paul tomorrow, and you and I will go to the toy store to pick one out, just the two of us."

"Can we get hangubers, too?"

"Hamburgers and french fries, too. We'll drop Paul off just before lunch, and go on our own little date."

"Can I buy a toy for Paul?"

That surprised me. "Sure. You can pick something out for your brother, too."

He snuggled back up against me. "Okay. But I'm still mad at daddy."

I couldn't fault him for that, not one bit.

I was already in bed with the lights out when the phone rang at ten o'clock. I fumbled in the dark, praying that it wasn't Mrs. Cooper saying that she couldn't watch Paul after all. I'd already told Nick that she could, and he was counting on having me to himself for an afternoon.

"I'm sorry," the voice on the other end grumbled. "I was acting like an ass."

"Doug. You were not."

"I snapped at you but I'm not pissed off at you," he said. "So I wanted to apologize."

"You didn't have to, but I appreciate it."

"This is just so fucking unbelievable. Why did I have to pick *now* to get a clue? Jesus, Terry, I'm a doctor, you'd think I would be the first to see something wrong."

I propped an extra pillow behind me. "Maybe you didn't see it until now because this is the first chance you've ever had to be so focused on Spider."

"I'm always focused on my kid," he grumbled.

"But not like you are now. Up until now Kris has been the one to deal with him the most. You work, then come home and your attention is divided between the two of them. Why *would* you notice, Doug? I'm willing to bet that when you come home you're more focused on Kris, and on playing or snuggling with him, not with looking to see if he has any flaws. He's your baby, our babies don't have any flaws."

"Yours swears."

"Yes, but he does it perfectly."

"Nick is an amazing kid," he said.

"Right now he's an angry kid."

"How so?"

I described Nick at dinner, the sadness that permeated his little eyes and the flare of anger that sent his fork flying across the room. My oldest son was big for his age and almost frightening in his intelligence, but at that moment he was just an unhappy three year old nursing resentment he didn't understand.

"Don't start crying on me," Doug said, catching the break in my voice.

"I'm just frustrated."

"You and me both. Is Nick okay now?"

"He was when I promised him an afternoon out, just the two of us. I'm being shanghaied to the toy store."

"New car?"

"Anything he wants," I said. "I don't care if it's wrong, but I just want him to feel completely special for a while."

"It's not wrong. I wish someone would take me to a grown up toy store and buy me a new car."

"If you went to a grown up toy store," I laughed, "you wouldn't be buying a car. You'd be buying something kinky that requires batteries or a VCR."

"Maybe," he chuckled.

"Or something that requires an inordinate amount of hot air for inflation?"

"Hmmm." He pretended to consider it. "I know a place right outside the air force base…"

"I just bet you do."

"Would Terry like someone to take her to a grown up toy store?"

"No!"

"But they have girl toys there, too."

"Oh my God, I do *not* want to hear about it."

He was laughing. "You're no fun."

"I'm fun, just not kinky."

"You might be a little fun. But I'm never shooting pool with you again."

"Chicken."

"No argument there. I'm just tired of losing to everyone else all the time! There's got to be something I'm good at."

"You're a good listener, Doug," I said. "And you're an even better friend."

"You must be sleepy," he grumbled, embarrassed.

"A little. But you are a good friend."

"So are you. You know, this whole thing may suck, but at least I got a chance to know you as yourself and not just as Chip's wife. I don't think we would have ever gotten to know each other this well otherwise."

"That's kind of sad, if you think about it."

We decided not to think about it. Brooding over them being gone wasn't going to change anything, it wasn't going to help me deal with Nick and it wasn't going to help Doug take Spider to another doctor. We agreed to be angry under the surface and try to be as hopeful for the kids as we possibly could.

"Just keep your fingers crossed," he said before I hung up. "I can deal with it if Spider is just deaf. I don't know what I'll do if it's something more."

I didn't ask what something more could be because I didn't want him lying awake dwelling on it.

In the middle of Toys R Us, I decided that my son was actually a salesman stuck in the body of a three year old. Nick stood there so seriously, arms folded in front of him and mouth skewed as he considered the possibilities, walking from one car back to another, peeking inside, weighing all the options.

He had convinced me that the standard hand-powered toy car was not enough; this time he wanted one he could ride in. One he and his brother could ride in. He mentioned Paul empathically, knowing that would seal the deal.

Either car was too damned expensive for a three year

old, but I didn't care. If it aggravated Chip, all the better.

"If I getted this one," he said, "I could make it go myself." He pointed to the manual pedals inside, a purely boy-powered operation. He pointed to the other car. "If I getted this one it goes by its ownself."

"Which do you like best?" I prompted.

He pointed to the first one, a red convertible with a white stripe down each side. "I like this. Paulie's feet would get hurted."

"How?" I looked inside, where he was pointing.

"It gots no floor, Mommy. He don't know to pick up his feet." We went to the other car, a beige, battery operated miniature Jeep. "This gots a floor and his feet won't fall out."

"Will it be as much fun for you?"

"Yeah."

"But you like the red one better, don't you?"

"Yeah." He shoved his hands into his pockets. "I like red. But I don't want Paulie to cry. I wanna get the brown one."

I looked at the price tag.

"Is that too many dimes?" he asked.

"Nope, it's just the right number of dimes." I pulled a tag from the shelf. "We have to take this up front and pay for it, then they'll bring us the car in a box."

"Okay."

He reached up and took my hand. "I'm very proud of you for thinking of something you could share with your brother," I told him. "You could have picked out something only for yourself."

"But that would make Paulie feel bad cause he didn't get to come with us."

I stopped before we got to the cash register. "Nicky, you

don't *have* to get something to share. We can buy you your own toy, and buy Paul something, too."

"But I want to play with him in the car."

"All right. I wanted to make sure you didn't think you had to get something to share just because he didn't get to come to the toy store."

He stood on his toes to see over the counter as I wrote out the check. "I know. But *I* get to drive it."

"No," Doug laughed, "we don't spoil our kids. Not ever. We would never think of spending a small fortune on a car one of them could use to drive over the neighbor's cat."

"You be quiet."

"What are you going to do when he decides to take it apart to figure out how it works? He will, you know."

Chip's younger brother Dave, took apart everything he could get his hands on, hoping to discover the magic that made things work. He was rarely able to get anything back together, his bedroom constantly scattered with the bits and pieces of wire and transistors he was never able to reassemble.

"Nick will take it apart, figure out how to make it go twice as fast, and *then* he'll run over the neighbor's cat."

"Before he's five, I'm sure."

Nick pulled the car up to Doug's feet. "I'm sorry, Uncle Doug."

"What for, squirt?"

"You won't fit in here." He squealed with laughter, hit the accelerator, and took off at a quarter of a mile an hour.

We were in the front yard, sitting on the porch steps, watching Nick take his opportunity to play with the car before I went to pick Paul up. Doug had driven up about the same time that I was pulling the car out of the box, while I was trying to explain to Nick that I probably needed to charge the battery before he could use it, and that might not be until tomorrow. Doug looked at the battery, told Nick to wait a minute, and disappeared into the garage. He came out a minute later with a six volt battery that looked like it was made to fit Nick's car perfectly. Chip, he explained. There had to be two dozen different batteries in on his workbench, all charged and ready "just in case."

"I can pick Paul up when I get Spider," he said. "Just get me his car seat."

I leaned back on an elbow. "Are you going to talk about it?"

He nodded, his head moving just a fraction of an inch. "I took him in to see my partner… as far as he can tell without further testing, Spider not only can't hear, his eardrums are nothing but tiny little mutated flaps and his vocal chords are only about half formed."

"God, Doug, didn't his pediatrician ever look inside his ears?"

"I never looked inside his ears," he said sadly.

"But you're not his doctor, you're his father! Dammit, Doug, you're always poking into Nick's and Paul's ears. If something were wrong you'd have seen it years ago. Why didn't Spider's doctor look?"

"I haven't asked yet," he sighed. "I will."

I sat up and slipped my arm around his shoulders. "I'm sorry, you don't need me jumping to conclusions."

"Just means that you care, is all." He leaned over and kissed me on the cheek. "I called my parents and told them a little while ago. They want to spend a day or two with him. And she says your mom has been whining about not getting to spend time with her grandkids, too. I think your folks want them for the weekend."

"A weekend without the kids? What will we do?"

"Sleep in," he groaned.

"Have you told your parents where Kris is?"

"No. I don't really have to, you know. I told my dad she was gone on business and that's all he needs to know. He remembers what it's like."

"Your mom must know how you feel right now, being the one left behind."

"She does," he agreed. "And you know what the first thing she thought of when I told her about Spider? It occurred to her that he would never get sucked into the agency. It was her first thought. 'Thank God, Steven will be kept safe.'"

We were watching Nick, both wondering if there would be anything to keep him safe from it, anything to dull the glimmer of curiosity the agency would surely dangle in front of him at some point. Doug was still a teenager when they approached him, his father an active agent working halfway across the world, far enough that he couldn't stop Doug before he signed his name to a contract.

"I was eighteen, I think," he told me. "They promised to pay off all my student loans, pay for the rest of med school, see me through my residency... And the pay they offered was so damned good, it was three or four times what I could make working in a hospital, and they were paying me while I was still in school."

"How do they get away with it? Chip swears they didn't know how old he was –"

"That's bullshit. Chip might *think* they had no clue because that's what they wanted him to think, but Christ, Terry, Ron was actively working when Chip was born. Somewhere in his file was a bright notation about the bouncing baby boy his mistress had given birth to. They damn well knew how old Chip was. You think they cared?"

"I would think they cared how legal it was…"

"If they cared about legalities, no one would have hung Dan Martin from the rafters, Ron never would have had to work his ass off as their personal little assassin, and we wouldn't have done half the things we did. Do you know how many things we outright *stole,* Terry? We'd walk into embassies and onto military installations all over the goddamned world and take what they wanted us to take like it was our God given right."

"Defense of the United States," I sighed.

"Yeah, right. At least that's what we always told ourselves. The sad part is that it was actually fun. I hate to admit it, but I got off on it most of the time. Pure, power driven emotion… it didn't matter how dangerous it could be, we all lived for it."

"Will you tell me now how dangerous this trip is for Chip and Kris?"

"I meant what I said before. I didn't think it was all that dangerous."

"But now?"

"Now I don't know. All I know for sure is the fact that no news is the best news in this case. As long as no one from the agency shows up with a priest in tow, they're probably okay."

"Do you swear?" I asked, tugging at his arm.

"Really," he replied, trying to smile. "As long as we hear nothing, then they're okay. Were you starting to worry they were dead somewhere?"

"Maybe."

"Don't. If you worry about anything, worry that they're enjoying it way too much."

My parents lived an hour away, in a suburb of Sacramento. They bought a house and moved there after my dad retired; I was eighteen and too stubborn to go with them, preferring to move into my own apartment so that I would be near friends. I'm sure my father thought that within six months I'd be crying to move in with them, my feminine ego bruised by the working world, or my bank book too light to carry me through.

They hadn't counted on Chip. My father was dimly aware of Chip's existence – that shiftless son of Kris's husband – but if he was upset with the knowledge that I had not only met him but was spending every possible moment with him, he never showed it. He treated Chip with the same uproarious gusto he did everyone.

My mother, on the other hand, hated Chip on sight. She reasoned he was up to no good – after all, she'd heard stories about him – and that he intended only to use me and discard me when he was done. When I let it slip that I had gone away with him for a weekend at his stepfather's beach house, her shrill explosion of temper could be heard a mile down the road. *He will break your heart.* She was sure of it.

She softened when Chip presented her with her first grandchild. He held Nick close to his heart, wrapped up in the baby blue blanket she'd sent, and very carefully, almost tenderly, turned his son to face his grandmother.

"Nicky," he said quietly, "I want you to meet the second most important woman in your life. This is your grandma." He pulled the blanket away from Nick's chubby red cheeks. "See?" he asked his son. "This is who your mommy gets that beautiful smile and those pretty blue eyes from."

My mother completely melted in that moment.

Chip placed Nicky in her arms and leaned over to kiss her on the cheek. "Thank you," he whispered. "Thank you for Terry, for raising such a perfect woman, thank you for Nick..."

He made my mother cry.

He made her fall in love with him.

She was also determined to be the World's Greatest Grandmother. A visit from her grandsons was An Event. The swing set I had always wanted as a child but never got was now firmly rooted into their back yard, she bought a sandbox and toys, painted one of the bedrooms in bright reds and blues and filled it with stuffed animals and books. She convinced my father to buy a VCR and rented videotapes of animals and cartoon characters when she knew the boys were coming, and always, without fail, made sure she had the ingredients to bake cookies.

I sat on the back porch with my father while Nick and Paul helped her mix cookie dough. It was a mild afternoon, warm enough that we could sit there and enjoy the afternoon sun. The back yard was lined with flowering bushes and perfectly trimmed, lush grass, the swing set on one side and a bird bath on the other.

"That will have to go," my dad surmised. "Before one of the boys pulls it over on himself."

I started to object and say that wasn't necessary, but yielded. It wouldn't matter. The mere idea that one of the kids could get hurt was reason enough for him to store it away until they were old enough to know better.

"Are you sure you don't mind letting us keep the boys for a couple days?" he asked. "I don't want you to get lonely down there. And you know your mother will spoil them rotten."

"Oh, mom will?" I laughed. "Grandpa wouldn't have anything to do with that, would he?"

"I would never spoil a child."

"I'll be fine. It might be nice to have the house all to myself. I can read an entire book without having little fingers rip it out of my hands. And I can take a long bath without someone throwing the door open and demanding to know what I'm doing."

"Lock the door," he suggested. "Any word on when Chip is coming home?"

"No. But Doug and I were talking about that yesterday. He says not hearing anything really is best. We'd only hear if something had gone wrong."

"Well then," he said.

"You never have asked what he's doing."

"Nope."

"Not curious?"

"Angel, I figured out a long time ago that when it comes to Chip there are some questions I had just better not ask. Especially if he's off doing something with Kris. We've always known not to ask questions about that."

"Did you know before I married him?"

"I suspected."

"Did Mom suspect?"

"No," he chuckled. "She was just furious that he was manhandling her little girl." He reached over and grabbed my hand. "He'll be all right, sweetheart. He's smart and he's strong. He'll be just fine."

I was grateful that my father didn't put me in the position of defending Chip for being gone, especially for being gone so long. I stayed long enough to have dinner with them, kissed the boys and told them to be good – not sure if my feelings should be hurt that they didn't seem to care that I was leaving – and left. I hadn't intended to stay so late; it was dark and beginning to sprinkle; I hated being on the freeway at night even when it was perfectly dry.

It hit me as I was leaving just how long four months was. Chip had been gone at least that long. He'd missed our anniversary and his own birthday, he hadn't seen the boys dressed up for Halloween, and Thanksgiving was just a few days away. My parents would bring the boys home and stay through the weekend, we'd fix a huge holiday meal and have Doug and Spider over; my dad would drag Doug into the living room to watch football while my mom and I cooked, and once in a while one or the other would poke their head in and ask if they could help, hoping, of course, that the answer would be no.

It would be a traditional family holiday, only part of the family would be missing.

My parents wouldn't say anything, but Nicky would be feeling it. Doug would be so caught up in everything going on with his own son that he wouldn't possibly be able to focus on much else. I'd be fighting to hold myself together until I could be alone and fall apart in private.

I drove down the freeway mentally chewing Chip out, alternating between being angry at him for being gone and being angry at him because it was raining and the windshield wipers needed to be replaced; he knew I was terrified of driving that stretch of road in the dark, and if he was home where he was supposed to be I wouldn't have had to. If he was home we would be curled up in front of the bedroom fireplace, the boys would be asleep in their own beds and we could plan the holidays together. If he was home I wouldn't have felt the need to leave my sons with their grandparents to be alone for a few days, I wouldn't be on that damned road, and I would have seen past the tears in my eyes to the car that spun out of control just ahead of me.

If he had been home, I never would have hit it head on.

The words flew out of Doug's mouth as quickly as he flew through the exam room door. "Oh my God, are you all right? Are you hurt? Did you break anything – ?"

With the door open I could hear the commotion of the emergency room, the wail of sirens outside and the moans of people shuffling down the hallway. Doug was breathless and a little disheveled, dressed in old sweatpants and a t-shirt, the laces from his shoes flapping behind him. "I'm fine, Doug. Just a little banged up, that's all."

He grabbed my chart from the holder on the door. "You hit your head."

"Small bruise." I tapped my forehead. "No bleeding, my eyeballs are not hanging out of their sockets, and I did not launch through the windshield."

He frowned and looked back at the chart. "Do they want to keep you over night?"

"No, when I said I would leave here with a genuine, certified physician, they said I could leave."

"Did you tell them I was certified or certifiable?"

I slid off the table and carefully set both feet on the floor. Every muscle was beginning to ache, my arms felt like someone had tried to rip them from my shoulders. "I'm not really sure," I told him. "Could have been either."

"Get back on that table," he demanded, serious. "I want to see for myself that you're really okay."

I hopped back on. "You just want to peek under my shirt."

"Well, that too." He lifted my shirt and looked at my back, pressing cool fingers into my skin, his hands running along my spine and my ribs, gently probing at my neck and shoulders. "Did any of that hurt?"

"Not really."

"Stand up."

I slid off the table again.

"Standing there, does anything hurt? Feet, hips, lower back?"

"My feelings are going to be hurt if you don't get me out of here in the next three minutes. I'm fine, Doug. My car is totaled and I broke a fingernail, but I swear, I'm fine."

He slipped his arms around me and hugged gently. "I'm sorry, I was just worried. The entire drive up here I kept thinking the worst."

"Thank you for coming to get me," I said, standing on my toes to kiss his cheek. "I didn't want to call my dad and then get the boys upset. I'm sorry if I pulled you away from anything fun."

"Laundry. Very fun. Did they give you anything for pain?"

"Motrin." I held up the bottle to show him. "But I haven't taken anything yet, I had other plans for pain tonight."

"Such as?"

"Take me to a bar," I said. "A good one."

The bar we wound up at was on the I-80 frontage road near the University of California in Davis. It was lodged between a string of car dealerships and cheap motels, so out of place that no one ever would have guessed it was there with a only quick glance when driving by on the freeway. It was a college hangout, a revolving door of students hoping to score a pitcher of beer long before their twenty first birthdays, manned by a surly, sleepy looking grad student who checked IDs and stamped the back of every other hand with "No Booze For Yooze." He waved Doug in and demanded to see my driver's license.

"I'm an old fart with a hot chick," Doug groaned. "I used to like it here."

It was too brightly lit, decorated like a fast food place gone very, very wrong. It was littered with tiny square red laminate tables and metal chairs that were too cold and hard, designed to get people in and out as quickly as possible. We chose a table as far away from the center of commotion as we could, away from the juke box and beat up pool table on the other side of the room.

I looked around while Doug went to the bar to get drinks; this place was everything Chip said a bar should not be. The bar in the Charybdis hinted at being upscale; it was immaculately clean with thickly padded booths and barstools designed to keep people there, let them smell the food from the dining room, make them hungry and happy at the same time. The lighting was understated and it felt warm; it was a place you could stay and relax, order food if you wanted, or a few drinks if you didn't.

Chip would hate the place Doug took me to.

All I wanted was to deaden the growing ache in my back and legs. The décor didn't matter, the alcohol did. Doug brought a pitcher of beer to the table and a very large glass of something blue.

"Blue Hawaiian," he said. "Trust me, you'll like it."

I liked it enough that I had three more before we left.

"What are your plans for tomorrow?" he asked. "Your first full kidless day."

"I'm sleeping in. If you call me before noon, you'd better be bleeding to death."

"I doubt I'll be up by then myself, but if I am I might wander over to the hospital and spend some time in the library to do a little research."

"Sounds like fun."

"It's necessary. I want to know a little more about what Spider is facing and what his options are before I start dragging him from doctor to doctor. I suspect there's not much that can be done."

He said it as if he had accepted the inevitable. It was too easy for me to brush it off with platitudes – "oh, you'll love him no matter what, etc. ad nauseum" – but I knew he was more conflicted than he was letting on. If not for the distraction of me smashing my car into someone else's brand new Chevy, though it wasn't completely my fault, he would be at home, sitting in front of a TV he wasn't watching, agonizing over his son's future.

Instead, he was deliberately getting me drunk, making small talk and munching on stale popcorn.

"My folks are already talking about Christmas," he said with a sigh. "Apologizing because they made plans to go on a cruise before they knew Kris might not be home. Now they want Spider and I to go with them."

"So go. It might be fun."

"Christmas on a boat with my parents doesn't sound like Christmas. Spider doesn't even know it's coming, but I'd still like to put up a tree for him, tease him with presents and get his picture taken with Santa."

"Nicky has already asked about going to see Santa," I said. "I don't know what I'll tell him when he asks if Chip will be home, and you know he's going to ask."

"Just tell him the truth, that you don't know."

"If I tell him that one more time the poor kid is liable to lose it altogether. If he could just talk to Chip, it would make all the difference in the world."

We both knew that wasn't going to happen and I didn't need for him to point that out. Wherever Chip was he wasn't going to dial home or even drop an anonymous postcard in the mail.

"You know, it's not really as hard as I thought it would be," I said, blinking the fuzz of three drinks away from my eyes. "I mean, I miss him, obviously, but it occurred to me that I was doing fine without him. I function perfectly well on my own."

Doug nodded his agreement. "Handling Spider alone isn't the monumental task I expected, either. But face it, we've had each other to lean on. You're there to watch my kid when Mrs. Cooper can't. I don't know how single parents without this kind of support do it. I'd be very lonely without you, you know."

"I'm sure you'd find things to do, Doug. You had a life before you got married, you know."

"Yeah, but I didn't have a two year old son, and I had Chip to hang around with."

"I don't want to hear about him having fun," I said.

"You'd prefer to hear about him miserable?"

"Right now? Damn straight."

He was looking into the bottom of his glass, staring at beer foam. "Not gonna do it. Not gonna say anything I might later get my ass kicked for."

"I won't kick your ass."

"Chip might."

"My lips are numb."

Doug laughed abruptly. "Darlin', yer drunk."

"I am," I admitted, "and my butt hurts from sitting here too long. We need to get out of here."

We left the noise of the bar and went out into the cold night, leaned up against his car, and stared into the sky. The rain clouds were already gone, leaving it crisp and twinkling with starlight. Doug sighed hard, turning his head to look at me.

"You are *so* plastered," he said. "And I had way too much to trust myself to drive."

"Then we have a problem."

"Yep," he grunted. "A cab from here would cost about a hundred dollars."

"We could walk but that would take, what, about a week?"

"Yep."

"Well… we don't have kids to get home for and no one else is waiting up for us. We could walk down to one of those motels and stay there, stretch out and watch some TV while we sober up."

"You'll be sober in about three days."

I grabbed him by the sleeve and started walking, hoping I wasn't weaving as horribly as it felt like I was. He trailed behind a few steps and then caught up, slipping an arm around my shoulders as we walked the rest of the way.

The room was cheap but warm, and the TV worked. I kicked off my shoes and flopped down on the bed, trying to find the right channel for the news. Doug stood in the middle of the room, looking lost, swaying from side to side.

"One bed," he grunted.

"So?"

"I told you before, I sleep nekkid, and I know you'll peek.

"I might. Just keep your sweatpants on for one night. Or sleep standing up. It doesn't matter to me."

He kicked his shoes off and sat down on the bed next to me. "I'm not wearing any underwear, you know."

"I know," I laughed. "Your sweats don't hide much."

He blinked rapidly, trying to keep his eyes open. "You better not hog all the blankets, either."

"I will," I promised.

If he had a comeback for that, I missed it because I fell asleep as soon as he turned out the light.

I woke later, dim buzzing of the TV filling the room. My head was on an unfamiliar shoulder, fingers pressed into the flesh of an unfamiliar stomach. He smelled like soap and baby shampoo, his skin much softer than I expected, baby fine hair splashed across his chest, trailing down his stomach. I lifted myself up onto an elbow, head still swimming with the after effects of so many drinks , and leaned over to look at him.

His eyes were open, blearily looking back at me; he reached up and pushed hair out from my face, fingers brushing against my cheek. I could still smell beer on his breath, tangy and almost sweet. I leaned over and kissed him on the lips, lightly at first, but when he began to kiss back it became more than casual; it was curious and needy, weeks of want that unfolded so quickly I pushed myself to not think. I tore at his clothes with the same kind of anguish that he tore at mine. I didn't stop to think that this wasn't the body I wanted in mine, those weren't the lips I hungered for, those weren't the arms that I wanted holding me, keeping me safe.

It was curious and angry, almost violently passionate, and over before either of us could collect a coherent thought.

By the time I caught my breath I was filled with more

dread than I could have ever imagined possible. Doug was looking at me with the startled expression of dog kicked in the head by its master, a mixture of fear and pleading that I wouldn't hate him. No matter what, just please don't hate me.

All I could do was cry. I rolled over and buried my face in the pillow and sobbed, so very aware that he was still laying there feeling helpless, not wanting to touch me but trying to figure out how to comfort me. He waited until I stopped crying, until my breathing was more even, and then whispered, "I am so sorry."

"Are you sober yet?" I sat up and reached for my clothes, trying to dress without looking at him, hoping he was looking anywhere but at me. "Can you drive now?"

"I think so."

We drove the rest of the way home in silence, forty five minutes peppered by my sniffles and his sighs. When he pulled up in front of my house he started to cut the engine off, but I shook my head.

"No, just go."

"I don't want to leave you alone, Terry."

"I have to be alone," I said, knowing that as soon as I stepped inside that front door I'd hit the floor and curl up to cry until I couldn't manage another tear. "Just go home."

He nodded weakly. "I am sorry," he started.

"I know. God, Doug, so I am."

He waited until I had the door unlocked and was inside before he left; I watched from the window until he turned the corner, and then sat down on the floor, my fingers grabbing at strands of carpet; it felt like something inside me had cracked open, burned and twisted as I spilled blood into my own chest, and I wailed until I fell asleep.

~

The doorbell rang a little after noon. I had managed to peel myself up off the floor an hour or two earlier and stood under a shower, as hot as I could stand it and for as long as I could stand it, scrubbing myself raw with soap and a washrag. I managed to get myself dressed and was trying to talk myself into eating something, even just some dry toast, when the doorbell rang.

I almost didn't answer it. The last thing I wanted to do was face another human being, but I walked to it on automatic pilot and flung it open.

Doug.

I wanted to tell him it was still a bad time and that I couldn't face him much less face myself, but the look on his face stopped me cold. He had his hands jammed into the pockets of his jeans, he hadn't shaved, and his hair was still wild and messed up. He took a breath that caught halfway down, and swallowed hard.

"Kris is home."

Everything – light, pain, joy, thought – drained in one long dark electric sheet from my head out through my fingers and toes.

I woke up on the sofa. Doug had propped my feet up on pillows and was sitting there beside me, his fingers on my wrist as he checked my pulse. Fatigue lined his face, the little cracks that normally come with age darting from the corners of his eyes, dark circles like half moons just above his cheeks. When I opened my eyes he looked up from my wrist, and waited to make sure I was really all right before he spoke. I couldn't stop the tears from slipping over my eyelashes, or the terror that he was going to tell me the one thing I didn't want to hear.

"She was waiting for me when I got home," he explained. "She'd been there since about midnight." And before I could ask he added, "She doesn't know where Chip is. They got separated about four days ago and his standing orders to her were to head straight home if they lost contact for more than twenty four hours."

I didn't know what to ask him, every thought spinning around inside my head refused to form well enough for me to get one out.

"She waited forty eight hours, contacted the agency and then left cash and passports at a prearranged location, and took the first flight she could get home. As far as anyone knows, Chip is alive and probably okay... they just don't know where he is."

"If they don't know where he is," I managed, "then they don't know if he's all right. He could be dead."

"Don't say that."

"But he could be."

He didn't have an answer. At some point his fingers slipped from my wrist and he was holding my hand, trying to offer what little comfort he could.

"Kris wanted to come over," he said. "I didn't think that would be a good idea, you opening the door and finding her there without him."

"Or seeing her after..." I couldn't say it, couldn't admit it out loud.

"She doesn't know," he said. "I told her I went to pick you up in Sacramento, that you'd wrecked the car. She didn't ask anything more than that."

I touched the wild red mark on his neck. "And you had to get her into bed before she noticed this, didn't you?"

"Terry..."

"Don't apologize, Doug. If it had been Chip who came home I know I wouldn't have given you a second thought for a good long time. Nothing personal." I sat up and gave him some space on the sofa. We both leaned back into the cushions, staring at the cold fireplace. "I'm sorry, Doug. I can't even begin to tell you how sorry I am."

"It's not like you tied me up and forced me, Terry."

"But I did start it, didn't I? Be honest, if I hadn't kissed you, would you have made so much as a move in my direction?"

"I don't know."

"You do too know."

"I wanted to," he admitted.

"Before you were drunk?"

"The impulse has hit me several times, yes."

"What do we do now?"

"We pretend it didn't happen. For Kris's sake, at the very least. I can't tell her 'oh yeah, honey, while you were sitting here last night waiting for me and wondering where I was, I was screwing your cousin.'"

"Screwing," I grunted.

"Sorry."

"No. That about covers it, doesn't it? Why try to paint a pretty picture out of mud and horse crap? We screwed our little brains out, Doug. And I'll be damned if I'll say it sucked. For a few minutes there, it was awesome. Goddammit, it was awesome."

Pretending wasn't as difficult as I imagined it would be. I was so hungry for details on where Chip had been – all over Europe it seemed – and what they'd done that facing Kris wasn't torture. She told me everything she could, that they started out in London and followed a trail that took them to Paris, Sicily, Rome, and back to London. That Chip worked with such intensity that getting him to rest was work itself, and that he had started smoking.

"But," she added, "he also quit. Five times."

I couldn't picture Chip with a cigarette dangling from his lips, but if that's what it took to get him home, I could live with it.

"He had a hot lead from a reliable source," she told me over dinner at the Charybdis. "Our guy had used a planted credit card in France and left a paper trail behind him. What we didn't know was whether or not our source had been set up. He wanted to go alone just in case, and told me to come home if he wasn't back in twenty four hours."

"So it was a set up?" Doug asked.

"We're still not sure. The source showed up just fine, he had new leads on the guy and hadn't heard from Chip, but there's nothing to even suggest that Chip was railroaded or that he walked into a trap."

"What," I asked, not sure I really wanted to know, "would suggest he had been caught?"

Kris looked at Doug uncertainly.

"A body," he said evenly. "Chip's body."

Kris's hand was suddenly covering mine. "It's not all that unusual for Chip to go off like this, Terry, not when he sees an opening that's just not obvious to everyone else. His source may have said France but he may have read something else into it and decided to approach from a different angle. If he thought our cover had been compromised he might have gone to Germany first and approached France from there, or he may have realized that the guy we were after wasn't using that credit card, but he had another clue. Once we separated there was no way he'd contact me. He wouldn't risk giving anyone a direct line back to me."

Familiar words, Doug's explanation for why I wouldn't hear from Chip.

So we kept pretending. We fell back into the pattern of picking up each other's kids, having lunch and dinners together, but this time the kids had their Aunt Kris, and Doug had his wife to help him wade through the muck of Spider's hearing problems.

She handled the news with a few tears, but also a stubborn resolution to do whatever she had to for her son.

Spider, they learned in short order, would never hear. He might learn to vocalize, but that wasn't something they could count on. As they prepared to face life with a deaf son, I realized I was preparing myself to face life without a husband.

On Christmas Eve I caved in to Nicky's reasonable and repeated requests that he be taken to the mall so that he could see Santa and tell him what he wanted for Christmas. A little voice in the back of my head grumbled "you're getting cars and books and Legos," but I kept it to myself, and resolved to pay attention when he related his wishes to Santa, and if there was something special I'd pick it up while I did some last minute shopping. I planned on dropping the kids off with Mrs. Cooper for the afternoon while I went grocery shopping, and a side trip to a busy toy store was no more aggravating than facing all the last minute people at Albertsons.

The line for Santa was, thankfully, only half as long as I expected, and Nick waited patiently, almost quietly, for his turn. Paul made it clear that he didn't want to leave my arms; Nicky could go up to that old man and take his chances, but

Paul wasn't going anywhere.

They went through the usual start; yes, Nicky said, I've been a good boy. Yes, that's my brother, but he's scared. He doesn't know what Christmas is, but if you bring him a toy he'll like it. When Santa asked Nick what he wanted for Christmas, he cocked his head and said thoughtfully, "I don't want no toys."

I could feel my breath catch and the lump start to form in my throat.

"All I want is for my Daddy to come home."

Santa looked at me helplessly, and I had no idea what to do.

"I wish I could, but I can't promise you that," Santa told him carefully. "I really wish I could. Isn't there some toy that you want?"

Nick slid off his lap. "No, just my daddy."

He walked away from Santa, who watched him until he reached me, the expression on his face screaming 'I'm sorry.'

I tried to explain to him that Santa could only bring toys, but he pretended not to hear me, and was quiet all the way to Mrs. Cooper's.

For the first time in my life I was dreading Christmas. I had no idea how I'd handle it when Nick would creep into the living room in the morning, hoping against hope that Santa had found a way to get Chip down the chimney and stuffed into his stocking. My parents wouldn't be there until late morning; the only thing standing between Nick and the biggest disappointment of his short life was me.

As I pulled the car out of the grocery store parking lot, I wondered at what point Nick would stop asking for his father. Would this seal it for him, would Chip cease to exist in his son's mind after tomorrow? Nicky wouldn't understand how it felt for me to sit in Chip's car, breath in and smell him there, the longing it gave me and the hope that as long as I could still smell him there, he was alive somewhere. Nicky didn't have the benefit of a closet full of Chip's clothes, wouldn't understand the luxury of putting one of his shirts on and feeling it brush against bare skin. It was a simple fact that the longer Chip was gone, the more likely it was that his oldest son would stop missing him, or forget about him altogether.

I suspected that Paul already had.

I hit every red light on the way home, and cursed each one under my breath. The traffic was heavy, all the last minute shoppers crowding the streets and parking lots, absent minded people not thinking about everyone else around them, pulling out of parking lots without looking, running red lights and stop signs; every single one of them was conspiring against me, I was sure of it. I wanted to get home and get the groceries put away so that I could have some time to myself before picking the boys up, and they were all blocking the way.

Did the world not know that I was in a very bad mood?

Chip's car coughed and sputtered when I pulled it into the driveway, running for a good five seconds after I turned the key. I didn't know if that was a bad thing or not, and had no clue what to do about it. Call Doug? Call a tow truck? Drive it again to get the boys and pray it doesn't break down?

I decided I'd put the groceries away and then call Doug or Kris, maybe one of them would know if it was something simple or serious, and if the latter, they could go get the boys.

Nick probably didn't want to see me, anyway.

I opened the trunk and lifted both bags out, making sure I had my keys in my hand before I slammed it shut. I started to reach up again, heard a soft cough, and feet scraping on the front porch.

The first thing I saw was those tired, worn, dirty white Reebok hightops that I hated so much, and then the long legs hanging off the front steps. He stood up and stepped off the porch, that little boy smile tugging at the corners of his mouth.

I dropped the groceries and practically flew from the car straight into his arms.

"I left my keys in London," he said against my hair. "I didn't feel like going back for them."

"I thought you were dead." Tears were streaming down my face, and I didn't want to let go.

"Not dead." He tilted my head back, his fingers gentle on my chin. "Just misplaced for a while. You gonna kiss me or what?"

"Or what." I ran for the door and unlocked it, grabbed his hand and pulled him inside and up the stairs.

'Ladies and gentlemen,' my father once said, paraphrasing Robert Heinlein, his favorite author, 'remove their dignity with their clothes.'

We left our dignity in a trail up the stairs.

Chip was gentle and sweet; I left scratches across his back and teeth marks on his shoulder.

"My God, I love you," he whispered afterward. "I missed you so much."

His lips lingered on mine, warm and wet. "I can't even begin to tell you how much I love you," I said against them. "I'll start crying again if I try."

"Don't cry." He sat up, pulling me with him. "Damn, you look good."

He hadn't shaved in at least a week, and had tiny flecks of gray in his beard. I ran a finger across his face, his whiskers bristling on my skin, one after another. "I kinda like this," I said, and then it hit me. "Oh my God, Nick is going to get his wish!"

"For his daddy to grow a beard?"

"No!" I told him about Nick and Santa, the pleading look in both their eyes. This would certainly confirm Nick's belief in Santa Claus for the next ten years.

"It's Christmas?" Chip asked, surprised. "Damn, I'm sorry, I lost track of time and forgot."

"Like it matters." I kissed him again, lingering with my fingers still playing with his whiskers. "The only thing we wanted was for you to be here, and you are."

"Nick thinks Santa is bringing me?"

"It's what he hopes more than anything."

"Cool." He grinned. "I'll hide in here until the boys go to bed, and in the morning I'll be sitting under the tree waiting for them."

I started to protest; it would be too hard to keep the kids out of the room.

"I have an ulterior motive, woman," he said. "I love my boys but I want one night alone with their mother. That's what I want for Christmas."

He showered while I went to get the boys, and shaved – "Nick expects the daddy who left, not some creature with fungus on his face," he explained – and then hid quietly the rest of the evening, He read while I wrestled the boys into baths and tried to get Nicky to sleep in spite of how excited he was over Christmas. We waited until long after they were asleep to creep down into the kitchen so that Chip could eat, and when we came back upstairs we made love as quietly as we could, as sweetly as we could, holding onto each other like we were afraid that if we let go, even for a moment, we'd discover it wasn't real after all. That we'd been there only in each others' dreams.

"You have to promise me you won't leave like this, ever

again," I said in the middle of the night, lying on top of him, our noses touching. "This has to be it."

"I don't plan on going anywhere."

"Promise."

"It would have to be something really big for me to even think about it," he said. "I never meant for you to be scared, Terry. I know I should have told you more of what to expect, but I didn't think it would take so long."

"Did you get him?"

"I did."

"And you didn't get hurt?"

"Not a scratch, I swear."

I touched the bite on his shoulder. "Well, you have a few now, mister."

"Rabid woman attacked me this afternoon. I was totally helpless, I swear. Besides, she was so beautiful and she felt so perfect in my arms that I just couldn't help myself. I'm weak that way, you know."

"I think that's what I like about you. Now if this woman were to start kissing you again, and touching you in places you really should have covered up in public" – I kissed his chin and his neck, working my lips down his chest – "would you try to stop her?"

"I don't think I could."

"Would you want to?"

"Well…" he laughed and moaned at the same time. "The woman should be aware that she's going to have to get up at the crack of dawn, and if she keeps up what she's doing, she's gonna be walking funny tomorrow."

"The woman will take it under advisement."

"Don't talk with your mouth full," he admonished.

"Chip!" I started laughing and had to rest my head on

his stomach. "I missed you. I missed this."

"You missed my winky?"

"I missed my Irishman's stupid sense of humor."

"Ah, is that what you're calling it now. I thought it was my winky."

"You dork."

He reached down and pulled me up, rolling until I was trapped under him. "Your Irishman would much prefer to be able to kiss his woman, and he can't do that if you're nibbling on his sense of humor."

"Then what," I murmured against his lips, "do you want to do while you're kissing me?"

He slipped inside me, sighing. "I just want to be with you, that's all. I just want to feel you all around me, and I want to feel you slide right over the edge. Just be with me. Just be with me."

He was quiet then, just the sound of his breath coming in quickening gasps, his lips near my ear, and the small sound that came from the back of his throat. I strained against him, trying to feel every inch of his body with mine, and when we were both able to breath again, to speak without moaning, he placed a kiss behind my ear and whispered, "Merry Christmas."

THREE

1994

Nick

Behind her back, Kevin sometimes referred to Mom as "Our Lady Of Perpetual Floodgates." It never took much to make her cry, and as she sat in the living room trying to tell me about the mistakes she'd made and a part of my father's life he never wanted me to know about – minus the horny details – her eyes filled with tears that stayed there, just a blink away from spilling over her eyelashes.

I wasn't about to justify what she'd done and forgiveness wasn't mine to impart; obviously Dad had managed that just fine without my input. Hearing her tell me everything, though, brought back bigger fragments of memory. I remembered him being gone and I remembered the tension that built steadily while he was away. I remembered missing him as desperately as she must have.

I remembered that Christmas morning, too.

"You shuffled down the stairs," she said. "Your little heart just wasn't in it and you couldn't have cared less. You came downstairs dragging a teddy bear and curled up on the sofa without even looking at the Christmas tree, not until Paul stopped dead in his tracks and then hid behind my legs."

Paul squealed, an uncertain whimper that caught my attention when he darted behind her, peeking around her when he was sure he was safe.

"You slid off the sofa in slow motion. Your father was sitting right in front of the tree and once your feet hit the floor you didn't budge until he held out his arms and told you it was okay, that he was really home. His voice was so even and gentle. 'It's okay, Tiger, I'm really here.'"

"I remember."

"As soon as Paul saw you leap at him, he got brave and let go of me and slowly made his way over... I don't know if he decided it was all right because you were so happy or if he knew what was happening, but he wasn't about to let you get all the hugs. And then it clicked – he remembered he had a father. He actually said 'Daddy.'"

"And you were crying your eyes out," I murmured.

"There were a lot of tears that Christmas, but it was all good."

"For how long?"

One tear finally made it. I looked over at her and she had a single tear slowly rolling over her cheek. "Two weeks. I had to tell him, Nick."

"Why? To ease your own guilt?"

"No, that wasn't even possible. I knew it would kill him, but I owed him the truth. He had to be able to decide if he could trust me even after knowing what I'd done. I couldn't make up his mind for him on something that big."

"So what? He just shrugged it off?"

"God, no. It took us a long time to get back everything I ripped apart."

"But you did."

She nodded. "We managed to work through it before Kevin and Eileen were born."

I looked over at the wall by the fireplace, filled with family pictures, Kevin and Eileen lumped together unwillingly in most of them. The Twins. Always a conjoined thought; it was always "KevinandEileen" or "the twins." They barely had their own identities. KevinandEileen graduated kindergarten. KevinandEileen learned to swim. KevinandEileen want a dog but will settle for a hamster. Eileen was born first, but it was always KevinandEileen.

Dad came home in late December.

They were born in early August.

"Is Uncle Doug their father? Kevin and Eileen's?"

Her deep, cultivated sigh. I heard it as her arm went around my shoulders. "No. Nicky. What made you think he might be?"

"Do the math, Mom."

"I know the math. But I can promise you, Doug is not their father. You can look at Kevin and see that, he looks just like your dad."

"Still."

"They're twins, Nick. Twins tend to come early. I had labor induced six weeks before they were due because I was so sick there towards the end. But I swear, all four of you have the same father."

"Okay." I got up and was going to head upstairs, but stopped when I saw a picture of Uncle Doug and Aunt Kris out of the corner of my eye. "How did they stay friends?" I asked, pointing at the picture.

"I wasn't sure they would. Your dad refused to speak to Doug for almost five months."

"Why did he?"

"It's what I wanted for my birthday," she said. "All I wanted was for life to get back to normal, or for him to at least try to mend things, so he sucked it up and invited them over. He and Doug went out back to fire up the grill and within five minutes got into a loud, explosive fist fight. Doug wound up with four broken ribs, and then it was over. I think he realized if he could forgive me, he could forgive Doug, too."

"What about Aunt Kris?"

"I don't really know, Nick. She never held it against me, not from the moment Doug told her. I don't know why."

I could believe Aunt Kris didn't hold it against her, but I didn't believe she didn't know why.

I went upstairs and looked in on Dad; Kevin was sitting on the bed next to him, reading out loud, his voice rumbling softly. She was right, they did look alike, twins born two and a half decades apart. If Kevin and Eileen were born six weeks early, they were probably just a belated Christmas present. Welcome Home, Merry Christmas, and a Happy New Year.

There was no way she forgot how badly she missed him those few months he was gone, and how exhilarated she was when he came home, showing up on the front porch in the middle of December. She could conjure up the feeling fifteen years later.

Why couldn't she conjure it up two years ago, when it really mattered?

Terry

I should have known that Nick would be able to blink and make the leap of logic that would have him questioning the twins' paternity. I could have related the same story to

Paul, or my parents even, and it would have been weeks before they started ticking the months off on their fingers.

Nick's brain functioned on a completely different level than anyone else's in the family. He talked practically before he could walk, could carry on coherent, complete conversations by the time he was two, taught himself to read before he was four, and blazed through school at a pace that left even his teachers breathless.

Early in his freshman year of high school the administration decided they didn't have enough to offer him and formulated a plan that had him graduating by the middle of what should have been his sophomore year. He hung on for an extra semester; he wanted to spend the rest of the school year his friends – specifically Katie – and that didn't seem unreasonable for a fifteen year old to request. A week after the school year ended he began summer classes at the community college, and by the next spring he was making the commute to the University in Davis.

He managed his higher education without the collective input of his parents; separately we gave him our opinions and allowed him to make his own decisions. If we'd had the guts to face each other and to help him make the transition into the university – if we had been talking from Day One – I doubt I would have felt compelled to tell Nick anything.

But he knew. As much as I felt obligated to give him the truth, for him to have some basic understanding of how screwed up I allowed things to become, I wondered if I hadn't given him more of a burden instead. He had insight into the too human frailties of his parents, and he had no one with whom he could share that.

I had to trust that he could take one look at Kevin and realize I was telling the truth; I had to pray that he didn't spend the next few years of his life searching the faces of his brother and sister for signs of Doug Stone, looking for something he didn't want to find but was sure was there.

Before they were born, I worried that Chip would spend the rest of his life looking and wondering, not trusting what his heart would already know.

The doubts began before I was four months pregnant with them; it had been at least a week since I had seen my feet, and it was too soon. At four months I looked closer to six, and felt as if I had surpassed the eight month point. Chip would jokingly tell me it was two slices of pizza too many, but doubt was flickering in his eyes. Doubt and pain, and a longing I couldn't quite put my finger on.

Like he had with Nick and with Paul, Chip whispered to my growing belly, he sang and rattled off silly stories, but the same incredulous joy wasn't there. He was doing it for the sake of the baby, a child he would claim as his no matter what.

I didn't realize how unsure he was until the night he brought Will Parker home.

Chip's intent was to introduce me to the priest who had been hearing his confessions and listening to him complain – about me, I was sure – for two months, and for the three of us to discuss the sign language classes the church's school ran every week. As determined as he was to never set eyes on Doug again, he loved his godson as much as his own children, and he fully intended that as Spider grew and learned to communicate that we would as well. Nick was old enough to begin learning, and he reasoned that Paul would, too.

"And your next munchkin," Will added. "When's the baby due?"

"Not soon enough," I grumbled.

Chip settled his hand on my stomach. "Would you be-lieve not for five more months? At this rate this kid will be born six feet tall with a basketball in one hand and an NBA contract in the other."

"And if it's a girl?" Will prompted.

The idea didn't faze Chip one bit. "Girls play basket-ball, too."

"He wants a daughter," I told Will. "In the worst way."

"Yep, and we're just going to keep having them until I get one."

We wanted a large family; after Paul was born we talked about how many, and when. I wanted them as close together as possible, in spite of Doug warning me to wait, and I wanted a houseful. Chip just wanted a daughter, and would have as many children as I wanted, as long as he got his little girl.

After Will left I wondered if it would ever happen; I had my doubts that Chip would even be able to touch me again after this baby was born.

We curled up on the couch together; he sat sideways and I wedged myself between his legs, leaning against him, my head tucked under his chin. "What," I asked him, "will you do if Kris tells you to stay out of it and to let them find teach-ers for Spider without your help?"

"Then I'll butt out, but we still have to learn to speak Spider's language if we want to be a big part of his life."

"And you do, don't you?"

"Of course I do." He slipped his hands over the largest part of my stomach, rubbing softly. "How're you feeling?"

"I'm fine, Chip. You need to quit worrying so much."

"It's my job to worry. You feel like crap more often than not... It's hard this time, isn't it?"

"A little."

"Have you told your doctor?"

Just say his name, I thought. *Doug*. You won't choke on it.

"Tell him what? That I'm tired because I have two little boys to raise and they can be a handful sometimes? Chip, it's harder this time because I have more to do than just sit back and watch myself blow up."

He wasn't buying it. "What about the cramps?"

"Ligaments."

"Bullshit. You've been in pain, Terry, and you're so damned huge. This isn't going the way it should."

"How's it supposed to be going?"

"It's not supposed to be so hard. Be honest, you're not enjoying this like you did with Nicky and with Paul."

"Not entirely."

His arms tightened around me. "Just tell me what to do to make it easier for you."

I reached over my head, fingers gently brushing against his cheek. "You're doing plenty already. Just keep spoiling me."

"And you'll tell him?"

I sighed hard. If I didn't give in he'd pester me until I went into labor. "Fine, yes, I'll tell him, but I think you're over reacting. I'm fine."

"So you keep saying."

"What about you?" I reached for his hand, winding my fingers through his. "You're going to confession a lot, and you have these long, deep conversations with Will, but you don't want to go to Mass?"

"No."

"I'd go with you."

"I'm not ready."

"It might help," I said, turning my head to look at him. "You wrestle with so much on your own, and you're obviously trying to ease back into it. I wouldn't mind making my way back to church, too. I'll go if it will help."

He averted his eyes.

"But, I'm part of the problem, right?"

"Don't say that."

"Truth hurts sometimes." I leaned back again. "This pregnancy isn't only hard on me."

"How so?"

"Because you're right, I'm a lot bigger than I was at this point with either Nick or Paul. You've been doing calculations in your head, and you're wondering if it's even yours, right?"

He swallowed hard. "No."

"Come on, Irish. Be honest with me. I've seen the look too many times to ignore it anymore. If this baby comes early, it will break your heart."

"You're my wife. That makes it my baby."

He didn't sound convincing, and I told him so. "It's a big baby, that's all," I murmured. "This is your child, not Doug's. Your flesh and blood. I promise you, Chip, you fathered this baby."

His answer was a warm kiss on the top of my head.

We sat there quietly for a long time; I could tell by the sound of his breathing that he was crying and fighting to stop.

"Are you okay?" I finally asked.

"Sure."

I reached over and ruffled his hair. "You know, Irish, I love you."

His breath caught. "I know," he whispered. His hand went back to my belly, rubbing softly, not even aware of it. "I know."

Nick

Paul kept himself locked in his room rather than face the family; his drunken stupidity wasn't a secret and he knew it. He was aware I'd told Kevin and Eileen and he didn't want to put himself through Kevin's obnoxious teasing, Eileen's stares of disappointment, and especially Mom's quiet disapproval.

He fucked up and he knew it.

He also knew he was lucky Dad was too sick to do much more than ground him.

I wanted someone to talk to, but I knew better than to knock on his bedroom door and feed him something that would make him feel worse than he already did. I couldn't tell Eileen or Kevin; I had no idea what Kevin would do. He would either have all the answers, wisdom far beyond his fourteen years, or he would cough up the most lame jokes he could think of and then go running to mom and tell her he knew.

It occurred to me I could vent at Aunt Kris – cheezus, how in the hell did you forgive her – or even talk to Uncle Doug. Dude, how *could* you? Seriously. How in God's name could you even get it up for my *mom*? Your wife's cousin. You're practically *family.*

Practically, hell, dammit, you *are* family.

The only other person I could talk to about anything this deeply personal was Katie, but she had no right to the knowledge of my parents' stupidities. My mom's secrets were not mine to tell, no matter how much I wanted to vent.

Katie was sitting across a library table from me; she was trying to work on a term paper and I was supposed to be studying for a Spanish test. I stared at my text book, pretending to absorb all the rules of preterite tense forms, occasionally turning the page so that she wouldn't suspect the words were swimming in front of my eyes.

The only thing I wanted to be able to say in Spanish was "Screw this."

All right, I did know how to say "fuck you" but so did Katie and she wouldn't appreciate it.

"Nick." She reached across the table and snatched my pencil out of my hand. "One, that's annoying."

"What is?"

"Tapping this on the table like it's a drum. And two, I've asked you the same question twice. Where are you?"

"I'm sorry. What was the question?"

She rolled the pencil back to me. "It doesn't matter. What's bugging you?"

"Spanish. Yo no quiero hablar español."

"Well, tomorrow you'll want to be able to speak Spanish. What's bugging you?"

"Something my mom said," I told her. "I need to digest it before I can talk about it."

"Sounds big."

I nodded. So big I may never be able to tell you, I thought. And if I did, you'd never look at my mom the same way.

"I can tell you this much," I said, closing my book, "it's making me think that maybe some things are things we shouldn't wait for. You can't count on things staying the same, and you can't count on things not changing or things happening when you think they will."

"That's a lot of things, Nicky."

"I know, I'm not terribly eloquent today."

"Or ever," she snickered.

"I get my point across most of the time."

"And you have a point?"

"At the top of my head," I said, beating her to the insult. "You know, by the end of the spring semester I'll have enough credits to be done with my sophomore year. And you're graduating and turning eighteen."

"And…?"

"And, I was thinking. I want to move out this summer, get an apartment of my own."

"Won't your mom will freak?"

"She won't fight it."

"Don't be so sure."

"No, she won't freak out over me wanting to move out. She might freak out when I tell her I want you to move in with me. If you want to, that is."

She shoved her own book aside. "You want to live together after the school year is over?"

"I'd do it now if I thought we could get away with it."

"Nicky, we always said we would wait until you finished college and I was at least halfway through. We said we weren't ready for that much."

"That's the line I give my parents when they worry that you and I are moving too fast. By the end of the school year I know I'll be ready for it. I was hoping you would be, too."

"My dad will do more than freak," she warned.

"Yeah, but once you turn eighteen there's not a whole lot he can do, is there?" I got out from my chair and slipped into one next to her, sliding my arm around her shoulders. "Think about it. No more sneaking around. No more sex in the back seat of my car. Katie, I'm tired of feeling like a goddamned little kid, trying to hide everything when I know we have every right to be together. I don't want to wait two more years, trying to make my mom think I'm still this freaky little virgin living in the room down the hall."

"You'd still be freaky," she said, kissing my cheek.

"But I'd be a happy freak. And sooner or later our parents will get used to the idea."

"My dad? Never."

"Not even if we got married?"

She pulled away, just a little. "Nick…"

"It's not a formal proposal, not yet. But it will be, I swear. There's not a single reason why we couldn't get married this summer."

"I can think of a few," she sighed. "Rent, groceries… tuition, because if I move out I know my dad won't help out with it."

"I can afford it."

"On what salary, Nick? The fifty dollars a month you get for gas and lunch?"

"You'll have to trust me," I said. "I can afford to support us both, tuition included unless you decide to go someplace like Harvard. And once I turn twenty one, it's definitely not a problem. I'll get my trust fund then."

"You have a trust fund?"

"My dad's pretty well endowed."

"Oh my God." She started laughing, burying her face in her hands. "Now *that* I didn't need to know."

"Pervert." I pulled her hands away from her face. "You know what I mean."

"Nicky, I will never be able to look him straight in the eye again."

"Now who's the freak… Will you just think about it? If you won't marry me this summer, at least move in with me?"

"Well," she ran one finger along my jaw, "the idea of sex someplace other than your car is kind of nice."

The picture of my dad sound asleep in my mom's bed popped into my head.

"Um, you know... we have a place we can go tonight. If you want to."

"Spending your millions on a motel room?"

I stood up, shoving my books into my backpack. "Nope, it's a freebie. Do you want to?"

She gathered up her books, too. "Ever the romantic, Nick. 'Oh yeah, I know a place. Wanna go get laid?'"

"Well, do you?"

"You better be glad I love you, or I'd probably kick you in the nads right now."

"Not if you want to have sex with me." I laughed when she rolled her eyes. "We don't even have to have sex. It's just someplace we can go to be alone without worrying some cop is going to knock on the window."

"We wouldn't want that to happen again, now would we?"

At least not while my pants were down around my ankles. Again.

She had second thoughts when I pulled into the parking space my dad's car usually occupied. She hesitated getting out of the car and very tentatively walked up the stairs. I tried reasoning with her – I need to check up on the place, anyway – but she was still uncertain.

"Katie," I said, once the door was unlocked, "my dad will never know. Paul brings girls here all the time and he's never been caught."

"That's not exactly it, Nick."

"Then what?" I flipped the light on and pulled her in, making sure I set the deadbolt and chain. "It's not like my dad will come home tonight."

She leaned against me, setting her forehead against my chest. "It just feel like this means a little more, that's all. This is real, not like a couple of kids fooling around."

"We're not fooling around."

"Besides…"

"Besides what?"

She laughed nervously. "I've never seen you naked, you know, not really. I know what you feel like, Nicky, I just don't know what you look like."

"All the more reason to leave the lights on."

"Nick!"

"Nick nothing. I'm not freaky looking. And I *do* want to see you naked." She didn't move. "We don't have to, Katie. Not if you don't want to."

"But I do."

"Then what's the matter?"

"Nothing." She finally pulled away. "You just have to promise me a couple things."

"Anything." My inner child was jumping up and down, and if she listened closely I'm sure she could hear him squealing 'yesssss, we're gonna *do it!*' "Just name it."

"You have to make sure I'm home by curfew."

"Not a problem."

"And you can't laugh if I stare. Cause I know I'm going to."

"You can stare," I said. "Personally, I'm going to gawk."

Terry

"Sprawled out like that, he almost looks innocent," Doug grunted, dropping into a chair by the fireplace. "His fever is down, which is good, but he's still somewhere between the Outer Limits and the Twilight Zone."

Chip stirred, rolling onto his side, his back to us.

"At least we know where the kids get it from," I said.

"Yours and mine. Is he still throwing up a lot?"

"A couple times a day. That and he spits food at me. Ever been doused with regurgitated jello? It's wonderful."

After four days Chip was the same. No better, no worse. He knew where he was only in the sense that he could stumble out of bed and into the bathroom, but he gave no hint that he knew I was there with him, no sign that he realized he was home.

The kids accepted his presence there as a given; where else would he be if he couldn't take care of himself? Kevin read to him constantly, interrupted only by school and the times I had to ask him to leave to make sure Chip was really getting some rest. Eileen came in a dozen times a day to feel his forehead and ask if she could do anything. With the exception of Paul, they all behaved as if life were teetering on returning to normal, that they weren't expecting a miracle when the flu passed and he was awake.

"Kris said Paul made it home all right the other night," Doug ventured.

"More or less. I don't know what the hell his problem is. On one hand I wish Spider's girlfriend had called the cops instead of just a cab, on the other..."

"Does he normally drink like that?"

"Not as far as I know. What the *hell* was he thinking? He won't talk to anyone, he just comes home and hides in his room until dinner, helps with the dishes and then hides again."

"Think drinking is his only vice?"

It took me a moment to digest that. "God, I hope so."

"I can test him, you know."

I was tempted; I wanted some explanation for Paul's

temper. Something had to make sense.

"Not yet," I finally said. "But if you could talk to him... he won't talk to me."

"And if in talking to him I think I need to pursue more?"

I nodded.

"You don't think that's it, though, do you?"

"No. The changes in him have been too sudden. One day he's fine, the next he's drunk and ripping into me so loudly that Chip struggles out of his stupor long enough to stumble out and ground the kid for a month. I almost wish I'd had a camera to capture the look on Paul's face when he realized Chip was there."

"Probably sobered him up quick."

"Whatever's bugging him may be my fault, Doug. The kids are all old enough to start asking intelligent questions and I'm not sure I want to give them the answers. I've already been raked over the coals by Nick."

"I'm surprised Nick never demanded answers before. Out of all of them he's the one I would have expected to get nosey and start pressuring you – "

"He knows," I said suddenly. "He overheard me talking to Brad and I had to explain to him... you need to be forewarned. I doubt he'd say anything to Spider, but you never know. He was pretty upset."

"What business is it of Brad's?"

"It's none of his business," I told him. "He doesn't know who, just that it happened. Come on, once in a while I need someone to talk to. I'm really not comfortable dwelling on it with you, and I'd never throw it back in Kris's face. Brad is a nice, neutral person, and I'm sorry if it bothers you, but that's just how it is."

"Okay, okay, okay. I don't have the right to tell you who

you can unload on, anyway."

"I'm wishing I hadn't told Nick. I had no business giving him details I knew would make him so uncomfortable. Yet at the same time I felt like I owed him the truth, all of it."

Doug was also wishing I hadn't told him. He was watching Chip and not looking at me.

"I worry about what I did to his relationship with you and with Kris, too," I added.

"We'll be fine. Just give him some time to think about everything."

I thought he needed more than time, and every adult he would normally be willing to confide in was involved. I ripped my son's support system right out from underneath his feet.

"He can talk to Kris," Doug said after a while. "It affected her as much as anyone and she was able to comes to terms with it before I even had the guts to tell her. She could help him wade through the confusion. Or Parker. He helped Chip get through it."

"Will has his hands full trying to get us all through this idiocy of a separation."

"Then I'll give Kris a heads up."

Chip was stirring uneasily; I began a mental countdown, because in less than ten seconds I knew he'd be out of bed, losing what little lunch I had managed to coax down him.

I'd never seen him this sick.

"He's this sick," Doug said after I helped Chip back into bed, "because he doesn't take care of himself. He eats like an eight year old. Macaroni and cheese for dinner, with a potato chip chaser. Donuts for breakfast. Real nutrition is a Snickers bar and a Diet Coke at lunch. He's just run down, Terry."

"Obviously he's still working out."

"You're peeking," he laughed.

"He's naked, I can't help it."

"And he'll be okay."

"Go talk to my middle son," I said, "and quit picking on me."

He got up, reaching for his bag. "Fine. I'll go. But I know what you're going to do. You're going to sit on the bed and pretend to read, and you're going to start peeking again."

Nick

Suddenly Stupid.

That's how I felt, anyway. I stumbled through classes and meals the rest of the week, barely able to focus on anything other than Katie. My brain was nothing but mush, coughing out these saccharine, pseudo-poetic thoughts about her and the evenings we were spending in my dad's apartment.

Snow in the middle of summer.

Sweet wine at the end of a long day.

If I'd said any of them out loud I would have been laughed off campus, from the dinner table, out of the line at the drug store, or anywhere else I was when the grossly sweet phrases hit me.

Katie would laugh her ass off. She'd be flattered, but it would only reinforce the notion that I was her own personal little dork.

The surging gag-me kind of thoughts made up for any residual guilt I had over a broken promise; I told myself that if anyone would understand, it would be my dad. Evenings at his apartment, alone with Katie, were giving me a much clearer picture of what I wanted, and I definitely wanted it to be with her.

Five nights playing house with Katie gave me a tiny glimpse of the passion my dad must have felt for my mom.

Of course he forgave her.

Absolving a moment of pent up terror and lust gave him the next decade and a half with someone he loved more than anything in the world. He had to forgive her; if he hadn't, he would have ceased to exist.

If I loved Katie as much as I did, how much had he loved my mom back then? And if he could forgive her, why couldn't I?

She still loved him. If she didn't he wouldn't be zonked out in her bed.

For all practical purposes, Dad had been asleep for six days. I had been little to no help at all.

I went home early for a Friday, reluctantly forgoing another night with Katie at the apartment. The relationship would not, I was determined, becoming nothing but sex whenever and wherever we could get it. I wanted there to be at least as much affection. I took her to a movie and then took her home, explaining that I needed to spend some time at home, give my mom a break from taking care of my dad.

She understood.

That shouldn't have surprised me, but it did. Any of Paul's girlfriends would have whined like crazy. "You don't loovvvve me."

Of course he didn't love them, but that was beside the point.

I found Mom sitting on the bed next to Dad, nose buried in some thick paperback book that she'd been trying to get through for a month. The bedroom door was open but I knocked lightly before going in.

"You're home early," she said, closing the book. "Didn't have an argument with Katie, did you?"

I sat at the edge of the bed, careful not to send waves

that would disturb Dad. "Are you kidding? If I fought with her she'd die of shock."

"You spoil her," she accused affectionately.

"Not too much." I hesitated; she was looking at me curiously, waiting for whatever I obviously wanted to say. "Look, I've been a real shit this week and I'm sorry. Whatever happened, happened, and it really doesn't matter. It just threw me for a loop, that's all. I guess for the last couple days I just wanted to blame you for every problem this family has ever had."

"I'm to blame for a lot of it," she said quietly, and before I could protest, she was shaking her head. "I am, Nick, and I know it. A big part of me believed your father would fight back and try to win me over. I forgot how insecure he can be."

"Him, insecure?"

"He's never understood why I love him so much. After everything had happened, he said he expected me to leave him, not the other way around. He blamed himself and thought he pushed me into it, and thought that if he hadn't left in the first place or if he was worthy of me, nothing ever would have happened. He loves without reserve, but he has a hard time letting people love him back. I think it's that insecurity that kept him from kicking the front door in, and I let my anger push that fact from my head... by the time I remembered it was too late. So, you see, I really am responsible for the way our family is falling apart."

Someone's voice was whispering in the back of my brain. It was gentle and warm, and definitely not mine. "It's not just your fault, Mom. He hasn't had the guts to face you at all. He never should have lied, should he? If you had known all along he was working with this agency, none of it would have happened. You might have had one hell of a fight, but that would have been it. Dad traded his secret for a few years of comfort, so don't shoulder all the blame yourself. You both made mistakes."

"Who are you, Nicky?" She tossed the book aside and pulled me into a tight, warm hug. When I'm forty I'll still like the way she hugs; simple, direct affection. "God, you're too smart to be my son."

"Grandpa says I mutated in the womb."

"My honeymoon baby," she laughed. "You were such a surprise. I didn't even realize I was pregnant with you for such a long time."

"It's your hair," I teased. "The roots tickle your brain and the blondeness leaks in."

"Very funny." She tugged at my hair. "Is that your problem? Already leaking?"

"No, it's strictly a female thing."

"Maybe it's Paul's problem."

"Paul won't say what his problem is, but I have to admit, I really haven't asked him much."

"You don't have to, Nicky. You're his brother, not his father."

"I don't mind."

"Is it hard?" she asked. "Being their big brother? You've always taken it so seriously."

"Not so that I've noticed. It helps that they're not all total morons."

All right, that was debatable.

"Mom, you have to quit worrying so much about Paul and start worrying about yourself. He's probably obsessing over a fight with Monica or a bad grade. Seems to me you have your own relationship to work out."

"Too late, Champ. Like Doug said, I fumbled on the ten yard line and there's no time out left."

"Bullshit. Don't short change him. You love him and he loves you. I've heard him say it enough."

"Still – "

"Draw the line, Mom. When he's coherent and has had a day or two to shake the grogginess away, tell him in no uncertain terms that you still love him and you want your marriage back in every sense of the word. He just might surprise you."

"It's not that easy."

"So it's not easy. What have you got to lose?"

"Nicholas…" Barely a whisper.

"You know, someday we'll be gone. I'll probably move out next summer, and Paul the year after that. Kevin and Eileen won't be far behind. You'd be alone in this house, Mom. Eight bedrooms to yourself. Grandpa's huge study and a pool table to play with, alone. A swimming pool to splash in, alone. You seem pretty determined that you'll never remarry and your religion will keep you from ever living with someone. What have you got?

"And what about Dad? Leave him in that little apartment with just a cat for company? Turning forty was hard enough on him. What about fifty? Or sixty? I don't think he'll live that long. He doesn't have anything to live *for*. Just Max and a picture of you that he keeps by his bed."

"Stop it, Nick."

I had reduced her to tears. Baby blue eyes running wildly. And, I hoped, the image of two old and lonely people was etched into her mind.

"If you ever loved him at all, Mom, you have to win him back. Chase after him like crazy, just don't give up. He'll surprise you, I know he will."

I got off the bed and headed for the door. When I turned around she had tears streaming down her face, but she was looking at Dad, not at me.

"Men like to be seduced, too, you know," I said before I closed the door.

I know she heard me.

I just hoped she would listen.

Terry

"All right, Irish. Wake up and tell me what the hell we're going to do. We can't very well go on like we have been, can we? Our kids won't put up with that anymore. We have to do something for them if we won't do it for ourselves. One of us has to find enough strength to reach out first and I don't know if I have it.

"It would be so easy for me to wrap myself around you and stay there until you woke up. Maybe you'd be mad as hell but you'd get my message, wouldn't you? Or would you think it was just a sleepy mistake, my guard down when I least expected it?

"And stolen kisses – your lips feel just as right to me now as they did years ago. You kiss back in your sleep, did you know that?

"I'm terrified of asking you to stay. If you said no I don't know what I'd do, and if you said yes... I just don't know. I'm terrified of living the rest of my life without you. Nick is so damned right. We're dooming ourselves to bitter, lonely lives.

"How can I even consider giving up on my Irishman? Who else is going to make me laugh when I'm ready to crawl inside myself? Who else could wake me from a nightmare and make me feel safe? Who else can make me feel safe when I'm awake and the whole world is spinning too fast for me to hold on?

"Eighteen years, Chip. We've wasted too many of them already. All these hits and misses, and look where we are now. We've made more mistakes than either of us can keep track of. There's enough hurt between us to keep us in therapy until we die. But we never stopped loving each other, did we?

"What the hell did I do to us?

"Is it too late to untangle this mess? Are the threads that hold us together strong enough to be tugged on while we try to straighten them out? We could survive if one or two of them frayed in our hands... what do we do if they snap at the lightest touch?

"What about our kids? God, Irish, I've been so wrapped up in my own self pity that I don't even know them anymore. We don't have nearly the relationships we once did. Nick grew up before I realized it. Paul is running from some private hell he won't share. Eileen is on the outside looking in, and Kevin has become so quiet and studious that it's surreal. He's crossing the line between piety and devotion.

"I never noticed. Our baby boy is chasing after God and we haven't been there to help him find the way. We gave him the keys to a powerful vehicle and didn't tell him how it worked. I don't know how to help him, Chip. I don't know how to help any of them.

"Eighteen years ago it seemed perfectly clear to me. I knew exactly what I wanted with my life and you helped me find it. When did I lose my confidence with you?

"Our kids used to think we were perverts, did you know that? We amused them. Nick grew up with affection being a matter of fact in his life. Paul never had to question whether or not we honestly loved each other. Eileen and Kevin watched it crumble when they were too young to comprehend what a phenomenal mistake I was making. They don't remember catching us necking on the couch or stumbling into the kitchen late at night to find me feeling you up.

"Nick remembers. He clings to that. He learned about love by watching us. If we can't right the wrongs in our marriage, what will that do to his confidence in his relationships? Are we giving him the message that it's perfectly all right to walk away from a commitment when it gets hard?

"I want our children to understand what a sacrament this is. I don't believe in divorce, you know that. I would cave in and let you have one if I thought you really wanted one, but I would never cooperate with an annulment. No one is going to tell me that we weren't really married.

"You're my life. God, why didn't I see it then? Haven't we spent enough nights whispering to each other, laying claim to our devotion?

"I want you home, Irish. I want your body in my bed and your soul reconnected to mine.

"Nick doesn't think I know the message I wanted you to hear on your birthday. I knew what I wanted you to think, and it didn't escape me that you're wearing it. I still have your old crucifix, but I'm afraid to touch it. I have a nasty feeling that if I set a finger on it Christ will come right off. I won't be the one to make the whole thing crumble.

"I love you. If nothing else I have to make you understand that.

"I'm not sure I have the strength for anything else. What if I reach out and you're not there?

"Recover my fumble, Irish. The game's not over yet."

Nick

Paul was stretched out on my bed, his feet propped up on the wall, and he was staring numbly at a poster near the ceiling. I didn't think he was all that interested in my collection of old movie posters and I didn't think his intent was to leave sweaty footprints on the white latex paint.

"Fight with Monica?"

"Something like that," he grunted, not looking over.

I kicked my shoes off and then shoved aside the pile of dirty clothes on my chair. My computer was running and logged online.

"My modem's fried," he said. "Hope you don't mind."

"I'll bill you later for the time. So what happened, did she give you your walking papers?"

He sat up and spun around, leaning where his feet had been. "We're not breaking up."

"I'm not a dentist, Paul. I'm not going to pull teeth to get it out of you."

"I never said I wanted to talk about it," he grumbled.

Fine. He was splayed out on my bed, using my computer, not making any effort to get up and go into his own bedroom. Of course he didn't want to talk about it.

"How come you're not out with Katie?" he asked.

"I thought I should come home for once."

"I suppose she accounts for your shit eating grin all week. What'd she do, learn some kinky new trick?"

"Mind your own business. Anything Katie and I do is personal."

"Yeah? Well, if Dad suspected you were shagging her in his apartment he'd have a fit. You're not real sly, Nick. Mom's probably the only one who doesn't know where you disappear to every night."

"So I'm not sly. Dad's never going to know. And you can't tell me you've never taken Monica there."

"Never said I didn't. Just don't get caught. Dad might be cool about what we do but he was pretty obvious how he felt about us using his apartment."

"He'll never know," I repeated.

Paul grabbed my pillow from the head of the bed and clutched it like a stuffed animal. All his confidence and self possession was gone. He looked more like my little brother than Kevin. "What do you think they'd do if I quit school?"

"Before or after they skinned you alive?"

"I'm serious."

"Mom would cry for about a week and Dad would go ballistic *if* he didn't have a coronary. What the hell, anyway?"

"I'd rather work."

"Doing what? Who the hell would even hire you? You've never even had a part time job. Busing tables for Dad once in a blue moon doesn't count."

He took a few deep breaths. "I'm in deep trouble, Nick. Up to my neck at least."

Paul the clown, the crazy, self-assured mediator of the few arguments our parents dared have where any of us could hear, had last cried in front of me when he was about five years old and had broken his leg when he missed the tree branch he was reaching for on a dangerous swing from a higher limb. Paul preferred to laugh, he followed our parents around and made obnoxious kissing noises when he knew they were angry with each other. He teased Eileen with kindergarten level jokes when she thought she was too mature to laugh at them. He hated tears and wasn't especially tolerant of anyone, other than Mom, who cried easily.

He curled up on my bed and I watched him fall apart,

crying harder and with more anguish than I had ever seen in my life.

If it had been Eileen I would have hugged her until the worst of it was over. I wasn't sure how to deal with a brother who was nearly my size and more wrapped up in being macho sobbing wildly. If he needed to be comforted like that, I wasn't able to do it for him.

I waited it out, staring down at my feet, until he calmed down and regained a measure of control.

And when he told me, at least I understood.

I wasn't sure anyone else would.

Chip

I woke to half of my fantasy; I was flat on my back in the waterbed, sunlight streaming through the open window and a dust mote or two floating over my face. The only thing missing was the small, lively blonde curled suggestively around my body.

My head was aching and it felt as if someone had slammed a bowling ball into my gut, but I was obviously home. The bed sloshed when I shifted; water was rushing through the pipes from the bathroom just a few yards away.

I wanted to know how I got there in the first place.

I settled back into the pillow and tried to remember. I was forty. That bare fact glared at me viciously. I spent my birthday struggling to keep my temper around all four of the kids, spent the rest of the evening in church, and then what? I went home and paid homage to the Porcelain God.

Then – nothing. I wake to find myself in a bed that had begun to exist only in my dreams.

My fantasy in flesh crept from the bathroom stark naked and dripping wet. I watched her cross the room to the dresser, an arm flung loosely over my eyes to protect her from the knowledge that she was being carefully scrutinized.

I was more than willing to compromise the lady's body; her dignity I preferred to leave intact.

With that same thought came the realization that I was sleeping in her bed and had no idea why. This was not a woman I was casually acquainted with; I knew her body as well as I knew my own. If it bothered her to be admired, that, I reasoned, was her problem.

I propped her pillow on top of mine and eased back, watching her quietly. If not for the time and distance between us it could have been a morning not unlike hundreds of others.

She was my wife, dammit. I ogled to my heart's content.

She was so intent on getting a comb through her hair that she didn't notice me watching her. This was better than any fantasy I had created. This was flesh and blood.

"Nice view," I muttered after a while, voice fuzzy from the cotton dryness of my mouth and lips. "I died and made it to heaven, didn't I?"

I expected the towel to be snatched up indignantly. To my delight she walked over to me quite naked and not a bit self conscious about it. "Not dead," she said softly, sitting on the edge of the bed. She touched cool fingers to my forehead. "You had us worried, though. You've never been this sick, Chip."

My disappointment was right on par with a ten year old who expects a new bike for his birthday but gets underwear instead. The grogginess clouding my head should have told me I wasn't there because of anything than might have passed between us. "Sick?" I managed.

"Nasty case of the flu. Nick found you passed out cold in your apartment."

"And he brought me here."

She nodded. "He couldn't have very well left you there. You were sick enough that Doug was close to sticking you in the hospital."

"How long have I been here?"

"A week."

I'd been out of it for a week. Sleeping right next to her, no doubt, the entire time. She was just nursing someone back to health. Nothing special. She'd do it for anyone. I would have swallowed my heart but my throat was too dry.

"Thirsty?"

I nodded. "Hungry, too."

My angel of mercy had a glass of water in my hand in less than a minute but refused to feed me until she talked to Doug.

"I've seen you throw up enough for one week," she reprimanded lightly. "Think you'll survive until he gets here?"

I thought I might.

"How are you feeling?"

"Don't know." I wasn't sure. My head felt stuffed with cotton and my gut felt like someone had a tight grip on my stomach. She was regarding me carefully; what was she hiding behind that cool demeanor? She was holding something back; perhaps, you're better so get the hell out of my house?

"The kids will be so glad to see you. Poor Kevin is going hoarse reading to you."

"Seriously?"

She slid off the bed and started dressing. I hid my disappointment as much as I could, though watching her dress was almost as nice as imagining the clothes coming off. "He's spent at least two hours a night reading to you. By now you should be able to recite half his homework, half of the novel he's reading for English, and about a quarter of the Bible. He thinks you'll soak it up subconsciously."

What else would two people who haven't seen each other for two of the longest years of their lives talk about?

Four goddamned teenagers.

I love my kids but they were the last thing I wanted to talk about.

"Do you need to go back to sleep?" she asked. "You're looking a little tired still."

"Groggy. I think I've had enough sleep for a while."

How in the hell, I wondered, watching the shirt fall over her shoulders, did we get so strained with each other? We should have been able to talk about anything.

"Mind if I borrow your shower?" I swung my legs over the edge of the bed, carefully gauging how much my head was swimming. "I probably look as bad as I feel."

She was about to tell me to stay put, but sighed and asked, "Need help?"

Foolishly, without thinking, I told her no. I could have had her out of those clothes and standing under a spray of hot water just by asking for a little help.

Shit for brains, as Paul would say.

I tried to tell myself that what I was thinking was wrong; I came out of the shower and spread myself over the bed, air drying and swallowing back the intermittent nausea. I wasn't above using my body as bait.

She tossed a pair of shorts at me.

"Your daughter might waltz through that door, Irish."

I sighed and slipped them on.

I had forgotten that I could be squeamish when it came

to baiting my hook. I had made a move, though, however awkward.

The next move was up to her.

Terry

As horrible and selfish as it was, I hoped Doug would tell him he was still too sick to get up. Anything to keep him there a little bit longer. I lingered in the back of the room while Doug performed a cursory exam, pronouncing Chip "fit enough."

Chip started to get out of the bed, only to be pushed back by the doctor's hand.

"Not today. Stay put for the time being."

Thank you, Doug.

"Enjoy the room service while you've got it. You're still pretty weak."

The smile that came to Chip was full of doubt. In the three hours he had been awake I saw his face turn from moments of weariness to contentment and back again. I wanted to know what was brewing behind those green eyes.

I regretted making him get dressed after his shower. It wasn't until he pulled the shorts on and let out a long, sad sigh that I realized he was making a pass, as weak as it was.

I blew my one and only chance. There were no more remote overtures the rest of the day. Any opportunities were destroyed by kids excited to see their father with his eyes actually open. We barely had a chance to make small talk, much less begin on the things that were bothering us. I sat on the bed and listened while Kevin read him the rest of the chapter he'd been working on the night before, and watched Chip drift off as soon as Kevin left.

His eyebrows were furrowed together furiously in his sleep.

In the morning, I promised myself, we would talk. I'd bar the door and lock the kids out if that's what it took, but I intended to have my say.

Chip

Waking up alone is hard; waking up next to a woman you alternately adore and loathe is excruciating.

I woke just before dawn, five thirty according to the clock by the bed, and rolled onto my side to watch her sleep. She was curled in a tight ball around her pillow, hair in thin wisps across her face. Not much had changed. I stirred once in the middle of the night and found her wrapped around me, one leg resting suggestively between mine, her face buried against my neck.

Close to my fantasy, anyway.

I made damn sure that I didn't move. I barely breathed, avoided any twitch or shiver that would make her move. An hour later she sighed and rolled away, onto her back, arms stretched out over her head.

I'd be lying if I didn't admit to stealing a long kiss.

Most of me wished she would wake in the middle of that kiss, but a part of me was terrified that she would. I was pushing at that invisible line she had drawn down the middle of the bed. It was better, I reasoned regretfully when I was fully awake, to avoid the inevitable confrontation. I crawled out of bed, careful to not make waves.

My clothes were folded neatly on top of the dresser, waiting as if she knew I would leave. I dressed in the dark, shoving socks into my shoes so that I could put them on downstairs and avoid the slap of my sneakers on the wood.

Leaving that bedroom was the most difficult thing I'd done since the last time I'd left. Staying would have been harder, not only on me, but on the kids, as well. I scribbled a note of thanks and left it on the pillow, stole one last kiss, and tiptoed out the door.

My wallet and keys were on the phone stand at the foot of the stairs, the same place I'd left them for years. I stuffed them into pockets and sat on the bottom stair to slip into my shoes.

I nearly froze when I heard the padding of soft footsteps behind me.

"Daddy?"

I sighed hard and reached out for her hand as she sat next to me. "You should be in bed, Eileen. It's too early to be wandering around the house."

She shrugged, slight shoulders framed by a mop of hair that tore at my heart. My baby girl, the daughter I had wanted from the very beginning, was growing up too damn fast. Hardly a little girl anymore.

"I have to get up in an hour anyway," she said. "Nick wants to be at the first Mass."

"Nick is a masochist."

"Why are you up so early? Where are you going?"

No one ever said fatherhood would be easy. No one warned me that I would break their hearts so often. "I've got to go home, sweetheart. Before I wear out my welcome."

"But…"

"I can't stay, Eileen. There's just too much Mom and I have to work out. She let me stay here because I was sick, but that's it."

"She said that?"

"No, of course not." Tears were welling in those green eyes and it was just about killing me. "I'm leaving before she feels like she has to do that. I don't want this to be hard for her. I'd like to make it as easy as possible."

She blinked hard, sending a flood over her eyelashes and down her cheeks. I felt like the biggest heel in the world.

"You're not even going to say goodbye?"

"I left her a note." This, I thought wildly, is why I only have one daughter. Soothing the bumps and bruises is too hard, especially when you can't see them and you know they're your fault. The best I could hope for was that a strong hug would make her feel better.

I pulled my daughter into my arms and held on tight. "I love you, you know that don't you?"

"It's not fair, Daddy. You were supposed to stay. We all thought you would!"

"I can't," I murmured. "It would be too hard on your mom." I put a finger under her chin and made her look up at me. "Baby, it would be too hard on me. I've hardly said ten words to her in two years. It wouldn't be fair for me to waltz back into her life after so long."

"What happened? I thought you loved each other."

"I don't know what happened," I said, still whispering. "I can be a pretty hard man to live with and she put up with an awful lot from me."

She brushed the tears away from her face, sniffing. "Are you going to divorce her?"

My memory shot back to the same question asked by a curious three year old Nick during dinner almost fifteen years before. Nick in all his innocent wisdom, wondering if the tension surrounding him was going to rip his little world apart.

The answer hadn't changed, not yet.

"I don't want a divorce, Eileen. I love your mom. It's not just lip service, I really do love her... which is why I'm going. I can't stand to see her crying, either, and if I stayed I know I'd have her in tears."

"Some tears are good, Daddy."

"I know. I'll make you a promise, though."

Wide eyes stared back at me expectantly.

"I won't stay away from the house so much. Maybe Mom can get used to the idea that I want to spend time with you here sometimes, not just at my apartment."

"Maybe you'll talk to her some, too."

"I hope so, angel."

"She dumped Brad, you know."

I swallowed the smile. "Give us a kiss," I said, hugging her again, "and call me later, okay? I think you and I need to spend some time together without your brothers."

"Okay."

She kissed me lightly on the lips and started back up the stairs. I headed for the door.

"Dad?"

"What, sweetheart?"

"Did I talk to you this morning, or not?"

"Of course you did. You don't need to keep secrets from her, Eileen. Mom isn't the enemy, and this isn't a war."

"I wonder sometimes."

Terry and I had our own little cold war, and our children were the casualties.

On the drive home I passed the Interstate turnoff that could take me to the nondescript building that served as the regional headquarters for the U.S. Defense Agency. Ten minutes down the road, that was all it would take.

I detoured at the next light and went back.

She'd locked me out when I left to do their bidding, two weeks of hell that left me disillusioned with everything I'd ever done for them and questioning how I handled any of it.

Maybe something could be salvaged from it.

I went inside, and took care of it once and for all.

Nick

My life was going too well to have it suddenly sour. The worst I expected from Sunday morning was trying to convince Katie that it was possible to take communion in spite of everything we'd done during the week. I wasn't entirely convinced that we had actually sinned. It was nothing we hadn't done before.

We just enjoyed it more.

The last thing I expected was to encounter a somber Eileen in the hallway.

"You'd better go in and see Mom," she said flatly.

"Why?"

"Dad left."

The wind sucked right out of my sails. "When?" I groaned, deciding that my parents were the world's biggest dumbasses.

"I caught him sneaking out an hour ago. He said he was leaving her a note."

"How thoughtful. She caters to him for the whole frigging week and he leaves her a goddamned note. The man has no balls, Eileen. If he were any kind of man he'd have stuck around."

"Don't be such a prick. He said he didn't want to hurt her and if he stayed he'd make her cry. And he didn't want to wear out his welcome."

"Stupid – " I bit it off, slapping my hand against the door frame. "Is it just me or are they both incredibly dense?"

"Dad's just being careful."

"Right." I sighed miserably and headed down the hall

for Mom's room, hoping she was awake and had already read his note.

No doubt about that. Awake, out of bed, and dressed.

"I don't want to talk about it," she snapped when I went into her room. "Just turn around and let me finish getting dressed."

The faint voice in the back of my head kicked in, and it was annoying the hell out of me. I wanted to do exactly what she said, leave and let her have her temper tantrum in private.

The damned voice made me lean against the door jamb.

"Dammit, Nicholas, get out!"

"What'd he say?"

"Nothing. He didn't say a goddamned thing. Now leave me alone."

His note was on top of the dresser near the door, within easy reach. When she went into her closet for shoes, I picked it up.

Ter, coward's way out, I know. I just thought it would be best if I left before you had to kick me out. And I'm not up to seeing those blue eyes filled with tears just yet. I appreciate what you did for me, more than I can say. If you need anything – anything at all – you know where I am. Tell the kids I'm sorry I couldn't stay to say goodbye. Love you, Chip.

I set it back on the dresser. Not a total jerk, after all, he did have the guts to say he loved her.

"Satisfied?"

"Did you even talk to him?" I asked, ignoring the fact that I was wading into dangerous territory.

"Keep out of it, Nick. It's finished."

"Seems pretty clear to me, Mom. He left you a clear option – don't be a stranger. Not to mention how he ended the note."

"Goddamned afterthought!"

"Scared to admit something you might not feel in return!" I shot back. "Hell, did you give him a chance? Did you talk to him at all last night?"

"He fell asleep!" she shouted. "I wasn't about to wake him up to play twenty questions. Now drop it!"

"You sucked me into this, Mom. You expected me to listen to your side of things and not have an opinion? Well get this. You're waiting for him to fall at your feet and apologize from some wrong he doesn't even know he committed. Yeah, you *could* have woken him up and asked him to stay. Or you could have kicked us out at any time yesterday so that you could talk to him while he was awake. But you didn't. I don't know what the fuck you're waiting for but if you don't get your panties out of a wad your marriage *will* be over. He made it pretty clear, you know where he is. So go get him already."

Terry

Nick was not the only one of my children blaming me because their father disappeared before breakfast. Paul glared, Eileen slammed doors and stomped through the house with the indignation that only a young teenage girl can muster. Kevin pointed out the obvious.

"You expected two years to vanish just because you cleaned up when he puked on the floor?"

Honestly, I had hoped they would. I had it in my head that if we were going to make a go of it we might as well start right then and there. I saw no sense in him going back to that apartment other than to get his clothes.

"Are you afraid of him now?"

I poured Kris another cup of coffee while we waited for

Nick and Spider to come back from the Wednesday night sign language class at the church. We suffered our kids together, our marriages together, and now we suffered my separation together.

"Why would I be afraid of Chip? The man is as gentle as they come."

"With you," she agreed. "Anyone else is a fair target for his temper."

"Been there, done that."

"To a degree."

He had a temper, I knew that. I'd heard enough stories, not just from Kris and Doug but from Chip himself, to know that I should never discount it. It just wasn't something I ever worried would be aimed at the kids or myself.

He had control when he needed it.

When he wanted it.

"I worry about your youngest," Kris said suddenly, looking out the back door to where Kevin and Eileen were wrestling by the pool.

"Which one?" I followed her gaze. Kevin had Eileen teetering at the end of the diving board and one slight shove would send her into the water. She was protesting loudly, but with a laugh that told me to stay out of it.

"The youngest of the young. Kevin. Eileen can take care of herself. But Kevin seems inordinately preoccupied with religion and death."

"The religion I've noticed." Eileen was in the water, splashing up at Kevin. "Death has never been an issue here. What do you know that I don't?"

"I know what I'm not supposed to know, and Doug would be telling you himself if he hadn't been sworn to secrecy."

"Kris…"

"He called Doug a while ago, Terry. He asked some very specific questions about autoerotic strangulation, and I'm telling you because I think you should worry about it."

"What the hell," I asked, heartbeat accountably increasing steadily, "is autoerotic strangulation? And why is my son deferring to your husband instead of his own father?"

"I don't know why he didn't go to Chip."

"What is it?"

"It's tying a noose around your neck to cut off blood while masturbating. It's a search for a bigger thrill, but dammit, too many people have killed themselves trying it."

"Christ." I looked out into the back yard again. My son, the possible future priest, asking Doug of all people. "What did Doug tell him?"

"That he'd be better off jumping the nearest cheerleader and catching the clap. Kevin was not amused."

"And neither am I. Just when the hell did this conversation take place?"

She glanced at her watch. "About three hours ago. I thought you might want to head him off at the pass. Doug doubts he'll try it now, but the fact that he's been thinking about it was enough for me to stick my nose in it and violate Kevin's confidence."

This was Chip's territory and it terrified me. I'd done a lousy job at preparing Eileen for the changes she was going to go through – Chip rescued me on that one, wound up at a drug store at two in the morning to buy her feminine hygiene supplies she didn't realize she needed, and took the time to explain to her what she had to look forward to for the next thirty some odd years – and I had never entertained the idea of talking to my youngest son. Chip talked to Nick and Paul, he kept an open line with them on sex and adolescence from the time they were very young. I had no idea what he'd discussed, if anything, with Kevin.

I failed to take into account that a part time father doesn't want to spend his time in delicate discussions. He wants to enjoy the time he has with his kids.

Nick.

I dismissed that idea as quickly as it came to me. I had forced him into growing up too fast as it was. Educating his brothers was not his responsibility, but he might be able to tell me how his father handled it.

"Please tell me," I said nervously, "that it's only sex he's interested in."

"It doesn't matter what it is, Terry. If he tries it he could kill himself."

Kris agreed that Nick should be consulted before sitting Kevin down. He might know what Kevin really wanted, his brothers confided in him often.

"Are the kids still planning on having their pool party Friday night?"

The last pool party of the year was an annual event, begun when Nick was in sixth grade. Between him and Paul there were usually fifty invited guests and a few stragglers, little swimming and more food than I could have imagined possible clogging the pool filters. Kids spilled all over the yard, kitchen, and study.

Once a year was enough.

"Please tell me you'll be here. Salvage my sanity and protect me from the throngs of teenage hornballs."

"Wouldn't miss it."

I had a sudden thought of who else might be interested, someone who failed to show at last year's party in spite of the pleading from his children.

"Could you put up with a little tension, Kris? Like watching two people itching to scream at each other?"

"I'll be the referee."

Despite the nerves that seemed to overpower my fingers as I reached for the phone, I managed to punch in the number before I could change my mind, half hoping he wasn't there or was too busy to talk, half hoping Ted would answer instead.

Wednesday night.

I knew damn well he'd be at work.

"Charybdis." Very tense voice.

"It's Terry, Chip. Do you have a minute?"

He hesitated. Yes, I knew he was busy. He was always busy on Wednesday night trying to get the mid week payroll done in time for Friday. His fingers were probably numb from all the paperwork and I wouldn't have been surprised to hear he was still refusing to learn to use a computer to get it done. "Not too busy," he said, softening. "What can I do for you?"

Pass the ball or drop back, as Doug would say. "Can you take off work Friday night?"

"Depends," he muttered, distracted, papers shuffling in the background. "If it's important I can."

"Not terribly," I admitted. "Your kids are having the annual pool party."

"That time of year again? Woman, my kids are important. I'll be there. Where's my cat?"

"He's still here... Chip, did you know that your cat is insane?"

"Max isn't a cat. He's Satan wrapped in fur."

"Funny," I laughed.

"I'm not kidding. Living with that little freak is like living with a toddler on speed. I think the cat food is laced with crack."

I couldn't argue. "Max has discovered a golf ball, and spends a good part of the day banging it down the stairs, carrying it back up in his mouth like a dog, and then rolling it back down. I don't really mind, except when he does it at three in the morning."

"He must be in kitty heaven with all that room to run."

"He does seem to exert most of his energy running from one end of the house to the other at top speed. He's either going at full tilt or he's asleep, there's no in between."

"Whose face is he sleeping on at night?"

"Eileen's, but she's not complaining."

"You realize I'm serious? He likes to lay across someone's head at night."

"As long as it's not mine. I suppose you can collect him Friday night."

"Do I have to?"

"I thought you were head over heels in love with this cat."

"As far as my daughter is concerned, I am. She gave him to me. But to Max I'm just He Who Feeds Me and not much more. Would I get into hot water with you if I told Eileen I just don't have as much time as he seems to need and he seems *so* much happier with her?"

"I don't mind as long as I never have to change a litter box."

"Are you sure? Sooner or later Max will decide that you'd make a mighty fine bed and bathtub. He'll stake a claim to your lap, and you'll never be able to sit down without him launching across the room to make sure it's warm enough for him."

"He is awfully adorable," I said. "He crawls into my lap and purrs, and sometimes reaches up with his paws to rub my cheeks."

"You wouldn't have liked that as much before I got him declawed," he grunted.

"He gives kisses too. He'll stand on my legs and stretch up to plant kitty kisses on my nose."

"Face it, woman, you're in love with my cat."

"Possibly."

"Heh. What time Friday?"

"I expect kids to start showing up around eight. Say, seven? I'll even feed you."

"I'll be there. Love ya."

He hung up before I could say anything else.

I agonized over the next two days. Yes, I heard him right, I didn't doubt that. Nothing was more important than his kids, not even the Friday night rush.

He was leaving his cat here

He called me "Woman."

He loved me. Not an afterthought after all.

The pathway was open, at least. With Doug and Kris as mediators we could at least begin to talk.

I should have expected someone to block my way.

I just didn't think it would be my son.

Nick

None of us felt like having a party; Mom expected the house to be overrun with our friends and friends of friends, but the last bang of the year was nothing more than a whimper with the four of us, Spider and his girlfriend, and Katie and Monica. I think we would have scrapped the whole thing if Paul hadn't been given a partial dispensation from being grounded for the evening, and he needed time away from school with Monica. And Dad was going to be there.

Paul was past the point where he could hide how miserable

he was. If Mom noticed she kept it to herself, but after thirty seconds in the house, Dad did.

He leaned against the breakfast bar in the kitchen, regarding Paul carefully. "You okay, son?"

"I'm fine," Paul sighed.

"You don't look it."

"I'm just tired, Dad."

He let it go at that, but watched Paul closely as he slid the back door open and went to sit with Monica by the pool.

They both looked like hell.

Katie and I sat together on the steps in the shallow end of the water, watching Kevin bouncing on the diving board while he tried to work up the nerve to jump into the cold water. Paul was wrapped around Monica in one of the lounge chairs, Spider and Janet were glued to a board game, and Eileen was at the edge of the pool, staring down at her own feet.

Definitely not a party.

"Don't, Katie," I whispered when her hand slid up my thigh, a little too suggestively for the company we were in. "Kevin…"

"You started these games, Mister Nick. I'm glad your dad isn't sick anymore but I miss having his apartment."

Kevin flipped off the diving board and she seized the chance for one good squeeze before he surfaced. "We'll figure something out," I muttered. "Maybe we could cut class once in a while. My mom works, you know. We could have the whole house to ourselves."

She rolled her eyes and pulled away, swimming towards Kevin. "How's it going, Kev?" she asked once he was back on the diving board.

"Bitchin', Katie," he snickered. "I've got 'em all fooled."

"What is it this week? Still the priest?"

"This week I'm a sex fiend. If I'm gonna psych 'em out, I may as well run the whole gamut."

Eileen snickered. "Kevin popped a hard on in the locker room yesterday. The whole school thinks he's a sex maniac."

"Kevin, no," I groaned.

He shrugged it off. "Consider the topic under discussion," he said coolly. "Lydia Freeman. Any normal male would have had the exact same reaction given my memories of the girl."

"Translation," Eileen offered. "He felt her up under the bleachers at the last football game and was the only guy there who can lay claim to first hand knowledge of whether or not she's for real or if she stuffs her bra."

I bit. "Well?"

"Every inch a lady," he laughed.

"Whatever happened to the kid reading to Dad for hours on end from the Bible? Eileen says you're going to be a priest."

"As to the first... pretentions at piety. Mom thinks I'm a goddamned little angel. As to the second... Maybe. I might have a vocation, but I also have hormones. In reality your little brother is a closet masturbator. Actually, in the shower, but what the hell."

Katie laughed and swam back to me. "I swear to God your entire family was born horny."

"Parents included," I said. "Are the guys razzing you now, Kev?"

"They're just jealous."

"Lydia did ask where you got the tumor with the bone," Eileen said. "She wanted to know if there were any more at home like you."

"I certainly hope you told her no," Katie said with mock

horror. "I don't share."

"Lydia's not Nick's type," Kevin offered. "He seems to prefer women who can stay out past ten o'clock."

"That's right," I agreed. "Why do you think I hang around you? Those midnight curfews turn me on."

She splashed water at me. "I *know* what turns you on. Curfew or not."

"Carnal knowledge," Kevin scoffed, sitting at the end of the board. "What would your mother say? Such decadence for a proper young woman."

"I approach all my decadence quite properly," she teased back. "And what my mother doesn't know won't hurt her."

"Irrepressible libido…"

"And what are you hiding from your mother?" Katie pressed.

"Not to fear." He sighed melodramatically. "My virginity, unlike almost everyone else here, is still intact."

"Aside from the wonders of Lydia's monumental breasts?" I pretended to study him seriously. "You had a girl like that right at your fingertips and chose to keep your sex life a solitary pursuit?"

"No performance anxiety," he pointed out. "I know what I like and I don't have to play traffic cop."

"When I was your age," I said, "I didn't have the guts to feel anyone up, much less admit to jerking off in the shower. I was pretty sure if I kept it up everyone would know by the hair sprouting from my palms."

Katie grabbed my hand and looked.

"Everybody masturbates," Kevin said simply. "How the hell do you think Dad got through the last couple of years?" He held up his hand, clenched into a tight ball. "Meet Fistina, every man's whore."

"Oh God, you're gross," Eileen groaned. She looked over at me. "Do you think Dad's telling the truth? He hasn't been with anyone since Mom?"

"He's got no reason to lie," I said. "Not that he doesn't lack for opportunity. Half the women who hang around that pool would love to get him in the sack."

"So," Kevin said, "would Mom."

"Agreed," Eileen said.

We all looked at her. "Well?" I asked. "Do you feel a proclamation coming on?"

"Dad won't push," she said, a touch sad. "I think we should worry more about whether or not they can learn to say hello and goodbye to each other than whether nor not they'll screw."

"Agreed," Kevin sighed. "Their relationship gives me a headache. Got the latest Playboy, Nick?"

"Check under Paul's bed," I chuckled, enduring a poke in the ribs from Katie.

"It's an addiction," he explained to Katie. "Some nights the hormones require an extra kick and Miss October would do nicely tonight…"

He was probably about to explain his strange solitary sexual practices in great detail, but he cut short when Monica wrenched away from Paul and bolted across the lawn. Janet followed her; Paul stayed in the lounge chair, his face buried against folded arms.

"Shit's gonna hit the fan soon," Kevin observed casually. "Safe to say that brother Paul can eliminate the priesthood from his list of possible occupations."

"Father Kevin," I muttered, "you have a gift for understatement."

Eileen got up and jumped onto the diving board, and

pushed Kevin into the water. "Obnoxious prick."

That, he admitted when he came up for air, was entirely accurate.

Doug

"What," Chip asked, pointing to a bowl on the counter, "is that?" He turned to Terry, who was pulling a six pack of soft drinks from the refrigerator. "Did it die?"

"Spinach dip. Your kids love it."

"Looks like it's already been barfed up."

"You don't have to eat it, Irish, though if you're inclined to try it, Eileen made it."

He grimaced and backed away. "If you're still alive five minutes after you take a bite, maybe then."

His sarcasm earned him an ice cold can in the middle of his back.

I hadn't looked forward to the evening. When Kris told me – as we were on our way out the door – that Chip would be there, I almost backed out. Friends to the end, maybe, but I didn't want to get caught in the middle any more than I already was.

So far, so good.

In the two hours we had been there, sitting at the dining room table with the lights low enough we could easily spy on the kids outside, they treated each other no differently than they used to, with the possible exception of Chip's hands staying within sight. And he didn't make an effort to corner her in the kitchen.

Heaven help us, he was acting his age.

"Your kids know how to throw one hell of a party," Kris deadpanned. "Much more of this and the neighbors will be calling the cops."

Chip dropped back into his chair. "I expected tons of teenagers. I prefer this. I don't have to play bouncer."

"They've all been quiet lately," Terry said.

Chip was staring out the patio door. "Has Paul been giving you much trouble? He seemed a little spaced out to me."

"He's not giving me any trouble, but he's not sleeping, Chip. He spends half the night reading and I don't think he's getting much rest the other half. He's moody, withdrawn... he's turning into Kevin at his worst."

"Drinking?" He looked away from the kids and back to his wife. "Aside from the one night?"

"If he is I don't know about it."

"Trouble in school?"

"No complaints from his teachers and every time I turn around he at least looks like he's studying. Whatever it is, he'll tell us when he's ready."

He didn't seem so certain.

"It was easy when they were little," he said. "They'd come in crying when they were hurt and a few kisses and a hug would take care of it. Now they won't cry and treat you like toxic waste if you get too close."

"Adolescence," Kris offered. "You were such a shit when you were their age, you know. Worse, even. No respect for your parents, you drank like a fish, and we never knew where you were or if you were even coming home. So don't complain."

"I'm not complaining, Kris. Our kids are terrific but they're not angels, either. I just regret losing the little kids in them. Christ, Nick is damn near grown."

"How do you think we'll feel? Letting go is hard enough, but how do we step back and let Spider take control of his own life? I'm torn between wanting him to be dependent on us and looking forward to seeing the grown man."

"I hear you. But I wanted babies, not these brooding pseudo-adults with acne and attitudes."

Terry was laughing. "The last time I told you I was pregnant you said, and I quote, 'Woman, I want a daughter, so that in sixteen years I can sit on the front porch with a shotgun to terrorize her boyfriends.' You had her grown before she was even born."

"I changed my mind. I can pretty much cope with the boys growing up but it'll kill me when she goes off on her own."

"Wake up, Pops," Kris said. "She's almost there and the boys are going to start hanging around her in droves. You'll have to watch her like a hawk."

His glance flicked towards Terry. Somebody would be watching her, all right, but he didn't think it would be him, and he was terrified at who else it might be.

"Tornado warning," she said, nodding towards the back yard. "Looks like the love birds are fighting."

"Dammit," Chip swore under his breath. "I was afraid of this."

"Of what?"

He was already up and at the door. "Of what's bugging Paul. I'll be back." He slid the door open. "I don't think you're going to like it, either."

Janet flew past him in pursuit of Monica; he watched them run around the corner of the house, but kept walking towards the pool. Paul was sitting at the edge of his chair, face buried against his arms. Chip stood in front of him for a moment, and when Paul didn't look up, he reached down and lifted his son to his feet by his arms.

Wisely, in spite of her growing curiosity – our curiosity

– she left it up to Chip. Hysterics at that point would have done no good, anyway.

Chip

It was a nice night to have your future blown apart. Late September, a warm breeze cutting through the back yard, crystal clear skies and stars beginning to twinkle above. There was only the emotional tornado spinning dust on the deck by the pool.

The distance from the house to the deck gave me just enough time to get a firm grip on the anger bubbling inside. My first impulse was to grab my son and heave him into the water; the closer I got, though, the younger he seemed, and the younger he seemed the more my heart ached for him.

It seemed pointless to ask the other kids to leave. They probably had Paul figured out before I did.

"Paul."

He shook his head without looking up at me.

"Come on, son. Look at me."

"I can't." Choking back tears; not ten minutes before I had said my kids wouldn't cry anymore. I reached down and lifted him by his arms, making him stand in front of me. He took a deep breath, straightened up, and faced me.

"You are one special kind of stupid," I said. "How far along is she?"

"Three months."

"I thought you said you were taking care of it."

He bit his lip and thought carefully. "I did say that," he admitted.

The last time he had cried that I could recall had been when he broke his leg in three places. He was trying hard to win the battle with the tears pooling in his eyes, determined he wouldn't give in to it. What had I told Kris and Terry? That it used to be a few kisses and a hug would take care of it?

I grabbed onto my son and held him tight. I didn't let go until I was sure he wasn't crying anymore.

"I'm sorry, Dad."

"I imagine you are." I pointed to the chairs behind him and told him to sit down, pulling one close to his. "I'm going to get really nosey, Paul. What happened?"

"I thought…" He swallowed hard and started again. "I got totally caught up in the moment unprepared and let myself get carried away."

Count to ten, I told myself, before you open your mouth and say something that will destroy your relationship with him. I thought it all and tried to not let any of it get out. *What about abstinence? What about waiting? What about using your fucking hands, for Christ's sake? You didn't have to go that far.*

It was too late for a lecture.

I groped for the last thread of my temper and waited for him to finish.

"I thought," he whispered, "that I could pull out in time."

"Goddammit!" That last thread was close to snapping. "How irresponsible are you? That has got to be the dumbest – "

I bit it off.

Yelling was pointless. Telling him the obvious was pointless. In spite of my best intentions, of the years of trying to be open with him, answering his questions, and making sure he understood what his responsibilities were, he'd taken a chance.

He didn't need me to be his judge.

I wasn't sure what he needed.

"Has she seen a doctor?"

"Couple weeks ago," he said numbly.

"Is everything all right?"

"I guess. He wouldn't tell me much other than what a lousy person I am for letting it happen in the first place. He had the audacity to say he'd make her an appointment at some clinic in San Francisco."

"An abortion clinic?"

"I told him to shove it up his ass. I won't let that happen."

Paul went from contrite to defiant in less than five seconds. He stood straighter, and was looking me in the eye.

"How does Monica feel about it?"

"She's scared, but she doesn't want to get rid of it. And she can't tell her parents. Her dad…"

"What about him?"

"He'd beat the hell out of her. She's terrified of him on a good day, what do you think he'd do to her if he found out? Monica's mom is a walking bag of bruises. He'd kill her!" His gaze shifted past me. "She's scared of you, too. I've tried to tell her not to be, but she is."

I turned around. She was coming around the corner with Janet, and hesitated when she saw me there, moving forward only with Janet's urging.

"It's all right," I told her. Paul scrambled to pull up another chair and held it for her as she sat down. "You need to see a different doctor, Monica. Spider's dad would be your best bet."

She stared at me, wide eyed.

"He'll take very good care of you, I promise."

She nodded, looking down at her hands.

"You have to tell me about your father," I pressed. "How big a risk would you be taking if you told him the truth?"

Softly, she replied, "I'd be better off having an abortion."

"No!" Paul shot out of his chair. "There is no fucking way I'll let that son of a bitch do this to us!"

"Sit down, Paul."

He did as I said.

"Do you want an abortion?"

"No." Still whispering, not looking at me.

"No one will force you to, Monica." I leaned forward, trying to coax her into looking up. "You're older than Paul, aren't you?"

"I'm eighteen."

Older than Nick, even. She could leave home if she wanted, and there wasn't a damn thing her father could do about it.

"Have you talked about what you want to do?"

"We want to get married," Paul said.

"You're barely sixteen," I reminded him. "A little young to be making that kind of decision."

"I already made the bigger decision, Dad," he pointed out. "I love her, I want our baby, and I know what I'm doing."

"Do you now? What about school, champ? You still have two years of high school to get through. Planning on chucking that out the window? Suppose you do, and get a job. What kind of work do you think you can get? Paul, I rarely hire anyone without a high school diploma to work as a busboy. The competition for jobs is just too stiff. If I saw your application and realized you couldn't even get through high school, I'd wonder how much effort you'd put into working for me. I'd wonder if you'd quit when you hit the first rough spot. I might not give you a chance.

"And if you did find a job, do you have any idea what it would cost you to support a family? It's not as simple as it looks. Marriage is damned hard even under the best circumstances."

He didn't seem fazed.

"Do you consider your marriage to be a mistake?" he asked.

"What? No, I don't."

"You couldn't hold it together. There were no guarantees for you going in either, and Mom was only nineteen."

"I was making over fifty thousand a year, Paul. Money was never our issue. And I was twenty two, a big difference from sixteen."

"You dropped out of school when you were sixteen," he added. "If you found a decent job what makes you think that I can't?"

"I quit school and have regretted it ever since. And the job was barely even legal. What about all your plans?"

"I stick them on the backburner."

"And get back to them when? In twenty years when all your kids are old enough for you to ease up?"

"I don't need your lectures, Dad. Just your permission."

I sank back into my chair At his age I was out of school and taking my first steps towards working with the agency. I was a cold hearted little bastard with a death wish, and if I had ever gotten someone pregnant, I know I wouldn't have had Paul's sense of honor.

I would have turned my back and walked away.

"Not yet, son," I said after a while. "We have to talk to your mom first and let her know what's going on. In any case," I turned to Monica, "I don't think you should tell your parents right now. When the time comes I want to be there, and I'll get you out of the house. Understand?"

They both nodded.

The relief that flooded Paul's face was as palpable as the tension had been. I left them sitting together, saw him reach for her hand as I got up and turned away. No one else said a word.

Hopefully Terry would be as restrained.

Nick

We breathed a collective sigh of relief when Dad got up and left, Paul still pretty much in one piece. There was no bloodshed, no physical violence or shouting loud enough to burst everyone's eardrums, nothing like Paul expected.

Then again, Mom still didn't know.

I pulled Katie up against me. There was no way, I promised myself, that I would take such a stupid chance with her. Knowing that Paul was about to become a father didn't cool the passions, but I swore I would never be so incredibly selfish.

Kevin jumped up, bouncing at the end of the diving board. "Coitus interruptus," he informed us, "is a myth."

Eileen shoved him in again.

"No shit, Sherlock."

Chip

I have to admit something incredibly immature. Part of me wanted Terry to cry; during that hour after Paul told me, while I waited for Doug and Kris to leave and for the boys to take their girlfriends home, I had it in my head that I'd tell her, and that she would – predictably – dissolve into tears. If she was crying, I'd be obligated to comfort her. If she needed comfort, she'd throw herself against me.

Selfish, yes. I wanted her in my arms and wasn't above using my son to get that. I could have waited for him to come home and made him tell his mother himself, let him be the one to break her heart, but in the middle of everything my motives were less than pure.

Instead, we stood in the kitchen loading the dishwasher, waiting for the sounds of Kevin and Eileen getting ready for bed to stop, for their TVs to click on and drown out our conversation. Water stopped rushing through the pipes, Kevin shouted at Eileen to get out of his room, and it was quiet.

She tossed the dishtowel aside and leaned against the counter on the other side of the kitchen. "So how bad is it?"

"Do you want it all at once, or bit by bit?"

"All at once."

"His girlfriend is pregnant, and they want to get married."

She leaned her head back against the cupboard door, closed her eyes, and sighed hard. "My God."

"She's not telling her parents yet, either."

"Of course not." She opened her eyes; there were no tears, no searing, sudden anguish that I could tap into. "I met her mother once. Chip, the woman is terrified of her own shadow and won't look a soul in the eye. I don't even want to meet her father."

"I do."

"Really? Why?"

She wasn't about to wrap herself around me in a disappointed rage. I nodded towards the living room and she followed, dropping next to me on the sofa. She sat close enough that we touched, but I didn't dare try to slide my arm around her. Not yet.

"Someone has to be there when she tells them, and if the

man is as much of a son of a bitch as Paul says, it'd better be me. He won't lay a finger on her if I'm there."

"Is Paul okay with that?"

I shrugged. "Don't know and I don't care. If he walks in there with Monica and tells her father that he got her pregnant, the man might try to rip him apart."

"And if he makes a move towards you, he'd regret it," she reasoned.

"If he makes a move towards any of them, he'll regret it, Terry." I shifted on the sofa so that I could look at her. "How angry are you?"

"I don't know that I am. I don't know what I feel right now."

"Right now I'm feeling extremely conflicted," I admitted. "I'm mad as hell, but…"

"But you're going to be a grandpa. Your testosterone is going into over drive, and all you want to do is protect your son and your grandchild."

"Maybe. You're going to be a grandma, you know."

"I'm not old enough to be a grandmother," she moaned. "You, you're forty. You're certainly old enough."

"Rub it in, why don'tcha?"

"What are they going to do, Chip?"

"I'm not sure that what they want to do and what they'll wind up doing are the same thing. He's sixteen years old, for Pete's sake. His biggest worry right now should be whether or not he can afford to take her to the homecoming dance, not whether or not he can afford rent and diapers."

"Obviously he can't afford condoms."

"Don't get me started."

She grabbed a pillow off the sofa and held it against tightly. "Chip, have you talked to Kevin at all? About sex?"

"Not really. But I will."

"I was going to talk to him, but I don't have a clue where to begin. I'm worried about him. He's been asking Doug some fairly peculiar questions."

"About sex?"

She filled me in on her conversation with Kris, my mind flooding with images of my youngest son lying there with a rope around his neck, eyes bulging and skin flushed red. Kevin didn't ask questions on a whim; he pondered things until he was sure he wanted more facts. He rarely did his thinking out loud.

I got up and headed for the stairs.

"Chip, it's almost one in the morning. He's probably asleep."

"It can't wait."

I took the stairs two at a time, leaving Terry sitting there alone, clutching her pillow.

Kevin was as much a mystery to me as I must have been to my own parents. I hardly knew my own son. His personality was elusive; at times he was quiet and studious, sometimes he was the practical joker, and sometimes – to use his own term – he was a real prick.

I crept into his room, opening the door gently, not wanting to wake Eileen in the next room. Kevin was asleep, bathed in light from the TV he'd left on, the sound nothing more than a dull buzz in the background. I sat at the edge of the bed carefully, and watched him sleep.

Where the hell was my little boy? This lanky kid looked nothing like him. Little Kevin had wide, curious eyes and a mischievous grin that made you wonder whether to laugh or check for property damage. The young man asleep there was more serious, and grown so tall he nearly spilled out the foot of the bed.

There was a Playboy magazine sticking out from under his bed, and a pack of cigarettes and a beer bottle just behind the nightstand. I kicked the magazine the rest of the way under the bed, then reached for the cigarettes.

I didn't know enough about him.

"Wake up, Kevin." I shook him gently. "Come on, wake up."

He groaned and opened his eyes. "What?"

"We have to talk."

He propped his pillow up against the headboard and sat up, rolling his eyes with a 'Jesus, do you have any fucking idea what time it is' sigh. "What?" he repeated.

I held up the cigarettes. "We'll start with these. When did you start smoking?"

"I don't smoke," he replied gruffly, still half asleep. "I tried it, hated it, not gonna do it."

"And I'm supposed to believe that."

"Yes."

"And the beer?"

"Now that I liked. Have a problem with that?"

"I have a lot of problems with that, Kevin. You're way too young to be drinking, even beer. I want your word that this was it, just the one."

He nodded. "Fine. No polluting the temple. What is it you really want, Dad?"

Perceptive little shit, I thought, wondering how to even bring the subject up. It would have been easier if I didn't suspect that the Kevin Terry and I saw was completely different than the Kevin everyone else did.

"We're long overdue to talk," I said. "And your mom is worried…"

"Does this have anything to do with Paul? I don't have a pregnant girlfriend. In fact, I don't even really have a girlfriend. I'm still in the observation stage. I'm really enjoying observing."

"I'll just bet you are. The idea is to keep you from getting into Paul's predicament."

"No sweat," he shrugged. "I have the benefit of two older brothers who don't have a problem discussing sex with their kid brother. I've had the canned lecture on birth control already. Never trust a girl. Come to us if you need to. Condoms are a guy's best friend, etcetera ad nauseum. I think they even talked to Eileen, though for her the message was if they ever caught her fooling around she could plan on attending her boyfriend's funeral."

"Kev – "

"Double standards work when you have a baby sister," he added, matter-of-factly.

I had to bite my tongue to keep from laughing, and I wasn't sure if he was serious or yanking on my shorts.

"I'll be honest, Kev. We're more worried about what you might do by yourself. Your Aunt Kris brought up something you talked with Doug about."

"Wait a minute!" he snapped. "I thought anything I said to him was as confidential as confession!"

"Normally it would be, but what you're thinking of... she had to say something."

His face twisted in a grimace, and as quickly as the anger had flashed it was gone. "I wasn't asking permission to do anything stupid, I swear," he said. "Uncle Doug didn't really listen to me, Dad. I just wanted to know why."

"Why what?"

"Why it does what it does and why anyone would want

to try it. He just got nervous and spouted something stupid about cheerleaders and a venereal disease. I didn't even try to get a straight answer after that."

I groped with what to tell him. The few answers I had were from my gut and not peppered with any real facts.

"People try it," I said, "because it supposedly feels great, *if* they survive it. No one ever thinks they're going to die."

"But *why* do they die?"

He was looking past me, staring at the white fuzz on the TV screen. "They die because they cut off the blood to their brains, and because the heart is beating so fast that the blood just has nowhere to go... I'm not a doctor, Kevin. I don't really know the biology. But I'm guessing that they pass out and either suffocate, or have heart attacks."

He barely nodded.

"Now tell me why you really wanted to know."

"Just a rumor," he said softly, looking away from the TV and down at the bed. Anywhere but at me. "A guy I know from school died last week. People keep saying that his mom found him hanging in his closet with his pants down around his ankles. I don't know if it's true or not, but if it is, I wanted to know why he died."

"A friend of yours?"

"Sort of. We had a few classes together. I've known him since kindergarten."

"Christ, Kevin, I'm sorry."

"I just wanted to know why, Dad, but Uncle Doug wasn't listening."

"Sometimes we're not that great at listening when we need to, Sport, especially when you catch us off guard." I reached for him, and he leaned forward long enough to let me hug him. Pacifying me. "Kevin, Your mom is terrified you'll try it."

"I won't."

"And I can tell her that?"

He pulled away from me and leaned back. "Yeah. But ask her not to bug me about it. Please? She gets all freaky and cries about stuff, and she doesn't need to get freaky about this. I'm okay, I swear. She's not gonna walk in here and find me all tied up with my hand in my shorts. Besides…"

"What?"

"I just don't want to talk about *that* with my mom, you know?"

"That's fine, but I hope you're okay with talking to me. If you have any questions, you can come to me. I won't laugh or try to make you feel stupid or awkward. I'll answer anything you ask."

"If I came to you and asked about glow in the dark vibrators, I bet you'd laugh."

I shrugged, trying to not smile.

"Does it glow in the dark?" he went on. "Yes it does, no it doesn't, yes it does, no it doesn't…"

"Go back to sleep," I groaned.

I got up and headed for the door, turning off his TV on my way out.

I just didn't know these kids well enough anymore, and it had to stop.

Terry

We agreed to wait things out for a few days before trying to sit down with Paul and Monica and figure out what to do next. Chip wasn't sure he could keep a grip on his temper much longer and I wasn't sure I could handle the aftermath if he cut loose.

Paul knew his father well enough that he could suck it up and not let it overwhelm him; Monica, Chip pointed out, would have a difficult time understanding that he was not like her father. He didn't want his anger to frighten her away, and in the process, take Paul with her.

Given the agreement we would meet on Wednesday, I was surprised to see him pull into the driveway before ten o'clock Saturday morning.

He didn't bother to say hello. He stepped inside and demanded his son with a gruff, "Where's Nick?"

"Taking a shower."

He slammed the door behind him and shouted up the stairs. "Nicholas! Get down here, now!"

Chip angry, truly angry, is frightening. His ice green eyes go dark, and the air around him feels electrified. His venom could make a person wonder – with extreme trepidation – whether or not he was suddenly going to sprout horns and a tail, shoot to ten feet tall, and command an eruption of fire.

I rarely saw his temper in full form, and was grateful for it.

"What's this about?" I asked, following him through the house into the kitchen. I noticed then the book he had in his hand. He tossed it onto the breakfast bar.

"This is between me and Nick," he snapped.

"Well, would you mind cluing me in?"

"If you're curious," he growled, "stick around. I only want to say this once, and once had better be enough."

Nick stumbled into the kitchen, hair wet and wild, looking like he had been pried from a deep sleep.

"Dad. Hey. What's up?"

Chip picked the book up off the counter. "We goddamn

well know what was up, don't we? What the hell were you thinking, Nick? You gave me your word!"

Nick went white and grabbed for the edge of the counter. "Where did you get that?"

"It was under my bed. Been wondering where you left it?"

Nick reached for the book but Chip pulled it back. "Dad."

"I want an explanation and I want it now. Dammit, Nick! I expected more out of you."

"Maybe you expect too much."

"Do I?" Chip was yelling, and was heard, I gathered by the surprised expression on Paul's face, clear out to the pool. "I don't think expecting my kids to keep a promise is expecting too much. When I gave you the key to my apartment it was with the understanding that you would *never* bring her there unless I was home. Son of a *bitch*, can't either of you keep your pants on?"

"Whatever happened to understanding, Dad? I thought if anyone would, it would be you."

Chip slammed the book onto the counter. "I understand, Nick, but *not in my bed*!" He took a few deep breaths. "You know, I half expected this out of Paul, but I counted on you. You've never lied to me before."

"If I hadn't left the book you never would have known."

"Goddammit, I'd ground you until judgment day if I thought it would do any good. You have me up against a wall because I can't even take the car away because you need it to get to school. So you get off Scott free. Are you proud of yourself? You let me down, son."

"Don't expect an apology." Nick slapped at the counter and started out of the room. "I'm not sorry."

Chip slammed his fist into the counter; the book rose

and then fell with a quiet pop. "Damn."

"Well, that didn't tell me anything," I said. "What did Nick do?"

He shoved the book at me. "Open it. See for yourself."

I reached for it, and when I opened it, I had an explanation for all the nights at the library, all the times when Chip was sick that Nick had a ton of homework and couldn't do it at home. The book was a hollowed out math text, and in it was half a roll of condoms and two mangled tubes of lubricating jelly.

"He took Katie to your apartment?"

"Apparently." He slumped against the counter. "Terry, I suspected they were sleeping together but I had his word he'd never bring her to the apartment when I wasn't there."

I didn't know what to say. That Nick was sleeping with her should have come as no surprise to me, but I never gave it much thought. Never considered it. Yet the evidence was undeniable.

"Chip, he loves her…"

"Fine. Wonderful. Katie's a terrific girl and he's being careful about it. He didn't have to take her there, though."

"What's the difference," I asked quietly, "to him taking her there as opposed to someplace else?"

"The difference is that I demand my right to privacy, Terry. I expect those kids to respect my rules."

"Chip, please. Nick worships you. He made a mistake. Let it go." I considered him intently for a moment. "It's been hard on all the kids. They are so confused… they need both of us and don't understand what happened."

I could almost feel the rage beginning to boil. His eyes went dark again and the scowl that crossed his face warned of the storm brewing inside. I braced myself for it, hoping that he could keep it down enough to spare the kids from over hearing.

"They don't understand? Well, that's not my fault now, is it? I didn't leave, Terry, you threw me out on my ass and never gave me one hint of an explanation! You think I like being a weekend father? I don't. I fucking hate it. My kids are total strangers to me now. You want to lay blame for their problems? Don't look at me, woman, because I'm doing the best I can!"

"So am I," I sighed. "We just need to be able to back each other up. They don't need to hear one thing from me and something else from you."

"You want me to back you up? Christ, I didn't see you for two years! I left here thinking you loved me as much as you ever did, I never had any goddamn warning at all. You locked me out of the house and never bothered to tell me why! You want me to back you up? Then start treating me like a person instead of a goddamned dog you got tired of!"

"I'm sorry…"

"How nice. You're sorry. So am I, Terry. For whatever atrocities I committed, whatever I did that made you so angry you couldn't stand the sight of me, I'm sorry. I'd have fixed it if I could have. All you ever had to do was ask. I'd have done anything in the world for you but you never gave me the chance."

I leaned against the other side of the counter, reaching out to touch his hand. "For what it's worth, I'm just as confused as the kids are. I made a huge mistake and we might have been able to fix it if I had kept the lines open."

The raw anger drained from his face, and he nodded sadly, then pulled away. "I'd better go patch the lines with Nick or I'll regret it. I'm sorry I yelled at you. It's Nick I'm angry with."

"I don't think you're half as mad at Nick as you are at me. It's all right. Maybe Nick let you down, but not as much as I did."

"Terry…"

"Go talk to your son," I said, not really ready to wander through the swamp I had created out of our marriage. "He's probably licking his wounds."

He barely nodded, and backed out of the room.

A start, anyway.

He was fighting back.

Monday morning the full weight of everything hit me with the depressed feeling of a thick, wet fog that settles in for the long haul.

Paul was going to be a father. Whether I liked it or not, whether I supported his decisions on how to handle it or not, there was going to be a baby.

I was going to be a grandmother.

Chip was as angry as I suspected he might be. He was also lonely, scared, and seemed filled with a sense of want.

Nick was running at full speed and there was no way I could catch up to him. There but for the grace of the wisdom to use a condom, he could be in Paul's shoes.

I didn't want to be at work. I wanted to go home and crawl back into bed, and stay there until everything was settled. I didn't want to have to think about it. I especially didn't want to have to face my son leaving home without his father there with me.

Brad kicked me out of the office just after lunch, swearing that I was presenting him with briefs filled with more typos than words, and that I was too distracted to be of any good. I picked up my things and headed for my car, realizing that home was the last place I really wanted to go. Nick and his bad mood and Paul's skittishness just weren't things I wanted to deal with.

I pulled into a grocery store parking lot, sat there behind the wheel, and waited.

For what, I wasn't sure. Divine inspiration maybe, a clear thought, anything but going home.

I was ready to fall apart and wanted to be with someone who would understand the feeling.

I knew who I wanted to be with.

When the idea came to me I smiled and looked up. "It's a great idea," I said to whomever might be listening, "but it's taking a chance. He used to take Mondays off, but that doesn't mean he's at home."

What the hell.

Never ignore a revelation.

Chip

Mondays were meant for sleeping in and then zoning out on the sofa. I never worked on Mondays for no other reason than I didn't like facing them. I spent the rest of the week at work, and Sundays I fulfilled religious obligations. With the kids in school and not draped over the edge of the balcony like hormonal wet towels all day long, I made it a point to sleep until noon, shower if I felt like it, or watch the news, and then decide if I wanted to sit out on the balcony and watch the little kids play in the pool or if I wanted to plaster myself to the sofa and watch cartoons. I watched soap operas for a while, but they were more depressing than entertaining.

During school hours the pool was usually littered with toddlers splashing in the shallow end, their mothers lined at the edge of the pool, a matriarchal army ready to reach out and grab the first kidlet to slip under water or get out of line. Red was inevitably there with the four kids she babysat, and her little boy was tucked safely into his playpen, an assortment of toys at his feet and a huge colorful umbrella shielding him from the sun. If I thought she looked overwhelmed I'd wander downstairs to keep her company or to play with the kids, but for the most part I preferred sitting on my solitary perch with a Diet Coke in hand, watching the smallest of the complex's residents splash merrily, listening to the squeals of laughter that sometimes gave way to tired whining.

By three in the afternoon the sounds from the pool would escalate into loud adolescent horseplay. The older kids weren't half as much fun to watch as the tiny ones; I'd go inside and crash, to either watch TV or read a book.

Before I met Terry I never willingly read anything other than the comics in the newspaper; in the two years we'd been apart I absorbed half the city library.

This Monday afternoon I decided on cartoons. I suffered through the Smurfs and was waiting for He-Man when the doorbell rang. For half a second I thought about not answering; never mess with the Master of the Universe.

But then, when I started swearing mentally I had no idea what sweaty body was waiting on the other side of the door.

"Hi," she said meekly. "Can I be a pest?"

Her face was flushed red and dripping with sweat; hair was plastered to her forehead and she looked like she was close to passing out on my doorstep. I opened the door all the way and invited her in, suddenly wondering if I'd picked up the dirty clothes off the floor and if the bathroom was halfway presentable.

"Don't get pissed at me for saying so, but you look like

shit," I said, guiding her into the living room.

"I feel like shit and you're forgiven for pointing it out. Do you still have keys to my car?"

"Sure. Why?" I sat next to her on the sofa.

"My car is at a grocery store about a mile down the street. Both my purse and my keys are in the trunk…"

"Again?" She'd done the same thing three years before; she set her purse in the trunk while she moved assorted junk around to make space for a box, and then shut the trunk without thinking about her purse. "You walked all the way in this heat?"

"September," she informed me, "is not supposed to be this hot. And you're closer than home."

I got up and went into the kitchen to get her a cold drink. "You could have called," I said. "I would have come to get you. No need to walk all that way in high heels."

"I don't carry spare change in my pantyhose, Chip. Payphones require money and all my change is in the trunk. And my cell phone is in my purse."

"Of course it is." She might have wanted to clobber me, but I couldn't help laughing. I brought her a glass of iced tea, heavy on the sugar; the sweeter the better, I remembered. "I'll spring your keys for you, but not right now. You need to cool off before you pass out. Or worse, puke in my car."

"Heaven forbid I should desecrate the bluebird of happiness."

"You still hate my car?" She'd been less than thrilled when I bought it. I had it in my head that I was letting Nick and Paul talk me into buying it. Sure, it was sporty and it was a convertible, but it was just a car. Transportation. Something to get me from point A to point B. She pointed out, bluntly, that it made me feel ten years younger and it was designed to so that women would notice. Young women.

"I never hated it. It amused me."

"I amused you a lot, didn't I?"

"You made me laugh," she said, swirling the tea in the glass. "I haven't laughed like that in a very long time."

Like what, I wondered, but the thought was interrupted by a banging against the balcony door. Someone's red and white striped beach ball was spinning in my lounge chair. I opened the door and Terry followed me out to get a peek at the view I had of the pool.

Red was standing down there, looking up, shielding her eyes from the sun with her hand. "Hey, Hermit! Toss that back, willya?"

I tossed the ball down, over her head and into the water.

"Thanks. Still bowling tonight?"

"Yup."

"All bets still on?"

"Yup. I'll meet you down there at nine tonight."

"I'll be here." She bounced off, wading into the water to get the ball.

"It must be nice to have the pool right there," Terry said.

I closed the door and shut the curtain. "It's nice to be able to sit there and watch the little kids. And the boys do their fair share of girl watching from here."

"Well, I assume they watch *her* an awful lot. Those boobs can't be real."

"I honestly don't know," I chuckled. "I could find out."

"I bet you could. Come on, show me the rest of your apartment."

There wasn't much to show. She'd seen the living room and from there the kitchen was in full view. The hallway was short and the kids' room was to the left, a small bedroom crammed with two bunk beds and a dresser. There wasn't much room for anything else. I'd let them paint the walls a bright blue, and they lined the corners and ceiling with Christmas lights. With the beds hogging the wall space they decided to plaster the ceiling with posters, a collection of cars and half dressed women.

"Eileen doesn't sleep in here," I told her. "When the kids are here she sleeps in my room" – I guided her into the room on the right – "and I sleep on the sofa. I didn't feel right making her share a room with the boys."

One wall of the room was covered from ceiling to floor with pictures of pop stars and actors, with lots of pink and purple and glitter splashed between them. "Well... I figured since she slept here she should have a wall..."

"It's nice," she said. "I think I expected it to be bigger, but I like it."

If I had known I was going to be there that long, I would have rented a bigger place.

"So what's this about bowling?" We were back in the living room, sitting at opposite ends of the sofa. "I had no idea you bowled."

"Ted got me started last year. He needed someone really bad on his team to give them lots of handicap... I don't think he could have found anyone worse at the time."

"But you like it?"

"Sure. Tonight's just practice. Just me and my sixteen pound balls."

"Are you any good now?"

"Maybe. Why don't you come with me and see? I've never taken you bowling before. It could be fun. I'll even buy you dinner."

"I'm not exactly dressed for it, Chip. And I'm still all sweaty."

"Eileen has clothes here. I don't think she'd have a stroke if you borrowed some."

"Still sweaty."

"I do have a shower, you know. Come on, call the kids and tell them you'll be late. It'll give us a chance to talk."

She hesitated as if she was looking for a good reason to say no. "All right, Irish. You dig through your daughter's things and see if she has something that's not too far out for me to wear, and I'll go scrape the grime off."

I pointed her in the direction of the bathroom in the master bedroom – that was only fair considering the kids were responsible for keeping the other one clean – and then started digging through Eileen's clothes. I found jeans that might fit, one of my t-shirts, and tossed them onto the bed were she could be sure to find them.

She'd left the bathroom door wide open; too tempting for a horny forty year old with no sex life for the last two years.

I forced myself out of the bedroom. She'd agreed to bowling and dinner, which was much better company than I had counted on for the evening. I wasn't about to blow the baby steps by taking a giant one.

"So what's the bet, Irish?" she asked as she came out of the bedroom, Eileen's grungy sneakers in hand. "Your bowling bet with the redhead."

"Um, just a bet on my score. I've never won."

"What's the payoff?"

She sat next to me on the sofa and slipped the shoes on. I didn't really want her to know.

"I lose and then cough up twenty bucks a couple times a week, that's all."

"What if you win?"

"Hmm, well," I mumbled nervously, "I get to personally inspect them." I held my hands out in front of me, cupped at my chest. "You know."

"Chip!"

"Come on. There isn't a man alive who wouldn't give a years' pay to see that woman naked. But that's it, Terry, just a peek. I haven't promised anything and I wouldn't…"

"You're rambling," she interrupted. "And you don't owe me an explanation."

She looked as though she meant it. "Maybe I feel like I do," I said. "We are still married. I won't compromise that. There hasn't been anyone else."

For just the briefest moment she wouldn't look at me. She stared at the laces on Eileen's shoes, but then looked up at me, a wan smile on her face. "I'm glad," she said. "Look, about Brad – "

"Anything you have going with him is your own business and I'm not especially comfortable discussing it."

She smiled and leaned back, our arms touching. "That's just it, there's nothing there. I'm sure the kids have moaned and groaned about him, but he's just a friend. He's my boss and an occasional dinner companion, but nothing more."

"Okay." I know I didn't sound convincing.

"I never slept with him. I never wanted to."

"Well, good, because that's a picture I didn't want in my head. Come on," I got up and held out my hand to help her up. "Let's go bowling."

When I said I'd buy her dinner, I meant it. I didn't intend for it to be a freebie at the Charybdis, but that's where she wanted to go. She hadn't been near it since she parked my car and my clothes there, and she missed it. She missed

Ted, missed the smells and the sounds of all the people in the dining room, conversations pinging off the walls. Ted was working behind the bar; he smiled and waved at her when we walked past, and I doubt he even noticed I was there.

"This place hasn't changed at all."

We sat on opposite sides of booth near the bar. The dinner rush was over and there were a few unoccupied tables; couples would come and go the rest of the evening, and it wouldn't be so loud that we'd have to shout to hear each other over all the commotion.

She was right; I hadn't changed anything in the restaurant in years. Other than fresh copies of the same menu and new employees, there was probably nothing there she had never seen before. The waiter who took our order had no clue who she was; he probably ran back into the kitchen to gossip about the babe the boss had landed.

Not landed yet.

"Who won the bet?" she asked over appetizers.

"Depends on who you ask. The general bet is if I bowl under two hundred, I pay up. If I can prove I bowled over, she flashes me."

Her eyes widened and mouth sagged. "You didn't have a game under two-ten," she muttered.

She didn't have a game over ninety. It was fun to sit back and watch her, her frustration and fits of laughter over barely being able to keep the ball out of the gutter.

"No, I didn't," I said. "Can I explain the bet to you? My side of it?"

"You have your golden opportunity and you're throwing it away? Is it because of me?"

Only marginally.

"Look, if I tell her the truth, the polite little friendship we have is over. She'll pay up and be so mortified I'll never see her again. If I lose, it's just twenty bucks a couple times a week. Besides" – I hesitated, not wanting to sound self righteous and smug – "Red's husband died a while back. She has a baby and she watches other peoples' kids all day long. I don't think it's enough. Forty dollars a week is no big deal to me, but to her it's the difference between making it and going on welfare. I'm never going to win that bet, Terry. Not ever."

She reached across the table and touched my hand. White heat. I could feel a spark when her finger traced over my thumb; she turned my hand over and continued to sketch invisible lines across my palm. It itched and tickled at the same time, but I didn't dare pull my hand away.

"You're pretty wonderful, Irish," she said gently.

"Doug thinks it's pretty pathetic."

"He would," she snickered. "So would all three of your sons, but they're all walking hormones still."

"So's Doug."

She was still laughing when the waiter brought our food, her eyes twinkling and mouth open in a wide smile. *The boss's babe has this fricking awesome smile*, he undoubtedly reported back to the kitchen staff.

She had that effect; every new waiter and every new busboy spent the first three months of their employment with a massive crush on her. She had a dozen new young men to enthrall now.

One old one.

"It's late," she said when the plates were cleared away and she'd declined dessert for the third time. "Don't you have a lady you need to go pay? It's almost nine."

She talked nonstop the entire ride back, but my head

was pounding so hard I barely heard a word she said. When we walked from the car to the pool where Red would be waiting, I was sure my knees were knocking together.

I felt like a kid on his first date.

Do I get a kiss at the door or not?

Terry waited just outside the pool gate while I went in. Red was sitting at the shallow end, dangling her feet in the water. Usually there were four or five late swimmers, but tonight it was just Red.

I dug into my pocket and waved the twenty at her. "One ninety at my best," I said. "I'm getting there."

"Another year at your rate, Hermit." She took the twenty and looked past me. "Is that your wife?"

"That's the one," I said, trying not to smile.

"Well, at least now I know where Nick gets his looks from. It couldn't have been from you."

"Bitch."

"That's right." She came a step closer, finger poking into my chest. "Don't you blow it, Hermit. You grab onto her and don't let go this time. At least tell her how you feel before she has a chance to leave."

She smiled at Terry and gave a little wave as she disappeared into the darkness on the other side of the pool.

Terry couldn't leave; she needed me to take her back to her car.

I reached for the gate; I knew I either had to drive her back and open the trunk of her car so that she could go home, alone, or find some way to keep her with me, at least for a little while. She didn't move as I latched the gate behind me; we were only inches apart, she didn't take a step back to protect her personal space, and I had no clue what to say.

Her head was cocked to one side; she certainly expected me to say something. Anything.

What else could I do?

Kiss her, for one.

It had to be a careful kiss; not too demanding, just enough to get my message across. I kept my hands stuffed into my pockets and leaned my head down towards her, very slowly and very deliberately melting my lips against hers.

She expected it; I felt a surge of relief when she not only kissed back, but slid her hands up my chest and around my neck, leaning in to get as close as she could. I would have put my arms around her but she had my hands pinned inside my pockets.

"God," I breathed when we finally parted. "Don't go home just yet. Come upstairs for a little while. We don't have any of the kids hanging around and we can talk in private for once. Please."

She nodded and turned to head up the stairs.

My mind raced as I followed her. 'Open the door, offer her something to drink, even a soda… watch the early news if she wants, just get her talking…'

I got the door open and she stepped inside; as soon as it was closed and locked she grabbed my hand and headed for the bedroom. Her arms were looped around my neck, lips locked on mine, and we were on the bed before my head cleared.

"This isn't what I meant, Terry," I whispered against her lips. "I really did mean we could talk. I didn't have this in mind."

"I know." Her hands were working to tug my shirt over my head. "This is what *I* had in mind. You can say no, my feelings won't be hurt."

I'm not a total idiot.

We fumbled with each other's clothing, trying hard to

undress without our lips losing contact; we were there, both naked and more than willing, silently debating our choices. It could be either serious passion or inept comedy, and after all that time we weren't sure what we wanted.

We settled on tender affection; it was awkward yet familiar, and the best we could manage for each other were soothing sighs of contentment.

It was enough.

"I love you," she murmured against my neck. "I never stopped loving you, and it was such a stupid mistake…"

I lifted my head and shoulders from her body, quieting her with a kiss. "Not now. I don't want to talk about what went wrong, or about the kids, or anything else even remotely serious. It can wait."

She kissed me back.

"And I know you love me," I told her. "I doubted it for a long time, but" – I fingered the crucifix around my neck – "What you couldn't say in words you said with this. It meant the world to me, Terry. I cried like a baby after I opened it."

"Don't you make me cry," she sniffed.

"I always do."

"Not always."

I rolled onto my side, pulling her with me, pushing hair from her face. "I have to ask, though… I don't want to push for too much too fast, but I have to know. Is this just a one time thing, or do you want more?"

She kissed the tip of my nose, and then my chin. "This means everything to me, Irish. It's a start, not a detour."

"Terry, I want to come home," I said suddenly, surprising myself. "It doesn't have to be like right now… we might want to give the kids time to adjust to it. Hell, I might want time to chase after you and win you all over again, but I want to come home."

"You'd better come home, mister. I'm counting on it."

"Ah, are ya, now."

"And you can chase me all you want, but do it from home. The kids will be relieved, they don't need time to get used to it. They want you home as much as I do."

"I miss my cat, too," I admitted.

She laughed and kissed me. "I don't care why you're coming home. You can miss Max more, but I promise, give me some time and I'll be the reason you stay."

She was the reason I did everything.

I thought she knew that.

I stirred to warm lips burning into mine, soft hair teasing my cheeks. I muddled through leftover bits and pieces of a dream, trying to decide if I really wanted to wake up or not. My body was screaming that it wasn't time yet. I needed a few more hours.

Then I remembered Terry.

I woke up.

"Crawled into bed with this really hot guy last night," she murmured against my lips. "I woke up thinking it was just a dream, but here you are."

I glanced at the clock. Four thirty.

Cool fingers ran from my chest to my thighs and back again. My body reacted before my brain had a chance to.

"Not bad for an old man," she snickered.

"Hmm. Horny old goat."

"Works for me."

"Did you wake me up with a specific purpose in mind?"

"You really must be getting old if you have to ask." She rolled on top of me. "You can go back to sleep if you really want to, but parts of you are already cooperating."

Not a single part of me would have considering closing my eyes and drifting off. Nothing in my dreams could compare to having her right there wrapped around me, laughing like she used to, her lips and hands familiar brushing across my skin.

There was a time, when Will was considering leaving the priesthood to chase after the woman who refused to be his reason for leaving, that I asked him how we knew when we'd crossed the Very Catholic Line of having far too much fun in bed.

"If someone has to call the paramedics and have them scrape you off the ceiling," he said, "then you've enjoyed it too much."

We managed better than contentment.

Another minute and Terry would have needed a spatula for me.

After she'd caught her breath she sat straight up. "Oh, God, Chip. I never called the kids last night to let them know I'd be late."

"I think they've figured it out by now."

"If they've even noticed." She shoved a pillow behind me and urged me to sit up. "Put your arms around me, Irish. It's been too long since you really held me."

"Am I going to be in trouble if I want to talk about Paul?"

"Fifteen minutes ago you would have been in trouble. Now it's okay."

"I need to know what you think. I've been thinking we should let them do what they want."

"Let them get married."

"I don't see any other way. She's not getting an abortion and to be honest, I wouldn't want her to. I want my grandchild. She can't stay with her parents… I'm more than willing to support her but Paul has every right to be there right from the beginning of his child's life."

"They could live together."

"And that would make it too easy for him to walk away when it gets rough, and you know it's going to get rough. They deserve to have a chance to be a family. Our grandchild deserves a chance at two parents committed to each other. And my gut tells me Paul needs our trust on this. He's not walking away from it, Terry. I would have, at his age."

She sat up, the sheet pooled around her waist. "If he weren't so young I'd agree, but I don't think they have a real chance."

"Paul asked me if I thought our marriage was a mistake. He didn't see us getting back together but he didn't think I believed it never should have happened. Marrying you was the smartest thing I've ever done. If you'd never wanted to see me again, it still would have been the most important time of my life. He's having a baby with her… he doesn't see it as a mistake."

"You want to give him permission."

"Not without your consent."

"I suppose they could stay with us for a while…"

I shook my head. "No. If they get married, it's for real. We can help, but they have to be on their own."

"How?"

"Paul can work part time at the restaurant, and I'll arrange for him to get a part of his trust fund every month. The deal breaker is school, though. If he doesn't swear he'll at least finish high school, he gets nothing, and that includes our consent."

"You've really been thinking about this."

I'd gone over every scenario I could conjure up. Moving from the small apartment to something bigger, and letting them live with me had crossed my mind. Converting the study in the house to an apartment merited brief consideration. Giving one of the vacant places in the apartment complex to Monica popped into my head more than once, but the greater impulse was to allow my son a chance to be the husband and father he wanted to be.

"You know," Terry said, snuggling back against me, "if this was Nick I wouldn't have a second thought. I don't think he and Katie will last another year."

"You think they'll break up?"

"No, I think they'll get married before the end of next summer. They talk a mean game about waiting, but I don't see that happening."

"This is a good thing?"

"It's a good thing. Why, do you have reservations about Katie?"

"Me? Hell no. I've always liked her and she's good for Nick."

She lifted her head and looked at the bedside clock, groaning. "All right, Irish, now you have to take me home. It's almost six."

"What's so magical about six?"

"Some of us have day jobs, mister. I need to get home and make sure the kids get up in time for school, and I need to change clothes for work."

"Call in sick."

"I can't." She kissed me and threw the blankets back. "I took too much time off when you were sick. If I take any more off I might lose my job."

The world would not come to an end if she wasn't working but I didn't bother pointing that out. She wanted to work; when Kevin and Eileen started school she felt lost. Brad Colt offered her the job she'd had with his father before we married, and she jumped at it. One of us, she joked, needed to teach the kids a work ethic.

"Should we tell the kids we're getting back together?" I asked as we dressed. "Or should I just move my stuff in one piece at a time and see if they notice?"

"I think they'll get a clue when you're still there tonight and I'm dragging you kicking and screaming up the stairs. Or when we manage to pop the waterbed. We do have a couple years to make up for, you know."

"Should I be frightened?"

"Possibly." She wiggled back into Eileen's jeans and tossed my t-shirt over her head. "Take a swim suit with you. I have time to watch you swim a few laps before I go into work."

"I can't skinny dip?"

"Just what your daughter needs to see."

On the way out the door she reminded me she needed to pick her car up on the way. I fished the keys out of a drawer in the kitchen and was locking the front door when she stopped on the front step.

"About the car...?"

"Out of gas?"

"No. I locked the keys in the trunk on purpose. Just so you know."

Nick

I don't know what I was expecting when I stumbled into the kitchen, groggy from not enough sleep. Mom lying on her stomach on the diving board wasn't it. Kevin sitting quietly at the table munching on cereal and studying wasn't it. I definitely wasn't expecting someone swimming laps in the pool.

"Don't ask me," Kevin said, barely glancing up from his book. "They were out there when I got up. I don't know when she finally decided to come home."

Paul wandered in looking as tired as I felt. He was dressed in old gym shorts and wasn't wearing a shirt. "You'll get your ass tossed out of school dressed like that," I said.

"Not going," he grunted.

He stared out the door, shaking his head. "Out all night and she has the guts to bring *him* here," he snapped. "And she complains we don't keep our pants on."

"You don't."

"Eat shit and choke on it, you little bastard."

Kevin looked up, face as innocent as a three year old. "Are you cooking for us? I appreciate the warning."

Eileen's entrance stopped the potential fist fight.

"Christ, look at that." We all turned and looked outside to see what Paul was grumbling about. The swimmer had lifted himself out of the water, gripping the end of the diving board, his lips most definitely locked onto Mom's. "She can't even keep her hands off him with all of her kids around."

"You need glasses," Kevin said. "It's not Brad. Look. Anything familiar about his build? Hair, even though it's wet?" He paused for effect. "The shamrock tattoo?"

We looked closer.

"They came in about an hour ago," Eileen told us.

Paul and I looked at each other at the same time. His mood changed quickly, and he allowed himself a grudging smile. "She was with Dad all night?"

I was as surprised as he was. "I guess so."

For four kids whose biggest wish had been to see exactly what was taking place out in the back yard, we were amazingly calm. Kevin finished his breakfast, Eileen poured out orange juice for the rest of us, and we stared. Dumbfounded.

Goddamn. They got laid.

"Do you think it means much?" Kevin asked when we sat down, shoving his book aside.

I had no idea. My hopes were up but I didn't want to raise his.

"They'll get back together," Eileen said.

"If they're back together," Kevin reasoned, "they can tag team and gang up on Paul."

"No shit," Paul muttered.

"Admit it. This is what you had in mind when you knocked her up. 'C'mon, baby, let's do it so my parents will start talking and get back together just so they can freak out in unison.'"

Paul almost smiled. "Learn from my mistakes, Kev. If you're gonna play like an adult, you have to pay like an adult."

"I don't think I'll play for a while. The rest of you can screw your brains out. I'm gonna remain pure and good and all that crap."

"Right."

"Really. It'll totally freak them out."

"He's staying pure until Lydia flashes those boobs at him again and says, 'touch 'em big boy,'" I laughed.

"Well yeah," he said. "That'd just be for research. You know, making *real* sure they really are all her. Pure research, and it's all good."

"You're a dork, Kevin," Eileen groaned.

The back door slid open and Dad stuck his head in, dripping water onto the floor. "Good, you're up," he said. "Paul, I want you to go to school and get Monica and bring her back here. I want to talk to both of you."

He closed the door.

Paul's face paled.

"It'll be okay," Eileen said. "If it were bad news he'd have ordered the rest of us out so he could talk to you now."

"No shit," Kevin added. "He didn't look irritated at all."

"They're right," I said. "If he was going to rip your head off he would have done it as soon as he got here. He wouldn't have bothered getting in the pool."

Paul didn't look too sure.

"I'd better get dressed and go get her," he said quietly.

The poor slob looked like he was about to face a firing squad. I didn't think so; the squad was in the back yard, Mom squealing at Dad to stop splashing her, Dad threatening to pull her in with him.

Kevin got up from the table, shoving his book into his backpack. "I'm claiming first rights," he said.

"To…?"

He grinned. "I'm gonna start calling her 'grandma.'"

Chip

I hadn't heard the words "Don't be fresh" since I was around twelve years old and had tried to kiss some girl in the cafeteria line. Eight hundred empty headed preteens screaming at the top of their lungs, food flying through the air, and I was trying to lock lips with the seventh grade Wonder Woman.

Twenty eight years later they still made me groan. Coming from my wife – in the middle of the restaurant – they sounded absurd.

"Watch your hands on the dance floor, Irish," she laughed lightly in my ear. "You're as bad as the boys."

"It's all those Davis hormones."

She took a step back from me, not missing a beat. "Oh, wow, you don't know. I kept meaning to tell you but always found a reason to not call…"

"You wanted to call me about my hormones?"

"Well, sometimes," she snickered. "No, the kids were cleaning stuff out of the study and ran across a stack of Grant's old papers. They found a name change certificate, Chip. His real name was Brennan."

I stopped dancing. "Are you serious?"

"They found it about six months ago. God, I can't remember what his first name was. But there's a huge stack of papers, and his journals. I didn't let the kids poke through any of it and I didn't open the journal, but I'm ashamed to admit, I thought about using it to lure you back to the house."

Where would we be now if you had, I wondered.

There was a stack of work sitting on my desk, food orders to sign and time cards to be approved, but we left the restaurant and headed home.

I had to say it to myself more than once. Not the apartment, my pit stop on the way to hell, but home. My wife, my kids, my cat. Home.

I hadn't ventured into the study, now a game room, in years. The kids used it constantly; it seemed like any time I had wandered in there at least two of them were arguing over the rules of eight ball or nine ball, or they were throwing darts at the wall. My father's huge oak desk and the bookshelves behind it were forbidden territory, though I could tell from the stray pieces of paper on top of the desk – someone's complicated math homework – that they had taken my absence as permission to use it.

I lifted one of the papers and studied it. None of it made sense to me.

"Kevin's," Terry said, digging into one of the drawers. "He sometimes studies in here when Paul or Eileen are blasting their stereos too loud. I didn't think you'd mind."

"Is this math or chemistry?"

She glanced up. "I have no idea. I'm not about to ask because he'll just try to explain it to me, and frankly, my brain can't take it."

My kids knew I had dropped out of high school; there were times I felt they wanted to throw that back at me when I was pounding the importance of an education into them.

Sure, Dad, we have to put our all into it when you gave up at sixteen. You want us to excel and get great paying jobs, you want us to think we'll get nowhere if we don't go to college, yet here you sit on top of millions. Doesn't look like dropping out hurt you any. Why should we bother?

If they'd ever asked, I had my answer ready.

Because I Said So.

Terry stacked the papers and Grant's journal on top of the desk and began sorting through them. I sat in his old leather chair, running my finger over the edge of his journal. It was leather bound, the cover cracked and faded, edges of the paper yellow with age. I had vague memories of seeing him sitting there, pen in hand, the furrow across his brow as he scratched out his thoughts. At the time I'd thought it an odd exercise in futility; who would care what this old man had to say? After a few weeks alone, when the realization hit that I needed not only the apartment but furniture and everything else to go along with it, I understood his impulse to chronicle, and bought a journal of my own.

No one ever had to read it. No one had to care what I thought. It was cathartic, and that was all that mattered.

"Here it is." She handed me the certificate, and neatly restacked the rest of the papers. "Check the date, Chip. He was in Los Angeles when he got it, just a few months after you were born."

"Michael Ian Brennan, Junior to Grant Alan Davis." I looked up at her. "I wonder why."

"Maybe it's in his journal," she suggested. "There are tons of certificates here, too. Their marriage license, I think."

I flipped through them, pulling out the least faded of the bunch.

"My birth certificate." I turned it over in my hand, not certain I had the right thing. It was not the certificate Grant had given me years before, and definitely not the one I presented to the world as proof that I existed. "Michael Ian Brennan, the third. Mother Patricia Madonna Elizabeth Cagney, father Michael Ian Brennan, Junior."

I set it down, only to pick it back up.

"Don't believe it?" she asked.

That wasn't it. Seeing the name in black and white brought to my mind the whisper of a comment made by a man I was learning to not trust. Then, I had thought it was a diversion, something to make me blink and give myself away. I'd never considered it was the truth.

"Well," she took the certificate from me, "I kind of like it. Chip Brennan. Has a better Irish ring to it."

"You really are hung up on the Irish thing, aren't you?"

"It's your brogue," she teased. "It does things to me."

"I've noticed." I picked the journal up, carefully thumbing through pages. "It makes you want to try to break my winky."

"You're not going to read that tonight, are you?"

"Not if you have something else in mind."

"I have a lot of things in mind… but the kids are all up and still wandering around the house, and I think they want some of your time, too."

"Selfish little bastards, aren't they?"

"Sometimes," she admitted. "Once they realize you're home I expect they'll barge in here."

"Be vewwwwy, vewwwwy quiet."

She reached for my hand and pulled me up. "Come on. Let's at least go sit in the living room for a while and give them a chance to drift downstairs and see what's up. Sooner or later we have to tell them you're staying."

"Do we have to?"

I let her drag me into the living room and plopped down on the couch while she went into the kitchen for sodas. Max was at the top of the stairs hollering – he had the sound of a hungry kitty whose food dish must be empty – and I could hear Kevin and Eileen squabbling upstairs. The only thing missing was one of the boys bounding down the stairs in search of someone who would either drag Kevin from his room, do his homework, or give him money.

Max padded his way down the stairs and into the living room, ears flat with anger. He stomped across the rug and jumped up onto my lap and hissed – get me food, dammit – and then curled up on my suit coat.

The sound of crinkling paper under his butt reminded me I had something to give to Terry.

I reached into the jacket for the envelope I'd tucked away in the pocket. Max took a swipe at my hand, indignant at the intrusion. "It's *my* coat," I told him. "You're getting hair all over it."

He didn't care.

"Got something for you," I said when she came back into the room. I took one of the cans of Diet Coke she had and handed her the envelope. "Open it."

She sat next to me and opened it, carefully pulling out the papers inside, flipping them over to be sure she understood what they were. "Your pension fund? Retirement?"

"I resigned from the agency," I said. "Fully resigned. I didn't allow for any chance that they could find a loophole in my contract that would let them drag me back for anything else."

"Chip…"

"I never really lied, Terry. I wasn't working for them all along, but I did do research when they asked and I did some consulting for them. They kept the contract open and I never did anything to close it. And for that I am deeply, deeply sorry. Never again, I swear to you."

She flipped to the last page, looking for my signature, and the signature of the Secretary General of the U.S. Defense Agency.

"George Barron," she muttered. "Not Alex Barstow?"

"No." I took the papers from her and shoved them back into the envelope. "Not Alex Barstow."

FOUR

1992

Chip

My first reaction to the phone call from the agency's Assistant Secretary General was to tell him to go hell; over the years I had allowed them to pick my brain, I had waded through mounds of paperwork looking for stray clues others had missed, and I shared my experiences on working the field at a young age with trainees. I did it quietly, and I did it behind my wife's back.

Enough was enough – anything the ASG would personally contact me for had to be something I wanted to avoid. His call was a direct plea: hear me out, give me ten minutes of your time. Ten minutes to tell you why you'll accept this assignment.

I was curious; I agreed to ten minutes.

Within five minutes he had me seriously considering his proposal. I promised him an answer by the end of the day, and left in search of someone who could help me reach a decision. Someone who would understand.

"Do you think," Kris asked, settling next to me onto a bench by the pond, "that this is something Ron would have wanted you to do?"

"Probably not. No, I know he wouldn't. Ron would be telling me to turn around and run and not look back."

"But...?"

"But in spite of everything, I feel like I owe Barstow this much."

She leaned forward, staring out at the water. "Alex Barstow turned Ron into an assassin. If not for him, Ron might still be alive. He cracked under the pressure, Chip. The man might have been my ex, but I still wish he had been here all along to see your kids grow up. He'd have been a hell of a grandfather... whether he was your father or not."

Ron would have been a terrific grandfather; finding out I was not his son, however, probably would have killed him as quickly as he killed himself.

"Barstow provided the means for me to find my son when he was kidnapped," I reminded her. "Who knows what might have happened to Nicky if he hadn't let me abuse the system. God, we found Nicky in a day, that never would have happened if Barstow hadn't opened everything up for me. He let me use agency resources to look for my brother, too."

"Haven't you ever wondered if they didn't know where David was from day one? If they could have saved his life?"

"No."

She wouldn't look at me. "Did you know," she said, "that this was the last place I saw Ron? I met him here to tell him I was marrying Doug, and that I was pregnant. I was sitting right here, watching him throw popcorn to the ducks, and I ripped his heart out. He wasn't expecting to hear that kind of news."

"And Ron is why you think I shouldn't do this?"

A barely perceptible nod. "For most of your life you thought he was your father, and he let them twist him into becoming an assassin to spare *you* being stuck working for the agency for the rest of your life. I'd think you'd want to honor that."

"And ignoring a debt owed would be honoring him? Kris, it doesn't matter what he was manipulated into doing. He would agree that I probably owe my son's life to Barstow, even if he'd want me to turn around and run."

"But doing this? Going on a wild goose chase halfway across the world on the slim chance that you can figure out who has him, and how to get him out alive?"

"They already have the intelligence. Go in and meet my contact, get Barstow and get out, it's a simple enough case."

"So simple that three men have died trying to get to him."

"Rookies."

"Bullshit."

"They still own my contract."

"And they won't hold you to it. If you had no choice Barron would have made it an order, not a request. Son of a bitch, you could have gotten out of that contract years ago. They've never done anything that would explain why you're so damned loyal."

Kris gave me exactly what I wanted: an argument for not going, and reasons why I should. Honor. Loyalty.

"Do you ever miss it?" I asked. "The whole team working together?"

"Sometimes. Every now and then I miss the excitement."

"But?"

"But mostly I miss our team. I miss Dan Martin and his

stuffed shirt, and how ticked off he'd get when we'd start screwing around. He wasn't the best team leader in the agency, but he was such a good person and it pisses me off that we never got to know the Dan he would have been when he retired. And God, don't you ever tell Doug, but I miss Ron, too."

"I'm pretty sure he knows that."

"Doug accepts the idea that I visit the grave of my ex-husband and I make sure it has flowers and that the headstone is clean. He accepts the idea that when I left I still loved Ron just a little bit, and that when Ron killed himself I was hurt and I grieved... Knowing that I actually miss the man might be like rubbing salt into a wound."

"Give him some credit, darlin'. Missing Ron and having loved him doesn't take anything away from what you've got going with Doug."

"It wouldn't exactly be a confidence builder, you know?"

She had me there. My past included a hooker I'd proposed to, a teenager who killed herself when the realization that I didn't love her and was only using her came thundering down on her. I could imagine that if Terry thought I missed Brenda, genuinely missed her, she might feel threatened by the ghost of her memory.

My only real worry that afternoon, though, was figuring out how to tell her and make her think it was a good idea.

"Your contact is a local," Barron said, handing me a credit card, cash, and a plane ticket. "You don't need a partner or a cover on this one. Hopefully you won't be there long enough to be noticeable."

It was four in the morning, we were in the back seat of a government sedan, my head was pounding from lack of sleep, and he was so chipper I wanted to body slam him through the window.

Terry obviously did not think this trip was a good idea.

"Where do I meet up with my contact?" I asked.

"He'll meet you in the hotel lobby an hour after you check in. Don't unpack anything, just dump it and get moving."

"Christ, can I pee first?"

"As long as you're done in time to meet him."

Barron instructed the driver to just drop me off; no one was there to send me off, wish me luck, whatever it was I wanted. Normally someone would be going with me, a partner, a team; I couldn't remember having ever ventured out on an assignment totally alone from the start.

I was, I reasoned as I walked into the terminal, perfectly capable of catching a flight all by myself. I had on my big boy pants and shoes without Velcro closures; surely I could handle checking in alone and getting myself onto an airplane.

Taking off for Brazil would have been better if it were with Terry.

I slept in fits and snatches on the connecting flight out of Miami, stuck in a window seat beside a younger couple intent on babbling the entire way. Taylor and Bobbie – "that's short for Barbara, you know!" – Fox. Their honeymoon, I learned without asking. They had been married for fifteen hours and were taking the trip of a lifetime while they were still young enough to enjoy it.

The implication being that I was obviously long past that point in life.

"First thing we're going to do is head for the beach," Taylor said emphatically. "Nothing but sun and sand and water for a whole week."

I glanced at my watch. "You'll be getting there at night," I reminded them. "Besides, first thing on my honeymoon going to the beach was the last thing on my mind."

That elicited a shy giggle from Bobbie. She was only about nineteen years old, and Taylor didn't strike me as being much older.

Terry was nineteen when we married.

It hadn't seemed so young then.

I watched them fawn all over each other and listened to them gush, and hoped to hell Terry and I had never been that cute.

"How long have you been married?" she asked, pointing to my wedding ring.

"Sixteen years."

"Kids?"

I nodded. "Four. One is fifteen, one just turned fourteen, and twelve year old twins."

"Wow. I can't even imagine that. What's the secret?"

Hell if I knew.

"The secret," I guessed, "is that she's always right, and as long as I remember that, things run smoothly."

They both laughed.

I wasn't joking. Not exactly. In that moment it occurred to me that I tended to give in most of the time. Life was just easier that way.

We shared a cab to the same hotel – on me, what the hell, they could count it as a wedding present from a stranger – and parted ways after they checked in. I did as I was ordered, I went up to my room, took just a few minutes to throw my bag onto the bed, shaved and brushed my teeth, and headed back for the lobby.

For half a second I entertained the idea of calling Terry

before I left the room. My brain was fogged and I wasn't sure what time it was at home, but my hand was reaching for the phone when I thought better of it.

No sense ticking her off even more by waking up the entire house for a phone call.

God, I wish I had called.

The hotel was not as upscale as the others that dotted the beaches of Rio. It was acceptable for a casual stay, but not a place I'd bring my wife and expect her to remember the trip as Something Special. I suspected it was special enough for the Foxes, who would be looking at it through very young eyes, but if I'd been there for any reason other than to bring Barstow home, I would have been disappointed.

I waited in the lobby, staking a claim to the lone sofa that was shoved against a wall facing the door. People drifted in and out of the hotel; late arrivals checking in, and late partiers stumbling back half drunk and not at all quiet about it. Clerks at the desk wore their boredom on their faces, housekeepers wandered past and disappeared into the elevators, the smell of disinfectant lingering after they were gone.

Every time the doors to the lobby opened the clerks looked up expectantly, as if they hoped for more late comers, anything to break up the monotony. Most people coming through the door headed for the elevators, others for the restaurant. No one bothered to look my way, or even seemed curious that I was there alone and obviously waiting.

I probably looked like someone who had just been dumped and was waiting for my woman to come slinking back to beg forgiveness.

Almost an hour to the minute that I checked in, the doors opened and two men came in, heading straight for me. They didn't look around, neither glanced at the clerks or the elevator. The taller of the two muttered, "Ése es el hombre que estamos buscando," and nodded in my general direction.

My brain kicked into gear and reached far back to the immersion languages I had been soaked with my first years with the agency. They had to be there somewhere.

Spanish.

That's the man we're looking for.

The shorter of them hung back while the other approached. I stood up, and he asked, in perfect English, if I was the person looking for the missing American. There was barely a trace of an accent. He was dressed casually but carried a familiar air of formality, like someone's Harvard educated pool boy. Someone trying to slum without having a clue how.

He sat on the far end of the sofa. "You had a long flight. I can take you to the American now, or wait until morning," he said. "It doesn't matter. He'll be where he is either way."

With fatigue ripping through me, my impulse was to wait until morning, but my orders were to move quickly. "We can go now."

He looked doubtful. "You should at least eat first," he suggested. "I can take you to him in less than an hour, and once you have him you may not have the time to stop. He's not going anywhere."

My stomach agreed with him. We went into the restaurant, and I ordered what I thought would be least likely to kick back on me, a sandwich and a Diet Coke. My contact – who hadn't offered his name, nor had I asked – ordered similarly, making small talk while we waited for the food. I didn't ask about his companion, who hovered in the distance like a bodyguard. I avoided questions about my family or my job, and only asked about the region. Where would be a good place to stay on a more social visit? How expensive is it? How tired do they get of all the tourists?

"Where is the American?" I finally asked, waving to the waiter for the check.

"Not far. We'll head past the *favelas* to a better residential area. More like what you would expect in your country."

"He's being held in suburbia?"

He nodded. "Not what you expected?"

I wasn't sure what I expected. He gestured to his companion and told him, in Spanish, to bring the car around. His companion nodded and left, leaving us in an awkward silence.

"Cuanto tiempo usted ha vivido en el Brasil?" I asked. *How long have you lived in Brazil?*

He grinned, surprised at my use of his language. "Toda mi vida." *All my life.* "You speak Spanish very well."

"I can get my point across."

His companion came back. "El coche es listo." *The car is ready.*

The hairs on the back of my neck prickled; this didn't feel right. "Quanto tempo você viveu em Brasil?" I asked.

"Qué?"

"Ah, see, my Spanish isn't as good as I thought. Never mind. I'm tired and not thinking straight."

"We can wait," he offered again.

I nodded. "Maybe we should. If I get some sleep I might be able to think clearly."

He paid the bill and left without hesitating.

"Would you like anything else?" the waiter asked.

"No, eu tive bastantes, mas agradeço-o."

"Your Portuguese is very good," he said, shades of the familiar.

I got up. "It comes in handy every twenty years or so," I said, dropping more money on the table to cover a tip.

Going to my room and to bed was the last thing I intended.

I waited near the elevator, where I could see through the lobby doors and watched them climb into their car. As they pulled away I headed for the door, looking for a taxi. I waved the first one past and grabbed the second one, telling the driver to follow the red sedan, and to keep a safe distance.

Shades of a bad B-movie, but it was the only thing I could think of.

The driver grunted but didn't protest. He just flipped the meter on and pulled away from the curb.

It was too dark for me to see where we were headed. I was vaguely aware of the changes in scenery, the long string of hotels and beach that faded into urban blight, homes crammed together, one damn near on top of another, cardboard construction that roared poverty and contrasted the tourist strip in screaming black and white. The cab driver kept a good measured distance from the sedan, matching his speed and maneuvering around corners before he could lose them to the dark.

Forty five minutes later we were in the heart of upper suburbia. The sedan pulled into a driveway and disappeared behind a heavy security gate. I directed the cab driver to pass the house and pull over a block down the street.

The only words I heard from him were to demand payment.

The property was more upscale than the average American middle class neighborhood. Homes were hidden behind thick wrought iron gates and surrounded by brick walls and cement borders. Several had signs posted, warning of guards and dogs.

It was what I would have grown up with, had the times been equitable. Our neighborhood was affluent, but existed in a time of relative safety; the kids played outside without worrying about cars screeching down the court, and we didn't worry about intruders who would creep into our lives in the middle of the night to snatch children from their beds.

That particular nightmare waited until Nick was nine months old. I understood then the raw terror that forces people behind fifteen foot high walls and barbed wire. When we moved into my father's house, the temptation to build a wall all around the neighborhood was strong; the idea stayed in the back of my head, as neighbors grew old and died, or wanted to move from their spacious houses as their children left home, that I could buy every house on the street and close it off to the world.

Terry refused to live in a prison. We bought the houses and left the court open.

I found a spot on the brick wall where I could lift myself up high enough to see into the yard and still be obscured by trees. The driveway curled around the front of the house; there were four cars parked by the garage, the entire area brightly lit. Light faded around the side of the house, and the interior perimeter of the wall was dark.

There was nothing to indicate that the house was secured by guard dogs.

I lifted myself all the way over and dropped onto the grass, creeping along in the darkest part of the yard, making sure I stayed near the wall, looking for an easy entrance to the house.

I made it about twenty feet before my head exploded in

a starburst of pain, and the lights from the house winked out.

It hurt too much to open my eyes; my head felt as if it were wrapped in cotton and I could hear muffled voices, but I didn't want to move, not even to blink. I took a deep breath, my head pounding with each pulse, and forced one eye open just enough to soak in the blinding white ceiling above.

Damn, had I ever screwed up.

Slowly, I tried opening both eyes, squinting in the brightness of white-white walls and fluorescent lighting. The room's walls were bare save one mirror, and besides the mattress I was laying on the only thing close to furniture was a metal folding chair. There were two doors, one halfway open that lead, as far as I could tell from where I was, to a bathroom. The other was closed and there were people arguing on the other side.

Familiar voices.

I closed my eyes again and strained to hear.

"You should have brought him straight here. My orders were simple enough. Meet him, tell him you would bring him, and come."

"He needed to rest."

"He could have done that *here*."

"I did what I thought best. He needed to eat, and he needed some sleep, and one night made no difference. And he did what I expected, anyway. He followed."

"*He didn't need to follow, you fool.*"

"Either way, he's here."

The door knob turned.

"Get Yakov."

I sat up as quickly as I could, the room spinning while my head screamed in protest.

Alex.

"My apologies," he said. "You were supposed to be escorted, not lead here on some insane hunting expedition."

I kept my mouth shut.

"I can't believe they sent you. Or maybe I can, at some point Barron must have realized he needed to send someone he could trust to go all out and finish the assignment. I have to admit, I'm honored that you agreed to do it."

Why was he not locked in another room?

I looked up, scanning the ceiling and corners for cameras, peering at the light fixtures for evidence that we were being filmed. When I was sure I could stand without falling over, I got up and went to the mirror, leaning in as close as I could, touching my finger to the glass.

The tip of my finger touched its image.

I looked into the bathroom. There didn't appear to be any cameras, and there was a nice millimeter between the tip of my finger and its image in the mirror. There was nothing in the toilet tank, the shower head was just a shower head, and there were clean towels.

Barstow watched quietly while I inspected the room.

"You have privacy in there," he said when I came out. "And yes, the other mirror is two-way, but you're not being watched."

I had my doubts.

He turned when the door opened; defiantly I dropped back onto the mattress, though the gray haired, wrinkled old man who came in did no more than glance at me.

"Yakov," Alex said.

"Is he the one you expected?"

Barstow nodded.

"He's the fourth man, Alex."

"He'll be the last. I know him. We can trust him."

Don't be so sure.

The old man looked at me again. "How long have you known him?"

"All his life. His name is Michael Brennan. I worked with his father, and later with him."

"Is he in Barron's pocket?"

"No." Barstow shook his head. "I can swear to that."

What game are you playing?

The old man looked at me and asked, "Do you need a doctor?"

I shook my head.

"Fine." He turned toward the door. "Brief him, and pray he's the person you think he is."

Alex picked up the chair and opened it, sitting in front of me. "Go ahead and ask. No one is listening."

I shook my head.

"You have my word."

There was a time I thought his word was worth something; now I wasn't so sure. My response was a slight shake of my head.

"Fine. You can listen," he said, shifting in his seat. He leaned forward, elbows on his knees, hands rubbing together. "You weren't sent here to rescue me, Chip. No matter what Barron told you, your job is to bring me back by any means and I can't allow that to happen. If I went with you, I'd be dead within a week."

He had my attention.

"It would be a very public and very tragic accident, I'm sure. The agency would be in official mourning, Barron would grieve openly and would accept the public condolences of everyone from the President on down, and privately would receive their accolades for crushing me."

"For what purpose?" I finally asked.

"For the purpose of ridding the Defense Agency of its highest ranking mole."

"Very funny."

He didn't smile.

"You *are* fucking joking, aren't you?"

"No," he said simply. "I was never an American citizen, Chip. I was always a Russian mole."

"Jesus Christ."

He sighed hard. "I was placed with the agency from its very beginning in the early fifties. I rose to the rank that was expected of me in the time that as expected, and I was ready to go home – only now there is no home to return to. Factions of the KGB still exist, but many of them are so closely associated with the Russian Mafia... I can't go home. I'm a liability on both sides. The United States wants me dead for obvious reasons, and I don't know enough about the inner workings of former Soviet Intelligence to be of any further use to them. Any former KGB will want me dead because I can implicate them. And they no longer need the information I was able to feed them over the years.

"My only choice was to leave before I could be eliminated. I thought we had gotten out safely and had left no traces, but the three agents preceding you proved my arrogance wrong. They tell me the assistant secretary general knows more than I ever gave him credit for... He wants me home so that I can be assassinated in a public enough manner that it can be called an accident. He wants no trace of me left."

"Who is 'we'?"

He waved me off. "No one else that matters."

"And who's the old guy?"

"My father." He allowed himself a small smile. "In spite of what you've thought over the years, I was neither hatched nor found under a rock.

"And speaking of fathers," he went on, "I made a promise to yours. I swore I would keep you safe, and keep your family safe, and I meant it. I'll give you the chance to get home to your family, but I'm not going with you."

"Then what…?"

"What I want is for you to produce evidence of my death to the ASG. Pictures of my dead body covered in blood. Claim that you personally saw my corpse, and that you took the pictures."

He stood and moved the chair back to its spot by the wall.

"Take some time to think about it. I know you'll make the right decision."

I understood the implications; if I didn't agree, I wouldn't live to see the end of the week. If I did what he asked, I would be as much of a traitor as he was. Neither seemed a viable option.

I promised Terry I would come home.

I swore I wouldn't die.

Barstow gave me four days to think about it; the only people who entered the room were there to bring food or clean towels, and at one point the clothes I had left in my hotel room were delivered, freshly laundered and neatly folded. A stack of newspaper clippings, all the comics out of the Sacramento Bee from the previous week.

I wasn't surprised that Barstow knew what parts of a newspaper I headed for first.

I also wasn't surprised that I was never offered a chance to go outside, even with guards. Barstow was not about to give me the chance to memorize the layout of the house or the yard. He wouldn't take a chance that I would find even a tiny crack in his armor that would give me a way out, not until I gave him my word I'd keep his secrets.

He shouldn't have worried. If I'd been up to snuff I wouldn't have been locked in that room in the first place.

Late on the fourth day – I'd pretty much lost track of the time and gauged it by what meals were brought to me – he returned, briefcase in hand. He looked hopeful, sitting in the chair with the case on his knees, fumbling through it while I pretended disinterest.

"Everything you need is in here," he said. "Your passport, wallet, money, and assorted papers to make it look legitimate enough." He held up a small camera. "On this film are pictures to prove my death. Just tell them the camera was in the briefcase and you used it. It's a standard issue, there should be no questions about it."

Bullshit, I thought, but stayed quiet.

He pulled out two photographs, holding them by the corners. In them he was in a heap on the floor, blood oozing from his nose and mouth, eyes open and glazed over, a blood soaked shirt hinting of a huge wound underneath. "These are what they'll find on the film. Me. Dead."

"What makes you think they'll take my word for it?" I asked.

"Barron has no reason to doubt you."

I nodded towards the pictures. "Forensics will blow those up and comb over them pixel by pixel. They'll figure out it's a fraud."

He snapped the briefcase shut. "I don't think so. On your

word alone Barron will believe that I'm dead. It's what he wants."

I sighed and shook my head.

"I'm an old man, Chip," he said. "I simply want the few years I have left to be quiet."

He didn't look old, but I realized then he must have been in his seventies. His father was probably pushing one hundred but didn't look anywhere near it. The years Barstow looked forward to could push thirty.

I reached for the briefcase and flipped the latches, pulling out my wallet and passport. "If they don't believe me," I said, shoving the wallet into my back pocket, "you know they'll come after you again. And you know they won't send a single agent. You'll be running from special ops contingents from both our agency and the CIA."

"Barron *will* believe you."

"You damn well better hope so."

"Just swear to him you saw me dead." He stood, looking at me hopefully. "Deliver the pictures and your word, and you'll be out of it forever, Chip. Barron will never ask you for another thing."

"Sure. And how the hell do I know I won't walk out of here only to have one of your guys will plug me through the back of my head?"

"You have my word."

"Like that's worth much these days." I shoved my shoes on, tying the laces with sharp jerks. "So I just walk out of here?"

He nodded. "As long as you have that briefcase in hand, no one will stop you. Walk out this door, go down the hall and out the front door, and there will be a blue car near the gate. There are keys in it, and a map that will show you the quickest route to the airport."

"It's too easy," I grumbled.

"It shouldn't always be hard," he said. "I've always respected you. Under other circumstances I would have considered you a friend. I did consider your father a friend."

"Not my – "

"I know who your father is," he said. "I'm trying to save your life, not destroy it. I owe you that much, and I owe him that much." His hands went to my shoulders. "Chip, you know what you have to do."

I nodded. "I need to be back with my family," I said quietly. I reached for his shoulders to return the gesture. "And you're right, I do know what I have to do. I owe you for a lot, Alex."

"Thank you."

I took a deep breath, nodding, trying to smile.

Then I broke his neck.

FIVE

1994

Chip

"Chip, my God…"

"I didn't have much of a choice. I either let him live and walk away as much of a traitor as he was, or kill him to keep him from taking any more of our intelligence to Russia. I didn't completely buy his story… my gut feeling said he was headed home and he would have spilled it all to whatever agency replaced the KGB."

"No Russian mafia?"

"There's a Russian mafia and I'm sure many are also former KGB, but he had no reason to live in fear of them. He had every reason to make it home and every reason to make sure no U.S. agent got close enough to bring him back here."

"Then why were you able to get so close?"

"He wanted me to. He assumed I would help him out of a sense of obligation."

"But he had to know how dedicated you were to your job."

"He hoped I was more loyal to him. I don't know… I

tore out of there like my ass was on fire and I didn't look back. I honestly expected to have my head blown off before the plane could get off the ground. All I can figure is that they didn't find his body in time to catch up to me. I had his damned briefcase, no one tried to stop me."

"So you flew home."

"I called Barron from the plane and told him to meet me in D.C."

I spent the next three days being debriefed. He was remote, formal, and distinctly cold as he lead the panel conducting what felt like an Inquisition. I was grilled from morning until late afternoon, asked the same questions repeatedly, until the details became a blur and I was no longer sure of anything.

I told them everything I could: where the house was located, how many men I presumed Barstow had, the existence of someone he claimed was his father, and how I had killed him.

Barron ordered me onto a chartered plane, and once we were in the air and headed back to California, he relaxed.

"I couldn't tell you. For that I apologize."

I shrugged it off. "I'm one of the grunts, Mr. Barron. I'm not entitled to the details."

"Satisfy my curiosity. Had you known the inevitable end result, would you have gone?"

"No. I'm not an assassin. I'm surprised you didn't send one instead."

"Alex knew them all," he said. "No one else would have gotten so close. But he trusted you."

"And you knew he'd let me in."

"I had hoped so."

"There's an entire network of his moles out there, you know."

"Undoubtedly. But that's not your problem now."

He wrote the last chapter on my involvement with the agency that day, yet it took me two years to close the book.

"They can never push you into working again?" Terry asked.

"They won't. They can always ask, but I'm not obligated for anything. And I won't, Terry, not ever."

She started to say something, but the front door opened and Paul came in. He didn't seem surprised to see me there; if he was, he hid it well, walking towards us with the gait of a tired, cranky little boy.

"Aren't you grounded?" I asked.

For a split second he thought I wasn't kidding. "I'm ignoring it," he said. "I can be a rebel that way."

"Sure you are."

"How's Monica?" Terry asked him.

"Completely freaked out." He sat at the edge of the fireplace, leaning forward with his elbows on his knees. "I think she's worried her dad will figure everything out before she has a chance to get out of there."

"Just another day or so, son," I said. "Did you look at apartments today?"

"A few. I'm not real thrilled with the neighborhoods they're in. We have an appointment to look at a townhouse tomorrow. I dunno, Dad, every manager we've talked to takes one look at us and I think they're figuring we're way too young to be serious about moving in."

"Say the word and I'll go with you."

"You can't miss too much school, Paul," Terry said.

"The appointment is after school, Mom." He looked at me. "Did you talk to the principal today?"

"I did. You won't have any problems with missing a

week and they won't keep Monica from finishing the school year and graduating."

"Even after the baby is born?"

"Even after."

"Cool." He got up and headed for the stairs. "If you wouldn't mind going with us tomorrow I think it'll help," he said. "And I think Monica will be okay once she's away from her dad."

I waited until he was all the way up the stairs. "It's more like he'll be okay once Monica is away from her dad," I said. "If the townhouse isn't any good, I'll steer them towards my apartment complex."

Terry leaned against my arm, resting her head on my shoulder. "You know Paul is looking at apartments with the bottom line in his head. He's trying so hard to figure out a way to manage it all without our help."

"He'll get over it. All I have to do is tell him to accept a little help or move in with us. He'll accept a little help getting started."

"I thought you wanted them completely on their own."

"I do, but he doesn't know that."

"You're too easy, Irish."

"He doesn't know that, either."

"Chip, even your cat knows you're a soft touch."

If Max thought I was easy, he didn't show it. He followed us up the stairs, yowling at the top of his lungs until Terry detoured and went down the hall to fill his dish.

"Which one of us is the easy touch?" I asked.

"I'm just being the responsible wife of a pet owner."

"Well, guess what," I said, kicking off my shoes. "He's your cat now, too."

"He can be my cat when he's being cute. He's your cat

when he's being a pain in the ass and rolling the damned golf ball down the stairs at three in the morning."

"Why don't you just take the golf ball away?"

It took her too long to answer.

"Never occurred to you, did it?" I laughed.

"Well…" She dropped onto the bed, reaching out for my hand. "I've had my mind on other things. I haven't exactly been thinking clearly."

"You've been saving your brain cells for plotting to get me to feel sorry for the poor blonde who locked her keys in her car."

"Something like that."

"You know," I said softly, pushing hair away from her face, "all you had to do was ring the doorbell and ask to stay. You didn't need any pretense."

"But I wasn't sure what *you* needed, Chip. I wasn't about to make it too easy for me to walk away or for you to kick me out."

I wouldn't have, but at the time I suppose she couldn't have known that.

"Listen."

"To…?" I asked, then heard the soft music coming from down the hall, strains of an awkward guitar and a deep voice singing along. "Who is it?"

"Kevin," she whispered. "I don't think he knows we can hear him all the way down here. Don't you tell him, either."

"He can really sing, can't he?"

"He gets better all the time. He writes his own songs but the only way I ever get to hear them is when he's practicing."

I laid back, staring at the ceiling, listening to my youngest son's voice drift down the hall. His voice was deeper than I expected, clear and unwavering, and so beautiful it almost hurt.

I see the stars in your eyes
We whisper words, songs of sweet surprise
The moon on your face
Out of time, feeling out of place
They're calling out your name, calling out your name...

"When did he start playing the guitar?" I asked, still whispering. It was something else I was out of touch on; I knew Eileen played the piano – I had suffered through the first few years of her practicing and tolerated it long enough to enjoy the rewards of her hard earned talent – but if the boys had any musical inclinations, I was woefully unaware.

"Last January. He needed a fine arts credit and settled on guitar instead of a painting class or drawing."

"This song is nice..."

"Kind of romantic. Makes me wonder who he wrote it for."

"The girl with the big boobs," I chuckled. "I think her name is Lydia."

Score one for me – something I knew about one of my kids that she didn't. Kevin had a crush on a girl he had known since second grade and was clueless about what to do with those feelings. He was, after all, "still in the observation stage," and trying to enjoy all the observing he could.

If Lydia could hear him sing that song, he wouldn't be observing anyone else for a while.

Terry rolled onto her side, lifting herself up on an elbow to look at me.

"You know," she said with a sigh, "I didn't pull you down on this bed only to have you fall asleep listening to Kevin sing."

"Ah, didn't you now?"

"We still have some making up to do."

"I'm kind of ripe. Don't you want me to shower first?"

She slid off the bed and held a hand out to me. "Nothing says we can't do both. Besides," she added, pulling me up, "if we can hear Kevin it's a sure bet he can hear us, and I don't intend to be quiet at all."

Terry

"He was a priest."

I barely opened my eyes; Chip was sitting on the bed, his father's journal in his hand, and Max was perched next to my pillow with his nose less than an inch away from mine, whiskers twitching as he sniffed my breath. I glanced at the clock; it was after three in the morning.

"Who?" I mumbled, trying to keep Max from sticking his entire face into my mouth.

"My father," he said, sounding somewhat awe-stricken. "Grant – no, Michael Brennan – was a priest."

"What?" I tried pushing Max away; he crawled over my hand and curled up on my stomach. "I'm not awake yet. Grant was a priest?"

He nodded.

"How? He was married, Chip. Your parents *were* married, weren't they? I mean, after all the manipulations with Ron... Of course they were married."

Chip rubbed his chin thoughtfully, watching Max wiggle as he tried to get comfortable. "Depends on how you look at it, I guess. I'm sure they considered themselves married. And they even married in the church. Yet Michael Brennan was never dispensed from his vows."

I sat up and let Max tumble onto the bed. He glared at

me and then crawled onto Chip's legs, using Chip's ankle as a pillow. "Chip, he didn't become Grant Davis until after you were born. He must have gotten a dispensation to marry your mother."

"It says here," Chip said, tapping a finger on the journal cover, "and my birth certificate supports it, that I was born in September nineteen fifty four, and he became Grant Alan Davis three months later. He married my mom in January the next year. I was four months old, Terry."

"Wow."

"Wow my ass. This raises a lot of questions. For starters, why? Why did he leave the priesthood, and why did he tempt fate by thumbing his nose at the church he *loved* and assume another identity to complete the act? Was she pregnant before or after he decided to leave? And especially why did she carry on an affair with Ron the entire time they were married if he gave up so much to be with her?"

Frowning, his mind running at top speed while he absently stroked Max's head, he shrugged. "She was never faithful. I assume he could have gone back to the church at any time. And am I legitimate or not? Not that it really matters, but hell, I've been using the Davis name all my life, but I was born before the fact. I'm a Brennan."

"I doubt the name change means anything for you legally," I told him, rubbing a finger under Max's chin. He purred loudly and closed his eyes, soaking in all the attention. "I can ask Brad to be sure, but you went all through school as Jeremy Davis, you voted under it, your driver's license and social security is under it…"

"I'm not really worried about my name… It just confuses me, that's all. I can't for the life of me figure out why she married Grant or why he married her, and where Ron fits into all this. If I had been conceived after they married, sure. But why would he marry her when she claimed I was Ron's? Why didn't Ron marry her?"

"There's nothing in the journal that answers that?"

"No. There are long stretches when he didn't write anything at all. There's a lot of raw pain over my mom and even more over me..." He tried to smile. "Grant wrote so eloquently. There are long passages about Dave and how he used to take apart all his toys. I always thought Grant was tolerant about it – hell, he even helped Dave half the time – but he was mostly frustrated and wondered if Dave would grow up to be someone who just broke everything he laid his hands on. He expected Dave to start blowing shit up by the time he was twenty five."

"And what" – Max wiggled until he was on his back, inviting one of us to rub his belly – "did he have to say about you?"

"He knew what I did for a living, Terry."

"What? How?"

He shook his head. "I'll be damned if I know. But I should have been suspicious. When Dave was missing and Grant wanted me to find him, he said something along the lines of 'I know you have people who can help.' That should have tipped me off. And something Alex Barstow said, one of the last things he said."

I waited, rubbing Max's chest and under his chin.

"He said he considered my father a friend. When I tried to tell him Ron wasn't my father after all, he cut me off and said he knew who my father was. He said he was trying to save my life, that he owed my father that much."

"How could he have known Grant?"

"I don't know. It doesn't make sense."

"And you're going to sit there until you figure it out."

He finally smiled. "No, I'll be nice and turn out the light so you can go back to sleep. I didn't really mean to wake you up, but I had to tell someone."

"You can wake me up anytime, Irish."

"But you'd like it if I turned the damned light out, right?"

"I don't think the cat is going to let you move."

He lifted Max off his legs and set him at the foot of the bed, then tossed Grant's journal onto the floor before turning the light out. Max paced back and forth, his tail flipping indignantly, but he gave up and curled up around my feet.

I scooted closer to Chip, setting my head on his shoulder, listening to him breath.

He was quiet for a long time, then sighed and whispered, "I won't use the agency to figure this out, Terry."

"Where did that come from?"

"Just in case you were worried, that's all."

I hugged him and then planted a kiss on his chin. "Use your friends if you can, Chip. Won't they help without you having to commit yourself all over again?"

"Sure, but…"

"But nothing. As long as I'm not going to lose you to that agency, do whatever you have to, otherwise it will drive you nuts."

"Short drive," he chuckled.

"Can I ask you something?"

"Anything."

"Would you be opposed to the two of us going to see Will? And not as friends…"

"You want him to help us find our way back?"

"I think we found the way back, but I think we need him to help us find something else. I'm not sure what it is."

Chip rolled onto his side, sliding down on the mattress until his face was in front of mine, noses touching. "God's not pissed at us, if that's what you're worried about. He won't ground us."

"No," I said, trying to not laugh at the image of us both stuck in a celestial corner. "We made God a lot of promises, though, and we screwed it up."

"You want that feeling of this being a sacrament back."

He nailed it.

"Can we get that?" I asked.

"At the risk of sounding so mushy you might barf" – he snuck a kiss in – "I adore you. I cherish you. I love you more than I love anyone or anything else God put on this earth. I'll do anything you want, even bare my soul to Will, to get us both back to where we were and to that feeling that we have God's blessing on our marriage."

"Don't you make me cry."

"I always seem to find a way, don't I?"

"You're not going to withhold sex until we get that back, are you?"

He chuckled, pulling back and looking at me as if he might consider it. "Maybe I should ask Father Willy if that's a good idea."

"Father Willy would tell you it's a very *bad* idea and completely counter productive to healing our marriage."

"Ah, would he now?"

"He would."

"Did you know Will got himself laid?"

"What!"

"Yep. And if she hadn't been so scared he would have left the priesthood to marry her."

The creaking of footsteps on the stairs stopped any more

talk of Will and his sex life; Chip stiffened and sat up, listening.

"Be right back," he said, slipping out from under the sheet.

He flipped on the hall light, leaning against the door frame, arms crossed at his chest. Whichever one was sneaking in, I felt sorry for them.

I hadn't considered someone sneaking out.

"Take her home," Chip grumbled, "and pray that her father doesn't chop your pecker off and serve it to you warm."

He turned back to the bed.

"Those kids never learn."

"Do I want to know?"

"It was Nick and Katie."

At seventeen, Chip – and he admits it, though to his credit is not proud of it – had gone through so many women he couldn't remember all their names. He lost his virginity in the back yard bushes when he was thirteen years old, and was caught with a girl in his bed when he was fourteen.

Nick wasn't doing anything his father never had. The difference I could see was that Nick was hopelessly in love and not only would he remember Katie's name, in ten years he would still be with her.

"How ticked are you?" I asked after he was back in bed.

I was answered with a whisper. "I'm not."

"Then what?"

"Disappointed. Sympathetic. I'm not sure how I feel."

"He loves her," I reminded him. "And they've been going together since they were fourteen. We had to know that it would happen sooner or later."

"Not here," he said. "And not in my apartment, either. Bringing her here is like telling us to both just kiss his ass. He had to know he'd get caught, and he probably expected you to be the one catching him."

"No, he just didn't realize your apartment was free tonight."

"This amuses you, doesn't it?"

"It shouldn't, but there's not much I can do about it, so what the hell."

"Your little boy is getting laid, woman."

"So is yours."

"And that doesn't bother you."

"I'm going to make a concentrated effort to just not think about it. Even after Paul gets married, and the baby is born, I'm going to pretend it's not happening. They're all little innocents, and have never touched a girl below the neck."

"Oh, come on," he laughed. "Even Kevin groped some poor girl under the bleachers at a football game."

"I didn't need to hear that."

"You just don't want to think about them having more fun that you."

I reached for his hand. "Maybe not. But that's what I have you for."

Smart man that he is, he didn't disagree.

Chip

The Russell's house was a two story apartment wedged in the middle of a row of faded brown townhouses. The token postage stamp sized yard, spanning the width of their front windows, was lush green and neatly trimmed, bordered by flowers near the walkway.

I don't know why, but I had the mental image of an old, decaying house out by the freeway, complete with a rusted car in the front yard and a pit bull chained by the door.

My personal enlightenment obviously had not wiped out

a tendency towards stereotypes.

Paul barely said two words on the drive over; he stared out the window, his hands flat on his thighs, and when I pulled into the carport in front of their house he seemed reluctant to get out. For half a second I considered waiting until he was ready, giving him time to work up the courage to face Monica's father, but thought better of it. He would either follow me, or not.

My finger was half an inch from the doorbell when I heard the car door slam.

Monica's mother answered the door; she recognized me instantly – although she didn't seem the least bit familiar to me – and invited us in, waving fingers at Paul, who was standing behind me.

"Her name is Elizabeth," Paul whispered before I stepped inside.

Monica's father was in the living room, stretched out in a recliner, the TV on, a newspaper spread out over his lap, and a beer on the end table next to him. As soon as he looked up, I remembered him. Jeffery Russell, high school football star, president of our sophomore class, and the one voted Most Likely To Do Time before turning thirty. His popularity was enigmatic; he abused his girlfriends in high school with the same fury Paul swore he abused his wife and daughter.

He rose from the recliner, newspaper drifting to the floor, and held out his hand to me.

"Chip, long time no see," he said, smiling. "I had no idea Paul was your kid."

"One of four," I said, shaking his hand. "And we need to talk about the kids, Jeff."

"Christ, what'd they do?"

Before I could answer, I heard a dull thud behind me,

and Jeff looked up, his eyes not on me but his daughter, who stood at the bottom of the stairs, a suitcase on either side of her legs.

"I should be the one to tell him," she said, voice wavering.

"Tell me what?" He looked confused, his eyes darting between Monica's suitcases and her face. "What the hell is going on?"

I watched his face; while he waited for an answer, anger began to cloud his eyes, he clenched his teeth together so hard that his jaw began a slow grind, and he breathed in sharp, shallow gasps.

"I'm pregnant, I'm moving out, and I'm marrying Paul," she said simply.

Jeff took a short step towards her, his hands balled into fists. I matched his step, making sure I stayed an arms' length from him.

"Like hell you are," he seethed. "You're going nowhere, and you're *not* having any goddamned baby."

"It's not your decision, Jeff," I said evenly. "It's Monica's. She's leaving, whether she marries Paul or not." I turned to look at Monica. She was trying not to cry, eyes red and wild with fear. "You two go out to the car and wait for me there."

She picked up the suitcases, handed one to Paul, and left without another word, without so much as a glance toward her father.

Elizabeth Russell watched her daughter leave; I expected tears, but the look on her face was one of victory. She fought to keep from smiling, biting her bottom lip, refusing to look at her husband.

"What the fuck do you think – ?" Jeff sputtered.

"At some point you might be allowed to know where

your daughter is living, Jeff, but not until you get some help. Get your temper under control and maybe then you can see her and your grandchild."

"Fucking hell."

"And if I find out that you've taken your frustration out on her" – I gestured to his wife – "you'll have to answer to me, and trust me, that will be *extremely* unpleasant. Elizabeth, if you ever need my help for anything, don't hesitate to call. I don't care what time of the day or night it is, call and I'll be there."

Monica and Paul were in the back seat, watching me as I came towards the car, quiet when I got in and started the engine.

I glanced back as I pulled the car out; no one bothered to close their door, and neither of them watched as I drove their daughter from one life into the next.

~

It was too much like watching children at play, my son standing at an altar promising to love and to honor a woman for the rest of his life. It was reality and fantasy wrapped up in one surreal package, two babies dressed up all in white for a sacrament they couldn't begin to understand.

Yet, I had hope.

Paul's intentions were good; he had made a huge error in judgment and was rectifying it in a manner befitting the man he wanted to be. He wasn't running away, which is what I would have done at his age.

"You're looking at one scared puppy," he admitted, pacing nervously before the ceremony. I sat in a hard wooden chair by the door, listening for the music that would cue him to go out to the altar. "I know you don't think I'm ready for this, and I might not be... but I really do love her."

"I never doubted that," I said.

"I want it to work, Dad. In twenty years I want her to be able to look at me the way Mom looks at you."

He had no concept of living through two decades.

I doubted he fathom any concept of being with someone for longer than two years.

"Then take my advice, and don't ever lie to her, Paul. Not ever, not even a lie of omission. If I had been completely open and honest with your Mom, we never would have split up." I got out of the chair to straighten his tie; truthfully, I got up to touch him and used the tie as an excuse. This was my son, after all, my flesh and blood and bone, a much bigger part of me than I had realized before that moment. "Women," I told him, "aren't as complicated as they want us to think. The only thing she really needs from you is to be loved the best you can. Do that and you'll be all right."

The door opened and Kevin stuck his head in. "You ready? They're about to start."

Paul tugged at his sleeves, straightening out his tux, sucked in a deep breath, and nodded. "I'm as ready as I'll ever be."

More ready than his father, who swore to himself that he would not cry at his son's wedding. Let Terry handle the family floodgates.

"Paul, in case I don't have a chance to talk to you after the wedding..."

He stopped at the door.

"I love you, son. You took us by surprise, but we're not disappointed in you. I just love you."

He hugged me back as hard as I hugged him. "I love you, too, Dad."

As I watched them exchange rings, I slipped my arm around Terry, sharing her sense of loss and joy, wishing that I felt the same freedom she did to let a few tears fall.

Paul bent to kiss his bride, mischief and adoration twinkling in his eyes.

God help me, I wasn't ready to let him go.

Terry

The line between fantasy and reality, my Irishman has said on more than one occasion, is subtle and not always clearly defined.

Our son's wedding day rode that line, never quite real, and never quite a dream. Chip watched Paul with his new wife under the soft lights of the Charybis dance floor with worried, troubled eyes. The words that came out of his mouth – "They'll be fine, it'll work" – didn't match the disturbed expression on his face.

The restaurant was crowded, not merely from the splash of late afternoon customers, but from the invited guests, almost all of them under the age of eighteen. There were few adults in attendance at both the wedding and the reception; Doug, Kris, my parents, Will, and us.

The bride's parents had not been invited.

"The boy hardly looks his age," my father observed, leaning back in his chair. No matter where he was, Paul Stevens had the look of a man relaxing in his back yard, planted in a lawn chair, cooler at his feet and a cold beer in his hand. Gregarious and friendly, my father was a firm believer in commitment and family, and the news that his sixteen year old grandson was getting married didn't seem to faze him one bit.

Chip was still watching them dance. "I keep seeing the

three year old who tried to paint his bedroom walls with peanut butter. I can't get my head around the idea that he's going to be a father himself." He turned in his seat, looking at me. "Maybe it's my imagination, but I think she's showing a little."

"It's a little early for that."

"She's almost four months along," he said. "She will be soon."

"What are their honeymoon plans?" my dad asked.

"A couple of days at the beach house, then back to school." Chip sighed sadly. "They decided they could afford to cut a couple of days of classes, but Monica has a psychology test on Thursday. They're taking their books with them, like they expect to actually study."

"You look," my mother said to him pointedly, "like you need to dance. Shock the hell out of them all and give the old lady a twirl around the floor."

He smiled and did just that.

The years had melted away her animosity towards Chip. In the beginning she had hated him with a passion, reasoning that he was moody – true – a lech – not true – and not good enough for me – very not true.

Four and a half years into our marriage the ice that had begun to drip away when Nick was born completely melted. Chip was her hero, he was the perfect husband and father, and I was not good enough for him most of the time.

After all, I was an adulteress. I had slept with his best friend and was – briefly, for perhaps ten minutes – the slut she could not possible have given birth to. Chip, for standing by me, defending me, and honoring his vows to the bitter end, could do no wrong.

When I threw him out, I became the family scum, depriving my children of their father, tarnishing the image they had of me as his adoring wife; they stuck by Chip more than they did me, and he saw more of them over the two years than I did.

My mother was in love with him, for Pete's sake. In her eyes he could do no wrong.

And she danced with him much too close for a mother in law.

"Speak to me, little girl"

My father's deep voice drew me away from them. "About what?"

"About him," he said flatly. "I didn't just keep my eyes glued to my grandson today, you know. You were clinging to Chip for dear life. I assume you're on speaking terms now?"

Rather than play the game, which he was skilled at and loved, I decided to answer all the questions before he could ask. Head him off at the pass. "Yes, we're speaking. Yes, I'm sleeping with him. Yes, he moved back home. And yes, it's permanent. No more flakiness. He won't allow it."

"Good for him. I approve."

"I thought you might. I think the kids approve, too, though they haven't said much."

"When?"

"When did he move back? Last Tuesday, more or less."

My father, never at a loss for words, nodded thought-fully, but kept whatever was spinning through his devious mind to himself. "Nicky and his girl seem to be getting along quite nicely."

I glanced over to where Nick was dancing – more or less, barely moving, effectively glued from the knees on up – with Katie. "They get along too well," I said.

"How so?"

"I suspect that Nick would have been a whole lot happier

if it had been him up at that altar with Katie today instead of Paul and Monica."

He sipped at his beer. "Nick has always been about five or six years ahead of himself."

"Are you suggesting we give him the same permission we gave Paul?"

"No, but I know for a fact he's ready for the responsibility. In a couple of years he'll be marrying the girl and you'll have none of these doubts."

"Dad," I sighed, "if Nick had been the one getting married today, I wouldn't have half the doubts that I do now, but as to his sense of responsibility... right now that's in question. He hasn't been using his head lately."

"Oh?"

"Chip caught him sneaking Katie out of the house at three in the morning."

He tried to not laugh. "Even Nick is allowed to act his age once in a while."

Any reply I could have come up with was cut off by my mother, winded, dropping into the chair next to my father. Chip grabbed my hand and pulled me to my feet and into his arms.

"Come on, woman. If Doug can keep Kris on the floor all afternoon, I should get a decent crack at you."

"Doug is dancing with Kris because he's horny and can't do anything about it here."

"I'm horny too, and I'm a better lay."

"Chip!"

"Well I am." He steered me out into the middle of the floor and came to a stop and kissed me, lips barely brushing at first, then demanding and soul scorching. Any longer and he could have had anything he wanted, in the middle of a crowd, no less.

Nick brushed by us, clinging – not quite so much as he had been before – to Katie. "They're unnatural," he scoffed, barely holding back his grin. "They're going to be grandparents, for Chrissake, and they're making out like a couple of kids."

"No one said you had to watch," Chip retorted, undoubtedly pleased with the fact that his kids, while they grumbled and poked fun, were not really embarrassed by their parents' affections.

"If you give her a hickey, you're grounded," Nick laughed as he danced away.

"Cool," Chip chuckled. "Can I give you a big one, so that we get sent to our room for a week?"

"Oh my God, if I say one damn thing about a big one, I won't be able to look at Nick at all for the rest of the day."

"Heh."

"Change the subject and start dancing with me again, or we'll get ourselves into trouble in the middle of Paul and Monica's reception."

"All right." He took a half step back and found the beat of the music. "Boy or girl? What do you want?"

"Either. But I suppose your male ego is screaming out for a grandson."

"Naw. But I think we should tell them that twins run in the family."

"Don't you dare!"

He was quiet for a long time after that, pulling me close and dancing away from everyone else, carefully avoiding contact with his two oldest sons. "You know, I kind of envy Paul. I loved it when you were pregnant."

"Wishing for more kids?"

"Not necessarily. I don't know if I'd want to go through

all the bottles and diapers and terrible twos again, but I miss watching you get big, and rubbing your stomach. I really miss feeling a baby kick against me in the middle of the night… I mean, I wouldn't be totally against the idea of more munchkins if it were possible."

I pulled back, just enough to look into his eyes. "Would you really want another baby, Irish? This isn't just age or envy talking?"

"It's a moot point."

"Tubes can be fixed, and we're not too old."

We stopped dancing.

"We're not on ground solid enough to even be thinking about it, Terry," he said, voice laced with sorrow and regret. "I've always wanted more kids, but dammit, you nearly died with Kevin and Eileen and I won't put you through that again. And shouldn't we worry more about getting us fixed instead of your tubes?"

"We can still think about it."

He was tempted, I could tell. He swayed a little, hovered at the peak, and then fell.

In the wrong direction.

"No. We can't."

"Is that an order?"

"No, but I'm begging you… let's just have fun being together and being grandparents. And let's try to make up the last two years to the kids we already have."

"You're allowed to change your mind at any point," I said, pulling him back towards the dance floor. "You say the word and I'll talk to Doug."

"A year from now," he said, resting his forehead against mine. "If you think you want more kids a year from now, and we're on solid ground, I would honestly consider adopting. I won't risk your life to have another baby, but there's nothing to keep us from adopting."

"Except the fact that you're so old."

"Very funny."

"If you don't want another baby now, how about another cat?"

He sighed and steered me towards the bar.

"I need a drink. I really need a drink."

Will

Chip's problems, marital and otherwise, were nearly always best solved on the basketball court. He was more at ease discussing his personal woes when the pressure and confines of my office were nowhere to be seen. He took a particular delight in trouncing me in uneven matches of one-on-one, and I always thought the competition gave him the courage to cough up whatever it was that bothered him.

We played off and on over the fifteen years I had known him; this was the first time, however, that Terry was there listening and watching me get humiliated.

After all, she was a former crush. I dated her occasionally in high school, when she was a freshman and I was a junior. She was precisely the kind of girl I knew could be a serious threat to my vocation, and after a while I avoided her.

Over twenty years later she still claimed, without serious conviction, that I broke her heart.

In any case, broken hearts or not, they were asking for my help and I wasn't about to say no. I liked them both; for the most part Chip baffled me, but he was a good and loyal friend. If he couldn't count on me for help, I didn't know who he could count on.

I first met him on a very warm January day, seven months

before Kevin and Eileen were born. He stumbled, quite literally, into the confessional to spew forth thirteen years of sins he seemed sure would have me running out of the church, and I was so taken aback by the intensity of his emotions and the content of his confession that I had to see who was on the other side of the confessional. I didn't consider it to be breaking the Seal of Confession; the man needed help and emotional support, and he needed more help than I could offer by mere absolution.

I took a chance that day and gained a friend.

Within a year he had returned to the church. They honored me with the request to preside over their canonical wedding, and thrilled me by allowing me to baptize each of their children.

Come hell or high water, I would help them hold it together, even if it did mean a former love seeing me wimp out on the basketball court.

"Happily ever after," I grunted, missing a shot, "happens only in cartoons and fairy tales."

Chip shot from mid-court and the ball sailed cleanly through the hoop. "Tell me about it."

Terry sat in the grass next to the court. "You don't have to be so blunt," she moaned.

"Just what is it you're afraid of?" I asked, swiping the ball from Chip's hands.

"Of trying and failing?" He shrugged. "I don't really know, but I'm not especially worried."

"But I am," Terry said. "Will, I tossed him out of his own house for no good reason. Do you honestly think he's not angry?"

I looked away and caught the ball in the side of my face. "You think he'll turn the tables on you and walk out?"

"I don't know."

"I'm not going anywhere," Chip lamented, and judging from the look on his face, it was not the first time he tried to reassure her.

I grabbed the ball and held onto it; I didn't dribble or take a shot, and didn't throw it back to Chip. "How's your sex life?"

Terry blushed wildly and Chip laughed.

"You're a little pervert," he chuckled.

"Only partially. I do have a point to the question."

"All right," he said. "It's fine. Better than ever, I think. But come on, even at our worst our sex life has been good."

"Not always. Fifteen years ago you were impotent half the time."

"Leave it to you to remember that," he grumbled.

"My fault again," Terry muttered.

The spark in Chip's eyes flared and he spun towards her. "Will you cut it out, for Christ's sake? You don't need to be a goddamned martyr!"

"I'm just trying to be honest. Look at it, Chip. I screwed it up then and I screwed it up now."

"Maybe."

"Dammit, Chip!"

"Hey, this isn't a blame game," I said, rolling the ball onto the grass. "My point is that you had a huge problem then and you solved it. You forgave each other, and if you both weren't in a forgiving mood right now, you'd probably be suffering the way you did then."

"Look, I'm just happy to be home," Chip said.

I plopped down onto the grass beside Terry. "I've listened to both of you wail and moan about how bad life was without each other... You're not trying to mend a broken relationship, only a wounded one. And wounds heal."

They were looking at each other, not at me.

"I wish you could believe that I can put it all behind me," he said softly, standing in front of her with his hands planted on his hips. "If anything, being apart taught me that I want you more than I need you, and I need you more than anything."

"You did just fine."

"Did I? Terry, I woke up nights fighting off major crying jags. I had absolutely no life other than when the kids came over or when Ted dragged me off to bowl. Didn't you wonder why Red called me 'Hermit'? It was because I rarely wandered out of the apartment. I had no social life. I could have – hell, Red was there for the asking. But I didn't. I told you years ago, there would never be another woman for me. If it's not you, then it's not anyone, and I'll live out the rest of my life alone. And it won't be much of a life."

I kept my mouth shut; he was doing fine without my interference.

"I didn't do fine at all. Hell, when I got sick, who took care of me? No one else would do that for me, woman, and I know it. You were pissed off at me, I presumed way too much, and it hurt you. We both let stubborn pride get in our way. If I'd been any kind of man I would have kicked the goddamn door in and fought it out with you."

"I should have called…"

"But you didn't. And I didn't call you, either. Terry, if we keep looking back on all the stupid things we've done, we're never going to enjoy our future."

"It can't be that easy."

He kneeled on the grass in front of her. "I told you once a long time ago, and I'll say it again. You are my blessing in life and you're God's gift to me. I love you and I will until the day I die. Nothing you ever say or do can change that."

It might work, I thought, watching her throw herself into Chip's arms, at least for a little while.

I had no doubt that Chip, even as deep as his anger probably ran, had forgiven her.

She needed to forgive herself.

Chip

We stumbled through the next two months, giving our attention to anything but the question of What To Do About Us. Too many other things provided distraction: kids, jobs, bills that were getting lost in the shuffle of my changing addresses again. Anything we could find that provided a reasonable excuse to back away from The Issue, we grabbed onto.

I wasn't in any hurry to examine our relationship.

With the holidays rushing at us, putting it off was easy. We amused ourselves with Paul's snowballing excitement and Monica's expanding girth, and we wallowed in memories of how elated we were when Terry first felt Nicky move, the wonder of holding each other tight in the middle of the night to feel his slow, luxurious somersaults and the knees and elbows I could feel poking out at me.

I reveled in seeing the same delight in Paul.

I fell in love with my daughter-in-law.

Knowing my son and his sometimes unpredictable moods coupled by a wild sense of humor, I worried about the first stages of his marriage, whether he would drive a wedge in between them before they had a chance to really begin, or if he would learn to embrace all the little mundane things in a relationship and make her feel as if they were special.

I'm a nosy son of a bitch. I cornered her in the kitchen just before Thanksgiving dinner and asked, bluntly, "How's he treating you, Monica? Honestly."

She was leaning against the counter, her hands resting on her growing belly. "Paul is wonderful."

"But how is he treating you?"

"He treats me," she said, smiling and blushing crimson, "like a piece of very expensive, very fine china, Mr. Davis."

"Chip. Mr. Davis was my father, and then only on a bad day."

"A year from now you'll still be telling me that," she laughed.

I doubted that. I figured in a year she'd be using my name liberally, and probably to seethe at me for the hours Paul worked and all the time he had to spend away from home.

I had my retirement hopes wrapped around a sixteen year old boy. He had his nose in everything and intended to learn it all. If he wanted it, the restaurant could be his some-day; in a year, maybe less, Ted could begin to train him to take over as an assistant manager. By the time I hit fifty he'd be more than ready to take over.

Presuming I survived Christmas.

Our traditions had already taken on a shadow of unfa-miliarity. Midnight mass, staying up until the sun started to rise while we assembled toys or just curled up on the sofa in front of the fireplace, talking until the kids came screaming down the stairs, the loud, excited breakfasts we made them suffer through after they had poked through their stockings and before we'd let them open gifts – I'd done none of it for just long enough that it felt awkward.

The Sunday before Christmas I realized I wasn't sure I was looking forward to it.

"So it feels awkward," Doug said, sitting in the pew behind me, waiting for our wives to stop flitting from one family to another, dispensing Merry Christmas wishes like fairy dust. "The real thing is, does it feel right?"

It felt right.

It just felt so far away.

"Last year at this time you and I were sitting in your office with a bottle of vodka while we pretended you didn't want to be here," he reminded me. "Even if it doesn't feel right, at least it's better than being alone. Right?"

"I don't know... if I was alone I wouldn't have to listen to you and Will and Kris and half the parish dissect my marriage."

"You love the attention and you know it," he laughed.

"I don't imagine the kids will be up at dawn this year," I mused, mostly to myself.

"So this Christmas you'll get laid instead."

"Jesus, Doug, you're in a fricking church, you know."

"I'm sure God knows you get laid once in a while."

"I take a whiz once in a while too, but that doesn't mean I'm talking about it *here*."

He shrugged. "Suit yourself."

"It just seems a little sacrilegious."

"But it's in your head now, and you're thinking 'hmmm, that would be a great way to celebrate Christmas.'"

"Oh, shut up."

"Fine, I won't remind you of all the kinky ways to ring in the holidays. How goes your search for info on your father the Father?"

"Other than his personal papers... I can't find a damned thing on him. It's like he didn't exist before he left the church. I even had Kevin and Eileen helping me dig through stuff in the attic, hoping he'd hidden more papers up there."

"Anything?"

"Only things that had those two asking question after question. By the time we were done they'd heard the whole damn story. Everything from my mom and Ron right down to finding out Grant was my real father just before he died. I didn't tell them anything about the agency, but I think we covered everything else."

"Do they know Kris was married to Ron?"

"Is it a problem if they do?"

He shook his head. "No, but I suppose if your kids know then we should tell Spider."

"You're kidding. Your own son doesn't know?"

"Never had a reason to tell him."

Our kids were standing near the back of the church, watching their mothers impatiently, occasionally looking to us for help in getting them out the door.

"I'll tell them not to say anything to him," I said, trying to see what Kevin was signing to Eileen and Spider. "When did he get so damned tall?"

Doug glanced over. "Who? Kevin or Spider?"

"Take your pick. Eileen looks tiny next to them now."

"Sucks when they grow up, doesn't it?"

"I think Terry wants another one. Or two or three. Can you see me with toddlers again, at my age? I'd be pushing sixty when they graduated high school. And forget all the things I used to do with the other kids. I wouldn't have the energy to do half of it."

"You might surprise yourself."

"Right. Would you want to start a second family at this stage of your life?"

"No, but I'm older than you are."

"All right, think about it, if you had a ten year old kid right now, could you do even half of what you did with Spider? The camping trips and coaching little league, or even all the hours rollerblading around the same stupid track at the park... Could you do it at your age?"

He considered it for a moment, looking back at the kids before shrugging and saying "Sure, I could do it. But I don't know how long I could do it, and I'd worry all the time about being around when the kid hit his twenties. Plus, you have something major you need to think about and discuss with Terry if you do decide on more kids."

"Aside from the age difference between a baby and the twins?"

"You have a strong family history of heart disease, Chip. And you have no idea what else... both of your parents died fairly young. I know you, you wouldn't want to leave a child in this world without you being there to be his father."

Terry was with the kids, laughing at something Spider had said, waving for Doug and me to get up and leave with them.

"Doug, what the hell do I do if she honestly wants more kids?"

"I don't know," he said, getting up and heading towards them. "Get a vasectomy? I've never had that problem. Kris has always been firm about not wanting more."

"You seemed okay with it."

"I was just grateful she had Spider."

"You were just grateful she had sex."

"Shame on you, still in church, using the 's' word."

"I notice you're not denying it."

He reached for Kris's hand. "Get me away from this cretin," he laughed. "All this dirty talk in the House of the Lord."

"And I can imagine who started it," she sighed.

Terry didn't ask for details, which was just as well with Kevin and Eileen half a step behind us.

"Nick never showed up?" I asked.

"If he did I never saw him."

I turned my head to look at Eileen. "Did you see Nick at all?"

"Nope."

"He said something about picking up Katie," Kevin volunteered. "Maybe they're going to a later Mass."

"I bet they ditched it and went to a movie," Eileen said.

"That's not like Nick," Terry said to me, after the kids were in the car. "If he intended to skip church he would have told one of us."

"If he'd planned on missing it, he would have. If something better came up, it might not have occurred to him to let us know."

"Something better being...?"

"If you really don't know," I laughed, "I'll show you when we get home."

Nick called at three in the afternoon – no, I'm not plastered all over the freeway, I missed church because something came up that Katie needed to talk about, I won't be home for dinner unless I have to be because I told Katie I'd take her out, sorry if you worried – and I didn't think much about it after I hung up; whatever Katie needed to talk about, judging from the fact that they were going out, must have been urgent only in a teenage it's earth shatteringly important right this minute sort of way.

According to Eileen, those moments were a matter of life and death.

"Kevin get off the phone I have to call Sherry *right now* because if I can't tell her what Mindy said about her during gym class today I swear I'm *going to die*."

My kids thought they were going to die at least twice a week.

I learned to not take their mortality so seriously.

When he still was not home at ten o'clock, I started to worry. I asked Terry if he had a cell phone; no, he had wanted one, but she wasn't about to pay the thirteen thousand dollars a month he would run up in over time minutes. I called Katie's house; no answer. I called Paul; no, Dad, I haven't talked to Nick in a couple of days.

"He'll be home by midnight," Terry said, kissing me goodnight before she wandered upstairs to go to bed. "He has classes in the morning."

"So?"

"So he probably took Katie to a movie, and he'll be home when it's over because he doesn't cut class. Your son is anal that way."

"He's your son tonight," I grumbled.

When she got up at six the next morning to get ready for work, Nick was still not home. I waited until she was dressed and downstairs before telling her; if she wanted to fly out the door in search of him she might as well have clothes on.

I was in the kitchen making coffee for her when she came down. She kissed me on the cheek, shoved bread into the toaster, and was reaching for the paper when I said, "He never came home."

"Nick?"

"I called VacaValley Hospital, North Bay Medical Center, the Fairfield police, the Vacaville police, and Katie's house again. No one answered her phone, and he wasn't anywhere else, either."

I could feel her heart lurch from where I was standing. She took a deep breath and sat in the closest chair at the table, fingers white as she pressed them hard against the wood of the chair. Her eyes were wide and dark, not looking at me – not looking anywhere in particular – and when she finally blinked she held them closed for a long few seconds, and then sighed when she opened them.

"If there were anything wrong," she said, "we would have heard. Someone would have called or shown up…"

"You'd think."

She looked up at me when I brought the coffee to the table. "Should we go look for him?"

"Look where?" I sat across from her, sliding the sugar bowl towards her. "For all we know he decided to drive to San Francisco and just didn't bother telling anyone."

We contemplated every possibility, from the chance that the Forrester's phone was simply out of order to the idea that Nick had taken off for the coast, following his father's proclivities towards hiding out at the beach house when things weren't going his way.

I didn't think I'd ever shared that with any of the kids and I wasn't sure Nick knew how to get there on his own.

"We have to do something," she said.

"You mean aside from nailing his ass to the wall when he gets home? You might as well go to work, Terry. Both of us sitting here isn't going to get him home any quicker. I promise, I'll call you when he gets here."

"You expect me to leave? Now?"

"What time does he normally get up?"

"Around eighty thirty."

"What time is his first class?"

"Ten. Why?"

"Because my guess is that he'll come slinking home around nine to change clothes before heading for school. If you haven't heard from me by nine-thirty, come home."

We argued for another ten minutes before she agreed that nothing productive would come from us both sitting there staring at the clock, and her still being there when Kevin and Eileen come downstairs would only have them asking questions.

After they scrambled downstairs and thundered out the door in time to catch the bus, I planted myself at the foot of the stairs, facing the front door, willing it to open. By that point I wasn't sure if I was worried or angry.

Lack of sleep was making me fuzzy. The days when I could stay up for forty eight straight hours working were long gone.

At eight forty five I was angry. I heard his key slide into the lock, and the door creaked open slowly. He slipped in with it only half open, looking towards the living room before heading up the stairs.

"Have fun?"

"Dad!"

"You don't have a curfew," I snapped, " but I damn well expect to know where you are and when you're coming home. Do you have any goddamned idea what we went through worrying about you? We had no clue where you were all night."

"I was with Katie."

"No shit. Do you know what a telephone is, Nick? Has anyone bothered to show you how to use one in the last six months?"

He stuffed his hands into his pockets. "I lost track of time."

"Bullshit. Losing track of time is wandering in an hour

later than you said you'd be. I don't want to hear any crap, I want to know where the hell you were and what you were doing."

"I wasn't doing what you think I was doing."

"Like hell."

"I wasn't," he said quietly. "We were at the restaurant until about midnight and then sat in the car out in front of her house. We were just talking, Dad. If you don't believe me, ask Ted. He saw us there."

"Fine, he saw you until midnight. You expect me to believe Damien Forrester would let you sit outside all night with his daughter?"

"You can think whatever you want, Dad. Katie's parents went out of town for the weekend. If I'd actually spent the night with her, I'd admit it. It's not like I'm ashamed of it."

"I don't think you've ever lied to me before, Nicky, but I have to tell you, I don't buy this for one minute. You call yesterday to say you're going to be late. Fine, I didn't mind that. But you knew we'd probably be in bed before midnight, you knew your mom would leave before seven, and you knew I'd probably sleep in until after you would normally get up. So it all works out for you – you come slinking in before nine and get ready to leave for school, and no one's the wiser."

"Classes ended last week, Dad. My semester is over."

"That's not the point and you know it."

"The point is that you don't believe me. And I really don't care."

He stomped up the stairs and slammed his bedroom door behind him. Other than calling Terry to let her know he was all right, I had no idea what to do.

My father's curse had come true.

I was getting back a taste of what I'd dished out.

Terry

"Chip is mad as hell," I told Kris. "I swear he's taking Nick's mood personally."

We were pushing our way through the masses of holiday shoppers at the mall; I felt like a pack mule, burdened down with packages, bags stuck inside other bags to make them easier to carry, the temptation to buy Paul and Monica a stroller growing with each step – I could stick the bags in the stroller and also have something to push people out of my way.

Kris was laughing. "I don't feel sorry for him one bit. I can't even tell you all the times we waited up for him and how much of the state Ron and Grant covered looking for him."

"You think he would remember that."

"Are you kidding? Do you consider all the crap you pulled when grounding the other kids?"

She had me there. I was no perfect angel; I was known to cut school once in a while but the few times I caught Paul at it I came down hard on him.

"It's just that Chip seems so focused on this one thing. Nick's entitled to screw up once in a while."

"What's Chip avoiding?"

"What?" I stopped to shift the bags in my hands. "What do you mean?"

"What is it he's using Nick for to avoid dealing with?"

"Us, I suppose."

"And why is he avoiding the two of you?"

I didn't know. But Chip was avoiding dealing with the huge elephant in the corner of our marriage, and I wasn't really sure why.

Chip

I sat in the living room Christmas Eve afternoon listening to Eileen playing Christmas Carols on the piano while Kevin bantered with his grandfather. Terry and her mother were in the kitchen deciding who would be responsible for what portion of Christmas dinner, allowing Monica in on their secrets, while Paul held fast to the TV remote, looking for a football game.

The only one missing was Nick. He hung around long enough to be hospitable to his grandparents, acknowledging them when they spoke to him, barely humoring anyone else. He left the house before four, yelling out that he'd see us at Mass as the door slammed shut.

"Nick," Kevin grunted, "is turning into an ass."

"And you've never been in a bad mood," Paul said.

"Bad mood, hell. If Nick were any worse he'd be homicidal. Yesterday I asked him to help me move my bed and he damn near punched me in the chest trying to shove me out of his room."

I couldn't argue with them. The few times over the week I tried talking to him I was met with vehement stares and one "get off my back, dammit."

"I hope," Terry said quietly, so that none of the kids would hear, "that we're not seeing a repeat of Paul and Monica. I'm too young to be this old."

The possibility had occurred to me, too. Nick's sense of responsibility seemed to be slipping; we worried that he might be jealous of Paul's wedding, that he wanted it to be him up there at that altar with Katie.

He was staying out until after two in the morning most of the time, and when he was home he was moody, argumentative, and sullen. Too much like me at my worst.

Terry was right. We were both too young to be that old. The idea of one grandchild at that stage in our lives was overwhelming enough. Two was mind boggling.

"He'll tell us when he tells us," I said, hoping that whatever demons Nick had poking at him would soon disappear.

I worried over the years how well I related to my kids. I sometimes feared being far too lenient with them, other times I thought I was being too strict. None of them were ever held back by the constraints of not enough money or their parents never having enough time; even they downplayed family wealth, and both Terry and I made the time they needed while growing up. The perks of being the boss included being able to take time off when I needed to, and I made liberal use of that.

I enjoyed their company, and spent as much time with them as they would tolerate. We searched for things we could do with the kids individually; I coached little league for Nick and Paul's baseball teams, and took Eileen to piano lessons. I took karate classes with Kevin. Terry and I both made a point of spending time with them individually and worked hard at making them feel special.

As a result, we tuned into their pain as well as their happiness. I hated seeing any of them fighting over personal torment, and watching Nick struggle with whatever was bothering him was beginning to border on heart breaking. The temper outbursts were not Nick. They were Paul, or Kevin on a bad day. They were me as a teenager. They just weren't Nick.

When he and Katie failed to show at Mass again, I worried as much as I ever had. Colonel Forrester and his wife and other two kids were there, Spider and the twins sat a pew ahead of us with Paul and Monica; Doug and Kris sat behind us. Everyone was there except for the two I most worried about.

"Damien didn't seem bothered by Katie not being there," Terry said on the way home, cutting through the silence, knowing what was on my mind.

"Probably because Katie misses church a lot," Eileen said. "She's not as religious as Nick is, you know."

I didn't know.

Another factoid of my kids' lives I was clueless about.

I was upstairs when Nick came home at three a.m. Terry was running water for a bath, the entire room lit by candles. I heard the front door open and stood in the middle of my bedroom debating; go check on Nick, or respond to the obvious invitation just a few feet away.

Another invitation would come my way again, I was sure. I headed downstairs.

Nick was in the living room and had turned on the Christmas tree lights. He was slouched on the sofa, eyes red and bleary. I took one look at him and my heart lurched.

I lingered in the doorway for a long time, not sure if I should intrude.

"She's leaving," he moaned when he realized I was there, "and I can't do a goddamned thing to stop it."

"Katie?" I sat next to him on the couch, relief flooding through me. No, not a baby. Just a broken heart. "Where's she going?"

"Washington. Her dad got short orders. They leave during her semester break."

I didn't know what to say.

"God, Dad, he won't even think about letting her stay."

"It's the middle of her senior year," I muttered.

"I know, and her mom even wants to stay so Katie can

graduate here and her brother and sister can finish the year here. He won't even think about it."

"Nick, he might not be able to afford it," I pointed out.

"I don't care. We had everything planned out…"

I knew the litany well. "I know. You finish college, she gets halfway through…"

He shook his head, slouching down further into the sofa cushions. "That used to be the plan. Don't get pissed, but we were talking about moving into an apartment together after she graduates."

That wasn't exactly a surprise.

"It was just an idea," he added. "I told Katie what I really want to do is to get married this summer. And I know no one will approve and we're going to have the hear the 'you're too young' speech over and over, but I know it's right and I know it's time, and why aren't you saying anything?"

"Because I expected it," I said. "I won't fight it. Yes, I do think you're both young and I wish you would wait, but I'm not going to push you away over something that's inevitable. And it's something I would want for your future. I think both your mom and I always more or less assumed that you and Katie would wind up together."

"How pissed will you get if I admit something really, really stupid?"

"No promises."

"For about ten minutes we played with the idea that Paul and Monica had the right idea…"

"No, they absolutely did not," I cut in.

"I know. And that's not what either of us want, not for a long time. But it crossed my mind."

I didn't tell him that was exactly what I was worried about.

"If Katie had a place to stay – and not with you – do you think her dad would consider it?" I asked.

"I think hell would be hosting the Winter Olympics before that would happen."

"Just an idea," I sighed. "I still have an empty apartment."

"This fucking sucks," he sighed.

"I know. And I don't mean to sound patronizing, but she'll be eighteen by the end of the school year, and you turn eighteen this summer. If she really wants to come back there's not much her father can do to stop her. And I doubt he would try, not if she's hell bent on getting back here."

"That's seems like such a frigging long time, Dad."

"Seven months, Nick, that's all."

It seemed like an eternity to him; I didn't point out that I had survived two years. Still, I understood how he felt. If he'd had more notice, if he understood the why of what was happening, he could have handled the disappointment better.

Hell, I still didn't know why.

SIX

1995

Will

I was exasperated. The two people sitting in front of me were too stubborn for their own good; they both wanted my help and were grasping at the proverbial straws, yet neither would take the first step to cover the gap between them.

They were living together and not talking. They allowed for too many excuses and looked for reasons to avoid anything more than cursory conversation.

I wanted to strangle them.

"I don't see a problem," Chip insisted. "Why can't we just let it be?"

"Because," I answered before Terry could, "your wife doesn't want to let just let it be. If she sees a problem, then there must be one. It's obviously real to her."

Sensing Chip would be more open if we talked privately, Terry excused herself.

"She sees something that isn't there," he said when the door clicked shut.

"Something is there, all right. She's living in fear, and

you refuse to discuss it. You two keep doing this strange little dance around each other and nothing gets solved. Do you want to lose her again?"

"No."

"Then what's the problem?"

"Will, we have a ton of other problems to concentrate on right now. She's worried that I might leave her, but we both know I'm not going anywhere. I don't care anymore what happened. I just want to forget it, and right now I've got a couple of kids who are hurting and I can't just put that aside."

I leaned back in my chair. January had brought a cold snap that forced us off the basketball court and into my office, where the level of tension was palpable. "What about the kids?" I asked, wanting to get the subject of them out of the way.

"I have one son who's less than three months away from being a father himself, and he's scared out of his mind. Another son is practically broken in half because he's positive he'll lose the only person in the world that matters to him on any tangible level. Could you worry about consoling your wife over some imagined fear when your kids are dragging themselves through these sticky swamps?"

"Honestly? I don't know."

"Paul will be all right if I can get him to stop working so many hours and get it into his head that he doesn't have to be an adult twenty four hours a day. Nick I'm not so sure about."

"Katie?"

He nodded. "You should see him, Will. He's lost interest in just about everything. He's hardly ever home, and when he is it's like he's just existing to get through the moment. Katie isn't even gone yet – what's it going to be like when she is?"

"He'll suffer for a while," I said.

"I know. And as long as he has liberal use of the phone and email they'll be all right. I can't get that through his head. He's terrified she'll get to Washington and meet someone else."

"It's a possibility."

He glared at me.

"If they asked you now," I ventured, "would you give Nick your permission to get married?"

He stared at me like it was a completely new idea, one he had never entertained himself, though I was sure it had crossed his mind a dozen times since Paul's wedding. "No," he said. "I'd prefer it if he waited until he was done with school, but I really have no say in it after he turns eighteen. Will, he's not going to lose her, he just thinks he might. It's grief talking, and I need to figure out how to deal with his grief."

"Has he given you any idea how close their relationship is?" I was going out on the proverbial limb, hoping it wouldn't break in two and alienate a son from his father and a boy from his kindly parish priest.

"You mean how intimate, don't you?"

I nodded.

"He's been sleeping with her for over a year that I know of. Their relationship is about as intimate as it can get. I suppose I encouraged it in my own way. I armed those kids with too much information way too young. I'm pretty sure I gave both of those boys the idea that I wasn't a great believer in waiting for marriage. I practically gave them permission to screw everything in sight."

"Did you?" I didn't believe it. "What you did was maintain some openness and honesty with your sons. Your kids understand more about respect and love than most kids their age. You supplied them with what they needed to know, and sex just happened to be a major part of what they questioned you on. You did the right thing, you answered the questions when they came up, and they learned about love by watching you and Terry.

"Look, Chip, the one thing I've noticed is that you've raised your kids to be independent and ready to face the world by the time they got out of high school. Nick is fully prepared to face anything the world can throw at him, and Paul is almost there. Kevin is as twisted as a corkscrew sometimes, but that's just his age showing. And Eileen – your daughter possesses more self assurance than a person has a right to. You've been a damn good father, and you shouldn't blame yourself for the things they trip over."

"You have a point?"

"Quit using your kids as something to hide behind. Paul will be fine. Nick will smart for a while and then he'll start counting the days until Katie comes home. If you worry about him at all, it should be about surviving how nuts he'll get in the week or so before they get married. Chip, if you worry about anything at all, worry about your wife."

"I would if I knew what it is I'm supposed to worry about!" he snapped. "Dammit, Will, what is it she wants to hear? One day she's talking about how shaky things are and the next she's talking about wanting another kid."

My eyebrows lifted in spite of myself. This was a new one.

"She wants to talk to Doug," he explained. "She thinks she can get her tubal reversed."

"Well, you two have always wanted a large family," I said.

"Wanted. Past tense. I just keep telling her to wait until we're on more solid ground before we even think about it."

"But you don't want another baby, do you?"

"A baby, yes. A child, no. I don't mind the diapers and bottles and being barfed on, but babies grow up. They become kids and then little people with tempers and issues of their own. I don't want to start a second family, Will. I want to spoil my grand kids, but I can't see me raising more. Christ, I even told her if a year from now she still wanted kids and we were doing okay, I'd consider adopting, but I don't think I can. I don't think I can be the sixty year old dad mistaken for grandpa at my own kid's high school graduation."

"Explain it to her."

"How? You want me to break her heart again? She's a perpetual mother, Will."

"You won't break her heart. I doubt what she wants is another baby. I think what she wants is that feeling you both had with each of the kids. All those warm fuzzies that made her think you'd be perfect forever. She's just scared."

"So am I."

"What is it you're afraid of?"

He looked around the room, eyes resting briefly on pictures he'd seen dozens of times. Family friends, his own children included, photos taken over the years at school plays and picnics. He was a much of an imp as they were.

"I'm afraid we'll never be the same," he said quietly.

"It's always going to be a part of your lives. The question is whether or not it's a transgression you can both forgive, or a shadow you're going to let hang over you for the rest of your life."

"How many times do I have to say it? I've forgiven her. I'm not so sure she's forgiven me for my part in it."

"Which is?" I pressed.

"Dammit, Will, I don't want to keep rehashing it. I just want to forget it, and I want her to trust me."

"Doesn't she?"

He shrugged. "Does she?"

"Do you trust her?"

He hesitated too long.

"You've got to talk to her," I insisted.

"She doesn't want to talk, she wants to fight."

It was my turn to shrug. "So fight. Get it over with."

"I don't want to hurt her."

"You're hurting her now, Chip. Every time you refuse to acknowledge her fears as legitimate, you hurt her. Every time you walk away from the issues that bother her most, she falls a little bit apart. So you love her, she knows that. Quit screwing around and start communicating with your wife. Lock yourselves in a room and go at it tooth and nail if that's what it takes, but dammit, give in and do it her way."

"You're full of shit," he seethed. "Fighting won't solve a goddamned thing between us."

"You can't solve your marital problems with the quick solution of sex, no matter how good it is. Sooner or later you're going to have to change the sheets, you know."

"I *always* give in, Will."

"You can pick something less important to take a stand on, Chip."

He rolled his eyes.

"All the years I've known you, you've described Terry as God's gift to you. A blessing. Are you willing to lose that kind of blessing again? Is God going to have to give you a cosmic kick in the ass before you swallow whatever pride you've got and whatever it is you're afraid of, and work it out on her terms? I know you've forgiven her, but she hasn't forgiven herself, and she senses that she lost your trust."

He flinched. "You think so?"

"If I can see it, you know she can."

He considered it, eyes shutting for a moment, lips drawn in a thin, tight line. "You know," he said when he opened them, "About fifteen years ago you tried to give me marital advice and I told you it'd do you some good to go out and find a good horny woman and screw your brains out, just to clear your head…"

"I tried it," I interrupted. "It didn't work, and it still hurts."

"Maybe I was wrong. I wound up taking your advice then and it worked. I just don't know if I can do it now."

"It'll be worth the effort."

"How did you get over the pain, Will? I know you were in love with her."

"I never said I got over it. If she walked through that door right now and said she'd thought it over and she still wanted me, I'd be out of here before you could blink, and screw the consequences. I doubt God intended me to be miserable. With her I was happy."

"And you're not as a priest?"

"Not as happy. Chip, if I were you I wouldn't waste the time you have together. It's not worth taking a stand on this one. You have a second chance. Don't fuck it up."

I watched out the window as he walked toward his car, an arm possessively around his wife. He had it all right there and was too frightened to examine it too closely just in case it exploded right in his face.

He couldn't see that leaving it alone would kill it just as easily.

For the first time in dealing with them, I was truly angry.

And for the first time, I was jealous.

Chip

"Nick's not coming home tonight, is he?"

I looked up from where I was sitting at the kitchen table and set down the newspaper I'd been flipping through. My wife, dressed in a very old, very thin white t-shirt, brushed past me on her way into the kitchen.

It was after two in the morning; Doug and Kris had come over for dinner and afterwards while Terry and Kris wandered into the living room to talk, Doug and I tried to teach the kids to play poker.

"We'll play poker," Doug told them, "because I don't want you to see me humiliated at the pool table."

"He sucks," Spider told Kevin and Eileen.

They left around midnight, and until Terry mentioned Nick, I hadn't given him much thought. He spent most of his free time away from the house, grabbing onto every minute he could with Katie. I doubted he would come home, and wondered what excuse she had given her parents to explain being out all night.

"He's okay," I muttered, distracted by a flash of red lace when she reached into the cupboard for a coffee mug.

"Do you know where he is, Chip?" She reached into the refrigerator for the milk. "He should have been home by now."

"Is it enough if I just tell you not to worry and he's all right?"

"No." She poured a liberal amount of milk into a saucepan and added several heaping spoons full of chocolate powder. "Want some?"

I nodded. "Nick is okay, Terry. And what he's doing is probably none of our business."

"Irish, if you know where he is you'd better tell me," she said, stirring the milk. "And I'd suggest you do it within the next ten seconds unless you want a handful of ice shoved down your shorts."

The question pinging around in my brain was who would she be the most angry with: Nick for staying out all night with Katie, or me for giving him the means?

I knew she didn't really mind Katie.

"Chip?"

There was no way out. "He's probably at my apartment. My guess is that they're spending the night there."

I waited for the tirade.

She turned her back to me and finished heating up the hot chocolate. I knew I was in trouble, though, just by the tight expression on her face when she finally turned around and came to sit with me at the table.

"Should I explain before you have to ask?"

"I'm already asking. What about not giving them blanket permission or the example he's setting for Kevin and Eileen? And I thought you took the keys away from the kids months ago."

"I gave him back a key on Christmas morning. He doesn't need any moral judgments on his relationship with Katie right now. All he needed was a quiet place they could go and not worry about brothers and sisters. Or parents."

She nodded as if she understood.

"Her father has orders to Washington," I said, sipping the hot chocolate carefully. "Nick is terrified of losing her, and she's leaving in a week. It was a snap decision, I just gave him the key and told him to be careful. It's not just a sex thing, Terry, they needed to be able to just hang out together and to talk…"

The sigh that escaped warned me of the storm brewing. She was too quiet and wouldn't look at me. She stared straight into her mug.

"Go ahead and say it," I said. "We might as well get this over with."

Another sigh.

I had a feeling I was about to get blasted with both barrels.

She set the mug down. "Why the hell did you have an apartment key to give him, Chip? Silly me, I assumed when you came home you'd give it up. Are you looking for an easy way out if it gets a little too uncomfortable here? I thought you were home to stay."

"I am."

"Then why keep the damned apartment? Unless you were thinking of keeping it in case you had to leave again, there's no reason for having it! None!"

"It's not what you think."

"Then enlighten me already."

"Well, for starters, I own it."

"That tiny place is a condo?"

"No. Christ, you're going to be pissed off" – not that she wasn't already – "but I bought the complex. It went up for sale a couple months after I moved in and I thought it had investment potential…"

"That doesn't explain why you still have your apartment, Chip," she snapped. "There's no return on vacant property."

"At first I kept it thinking that if Paul and Monica couldn't find an apartment on their own, I'd offer it to them. The market is tight for rentals, Terry."

She was shaking her head.

"Look, we gave them enough help by making sure they got money from the trust fund and giving him a job. I wasn't going to make it even easier by giving them a place to live without some kind of effort on their part."

"You are so full of shit," she grumbled, taking the mugs to the kitchen.

"What do you want?"

"I want the truth."

"The truth is that I did *not* hang onto it as a place to escape. That never occurred to me." She sat down at the table again, but refused to look at me. "It did occur to me that we could use the apartment if we wanted to get away from the kids."

She looked up, finally, blue eyes bright with anger. "Tell me the truth, goddammit!"

"I am."

"No, if it were the truth you'd have told me upfront. I would have known within a few days that you were keeping it and that you owned the entire damned complex. It's your 'in case' backup plan."

"I swear to God..." I reached across the table for her hand, surprised that she didn't pull it away. "If I thought that at all, it wasn't consciously. I don't need a backup plan, Terry. I'm not leaving you, and I'm not going to let you make me go." I let go of her hand and leaned back in the chair. "If you *really* wanted me to go, and if you don't think it's working out and you want someone else..."

"No. Stop that, Chip. Whether we work it our or not, we stay together."

"I don't want you to be miserable."

She sighed again, a light, airy lamentation of the pesky little boy reciting a worn out catechism. "Do I look miserable?"

Did she want honesty or not?

"Sometimes," I admitted.

"Then I must have looked like hell when you weren't here." She reached for my hand again and held it tightly. "Why won't you talk to me?"

"Why won't you just let it go?"

"Don't answer a question with a question. We'll never get anywhere if we don't talk."

I wasn't sure if I wanted to get anywhere, and I wasn't sure what was expected to come of it, other than a fight, which I didn't want.

Why couldn't she accept me back the way things were?

All right, fine, things were not perfect. Our marriage was nothing but sex at that point. Other than in bed we had little to do with each other; when we talked, it inevitably had something to do with the kids. She had her work, I had mine, and that was it.

Sounded like a pretty average marriage to me.

Only we had never been average before.

I thought about what we had before we split. Looking back, most of what we had then was sex. Lots of it. We had sex in every place we could and in every position we could think of. But there was also something else back then. We had more in common than the kids. Sometimes it was enough to just sit and look at each other, to be in the same room together. We didn't have to touch to be connected.

We talked a lot about the kids, but we also talked about our dreams for the future; we planned for the day when the house wasn't overrun with temperamental munchkins and loud music vibrating the walls.

More than anything, we laughed together, about anything and everything. We laughed about the stupid, wonderful things the kids did, about the eccentricities of some of my regular customers and my employees, Doug and Kris and her parents, snoopy neighbors.

We laughed about everything.

What we had in the aftermath was raw, desperate sex. It was as passionate as anything we could hope for; the sight of her sitting in the kitchen with me at nearly three in the morning stirred my desire as much as her curiosity had when we first married.

But, our loving was only fun. Never funny.

All right, I could see why she wanted to talk, even to fight. She wanted the laughter back in our lives as much as I did.

Terry wanted substance with the sex.

A decent husband would have given her that and more.

I just didn't know how.

Nick

Dear Katie,

I'm writing this to you now because I know that when it comes right down to it I won't be able to say it when I want to. There's a lot I want to say, too.

Six months seems like a long time, and what we make out of the time we have to spend apart will mark the rest of our lives. I'm praying that it will be all right and that it will only be six months.

I'm not offering up prayer as lip service, either. You know me better than that.

You know, when I was about fifteen, almost sixteen, I asked my dad how I could learn how to treat a woman the right way. You know my dad – he knew it was partly about sex and it didn't faze him one bit. He cut a rose off one of my mom's bushes and plucked off a petal, then handed it to me, telling me to run a finger over it. Like a clod I ripped the petal in half.

He picked a second petal, but before he handed it to me he told me to touch it as if I was reaching out to touch a newborn baby's cheek for the first time, to close my eyes and brush against it feather soft. He wanted me to feel the magic and the beauty, and to breathe in the sweetness of its fragrance. He reasoned that if I could learn to treat a woman with the same awe, I would be treating her right no matter how inexperienced I was.

You're my rose, Katie. I hope I always treated you with the respect you deserve and as much love as you needed. I always tried to make sure the petals stayed in place and the thorns not so sharp. And the fragrance – you filled me with so much wonder it never took perfumes of anything else to make my head spin.

We can still have a perfect life together. None of our plans have to change. Six months and the distance of an entire continent can't possibly change what I feel for you.

Consider this the formal proposal I said you could expect: I love you more than anyone or anything. I have since the day you walked into the freshman biology class looking pale and scared and hopelessly lost. I want the rest of my life to be with you. I want all the romantic fantasy and every minute of dull reality. I can't promise you the moon and the stars, and heaven will have to wait until the end of everything, but without you what's left on earth means nothing to me.

Marry me in June, Katie.

In six months I'll still be here, waiting. And I promise, no rose will ever be treated as delicately or treasured as much.

All my love
Nicky

~

Navigating through the dimly lit streets was more than a chore; winter had finally arrived, the bite of cold penetrating deep, my bones aching and muscles taut and trembling. Driving home was a monumental task I had not prepared myself for.

I hadn't prepared myself for much that night.

Going well under the speed limit, not trusting my reflexes or night vision, I suppose I was more in danger of getting pulled over for impeding traffic than anything else.

Sorry, Officer, it's kind of hard to see with tears in your eyes.

I promised myself I wouldn't cry. Letting Katie go was hard enough as it was, and I didn't want to complicate matters by reducing her to tears as well.

I should have known better.

Everything we did that night was slow and affectionate, two desperate people trying to touch the deepest parts of one another. The soft music drifting in from the stereo in the living room and the amber light streaking through the bedroom door added to an already melancholy mood.

"Awfully quiet tonight, Nicky," she said, cuddled in my arms.

"You're not real vocal yourself," I whispered, hoping to hell my voice wouldn't break. "I'm sorry, I'm not at my best tonight. I'd hope I'd do a little better."

"Better than what? You let me be the judge of when you're at your best or not."

It was hard to not be gloomy with her warm body pressed up against mine, the thought picking away at me that it could be the last time.

The last time you make love with someone should be

something to remember.

"My dad's giving up the apartment soon," I said absently. "I guess my mom took it personally."

"I can't blame her."

My watch began to beep. Midnight. I should have had her home by then.

"Don't worry," she murmured. "What can they do? Ground me? So I spend the first month in Washington stuck in the house. Big deal."

"You'll make friends fast," I said dully.

She lifted onto an elbow to look into my face. "Don't be so grim, Mister Nick. You have friends here, too, you know. And I won't freak out if you date a little."

"Not a chance."

"I don't want you to sit home all the time."

"Let me deal with it my own way, Katie. I loaded my class schedule this semester and I haven't left time for anything much except classes and studying."

"Sounds kind of dull."

"I want it that way."

She laid back down, fingers trailing across my chest. "Remember when we met? You were so short then. I walked into class and there was this little squirt with these thick glasses ogling me."

"Hey, I grew six inches just for you, and got contacts to boot."

"I was so scared then. I didn't know anybody."

"Which is why," I added, "you went out with me in the first place. Must've figured I was harmless."

"Nicky, you *are* harmless. Sometimes you can be such a dork."

I pretended to take offense.

"You're my dork, though," she said softly. "I'll miss you like crazy Saint Nick."

"Don't…"

"It's not forever. Just crook your finger and I'll come running."

God, I hoped so.

Colonel Forrester was waiting when we drove up to their house, standing at the window, a frown practically tattooed on his face. I hated him.

Yet, I also understood him. She was his daughter and still his little girl.

The sidewalk to their front porch felt like it was a mile and a half long. They had a small bench under the window – her father finally closed the curtains – and we sat there together, clinging like we would drown if either of us let go.

I reached into my back pocket for the letter that had been burning a hole there all night.

"Don't read it yet," I said.

And God, don't cry.

It was too late, the floodgates were already open, silky, silent tears slipping over her eyelashes and down her cheeks.

"Nicky, I…"

"Tell me when you come home." I stood on rubbery legs, knees practically water. "Go in before your dad comes after me."

"He won't." She jumped up and grabbed me, head buried against my chest. I could feel her tears soak through my shirt. "Nicky."

"Give me a kiss, and then go inside."

When we parted she stepped back, hand on the doorknob. "God, I love you, Nick."

"I love you, too. Six months, that's all, just six months."

That echoed in my head all the way home.

Six months.

Just six months.

I should have expected my dad to still be up when I got home, pretending to be doing anything other than waiting for me. I shut the front door quietly and locked it, starting up the stairs before I noticed the light coming in from the study.

It was still his father's study. The man had been dead since I was a baby, there was a pool table taking up most of the space, and it was still his study.

He was at the desk, pouring over the journal.

"Hey, Dad."

He looked into my eyes and knew.

"I'm really sorry, Nick."

I shrugged, trying to pretend it wasn't killing me. "How's the search for stuff on your dad going?"

He took the change of subject without missing a beat. "Slow. Your mom gave some of the documents to Brad. He's got some hotshot P.I. who's tracking a few of the particulars down."

"Don't you have friends who can do that?"

"Wouldn't be a good idea," he said.

"What's the worst that can happen? We all have to change our names. No sweat."

"It's just a matter of curiosity for me, son. It won't change a thing." He rose from the plush leather chair and beckoned me to follow him into the living room. As I sat on the sofa he fumbled around the bar, clattering ice cubes and glasses together.

I didn't expect him to bring me a drink.

"Here's to the women we don't understand."

I drank to it, though I thought I understood Katie. I could

see why my mom confused him, but I suspected that was part of the magic of their marriage. She was designed to delight him and to distract him. It wasn't necessary that he understand her.

"Did it hurt this much when you and mom split up?" I asked, using a considerable amount of strength to just look over at him. "I feel completely lost."

He nodded thoughtfully and sank back into the cushions. "I wanted to fold up and die, Nick. I won't give you any crap about the pain going away. It's going to hurt for a while."

Six months.

"I sort of made myself a promise. If she still wants me after her birthday, I'll fly out there myself to bring her back if that's what it takes."

"Me Tarzan, You Jane?" He laughed appreciatively. "I should have done that with your mom."

"You know nothing seems to be working out? Katie will be gone in a few hours, you and mom obviously aren't in synch yet, Spider broke up with Janet…"

"Really now. Spider let another one go?"

"Well, she broke up with him. No notice or anything. She just told him in front of the whole damned cafeteria that at the rate they were going she'd still be a virgin when she was thirty."

"Poor kid. She said it out loud?"

"Yeah, but he doesn't seem too broken up about it. I think he has his eye on someone else already."

"Now that doesn't surprise me."

He took my glass and went over to the bar for a refill. "Take it easy with this, Nick," he said when he returned. "I don't get hangovers, but you might."

"Really, Dad, I don't think I'll notice."

If it was a hangover I woke up with, it lasted eight weeks.

Will

With winter coming to an end, Chip was becoming a jumble of nerves and distractions, distracted enough that I could easily take him on the basketball court.

The warm weather returned in March so quietly I barely noticed it hadn't been there all along. I realized spring had snuck up on me when we sat on the steps in front of the church and watched women parade past us in shorts and skin tight t-shirts.

"I'm getting old," Chip declared when the twenty first point sailed through the basket and it wasn't his. "A few years ago you couldn't have done that."

"A few years ago you could keep your head in the game."

"Kids," he sighed. "Kids having kids, kids moping around the house. All four of them are driving me nuts."

"Let's see. Paul's on edge because the baby is due soon. Nick still misses Katie. Kevin can't decide if he's perverted or pious. What about Eileen?"

He rolled his eyes. "Terry claims she's just being fourteen. I keep getting these offhanded hints that there's a boy at school she likes but I haven't met him and she won't tell anyone who he is."

"Maybe she's worshiping him from afar," I chuckled.

"Don't laugh. This is my baby girl we're talking about."

"It's about time she started throwing a few curve balls your way."

Chip scooped up the ball and we headed back towards the church. "You know," he said, bouncing the ball as we walked, "none of the boys have made fun of her yet? I really thought when she started showing a real interest in boys they'd ride her hard. But there hasn't been any teasing at all."

"Your two oldest are past that stage. And Kevin, as

baffling as he'd like us to think he is, is a very sensitive young man. Where he complains to you about his twin sister, he praises her to me. And wishes he was more like her."

"They're good kids, Will. I don't know how or why, but they're all good kids."

"Must be the milk man's offspring."

"Must be."

We slumped onto the front steps of the church, and he continued to bounce the ball between his legs, staring into the street.

"Where's your wife today?" I finally asked, having avoided the question for over an hour.

"Work."

"This wasn't more important?"

He stopped dribbling the ball and looked at me. "She doesn't think it's doing any good, Will. Other than stimulating her already over-stimulated hormones when we play ball without shirts, she doesn't think she's getting anything out of it."

"Surging hormones is better than nothing," I reasoned.

Anything to keep them talking.

"You would think," he muttered, staring off into the distance, the basketball spinning slowly between his hands, "that after nearly twenty years we'd have settled into the same predictable pattern that everyone else does."

He laughed lightly and smiled.

"Hell, Will, she still carbonates my hormones."

"If it wasn't for the sex, would you stay with her?"

I expected him to think about it, at least for a moment. He just nodded and said, "I think so."

"Why?"

"Because" – he handed the ball to me – "when I'm with

her, I'm happy. It doesn't need to be more than that, does it?"

I heard those words once. In the middle of the night, mumbled through a haze of not enough sleep and raw, animal hunger; I still hear them when I awake with a sudden start, abandoned dreams still teasing my memory.

"I'm happy when I'm with you."

I was happier than I had ever been.

I wondered where she was.

I also wondered where I had blown it. Not enough tender words at the right time, not enough time to show her what I meant by what I said? Did I not tell her I loved her enough, or maybe too often?

She was simply afraid.

I couldn't make her believe that God would understand. She couldn't accept that He wasn't something she shouldn't be afraid of.

And deep inside, I knew He brought her to me, and if I were half the man I was encouraging Chip to be, I would go after her.

I was as lousy a priest as I was a psychologist, as ineffective at the pulpit as I was a lover.

I was so damned happy then.

"Kiss the blarney stone, Padre," Chip said, pulling me out of my reverie. "You look like my daughter does half the time."

"Just thinking."

At least Nick had hope.

"Lisa?"

I nodded soberly.

"Regrets?"

"More than I can count. Every day I think of another reason to go after her. I haven't made it work, Chip, not really."

"I think you have. Maybe not in the way you mean, though."

"I've got no business counseling you and Terry. I don't even have my own act together. God, I haven't even said Mass since September, I think. Everyone else covers for my sorry ass."

"What would you tell me to do?" he asked. "Hell, what *did* you tell me to do? When I was at my lowest, all the times I bitched and moaned about not having Terry, what did you tell me to do?"

"To go see her," I sighed. "I don't even know where she is now. And I doubt she'd see me if I could find her."

He was quiet for a long time, staring at me, judging every little movement and twitch of my facial expression. "You won't last another year in the priesthood," he said after a while. "You've given them your entire adult life, Will. Let go of it now before you turn into one of those bitter, hateful religious martyrs who ruins the experience for the entire parish."

"I made a commitment, Chip."

"And you fulfilled it. Don't use any of Lisa's arguments on me. I know better. No one will think any less of you."

Too many people would think much less of me.

My confessor had argued with me on that, more than once.

"Go with grace," he'd said. "You'll be no less the man for following your heart."

And I argued about commitment and the mass exodus of priests from the church. If we kept leaving to follow our hearts, who would be left? The vows were never meant to be easy, and they were never meant to be broken.

I was happy as a priest.

I was happier with Lisa.

Chip stood up, brushing dirt from his shorts and legs. "I'm going home to take a shower. I'll wait for my wife to come home, and if we don't sulk at each other or tumble into bed, I might even tell her she makes me happy." He shrugged. "I'll tell you what, going to bed with a woman you love, even if things aren't easy, is a hell of a lot better than going to bed alone."

"I don't doubt it."

"Lisa's working at that new, ritzy little nursing home down the street from the Charybdis. Her shift starts at three this afternoon, just go into the lobby and she'll be there at the reception desk. She's not married, and if I gather correctly, she's not seeing anyone."

Damn him anyway.

Would she accept accomplished fact? If I left because I knew it was no longer my life's calling, would she consider me a part of her life again, without the all-consuming fear that God was about to strike us both dead?

Did I have the guts?

How many times since they started crawling towards each other had I told Chip and Terry to deal with each other, and wasn't I pushing them towards a discussion that could blow them apart for good? Talk, dammit, no matter what the consequences?

I wanted Lisa more than anything.

A year ago the Bishop told me to get out while I could, and now Chip was warning me I had the potential to become a bitter man.

"Where," I whispered, looking up, "does my biggest responsibility lie?"

I got up and headed towards the rectory. I didn't have to wait for the answer I already knew.

My first responsibility was for the truth.

I packed as many clothes as I could and headed out the back door, got into my car, and drove to the closest motel to Chip's restaurant I could find.

Terry

For the most part, instead of working, I watched the clock and ticked off the things I thought Chip and Will would be doing. Macho hand slapping and boasting about who would run whom into the ground first. Will trying to get Chip to answer questions with more than a grunt. Chip insisting there was nothing he needed or wanted to talk about. At some point Chip would tease Will about his athletic prowess, his nosiness, or about women who made passes at him even after they knew he was a priest.

I began to regret telling Chip to go with out me. Even if it was doing no good, being there certainly didn't do any harm. Being with them gave me an appreciation for the friendship they'd built up over the years. They teased each other and squabbled like brothers; Chip had with Will the relationship he should have had with his own brother. Will helped fill a void that David's death created.

Brad came back from a lunch meeting half an hour earlier than expected, and waved for me to follow him into his office. "I've got some of the stuff Chip asked for," he said as I closed the door. "It's not bad for a quickie investigation."

"Anything worthwhile?" I asked.

He dropped into the high back chair behind his desk and pointed to the chair in front of it. I sat and waited while he spread papers out on his desk.

"Well, for starters, most of the certificates are forgeries. Baptism certificates, name changes…" He glanced up. "That's not a problem for Chip, you know. Simple usage is enough. His father never went through any legal process to change his name, and we can't make any substantial connection to a reason why he forged a document stating he had. All we have are guesses."

"Anything else?"

"Michael Brennan's existence stops right after he left his parish. No one from the church ever heard from him or saw him again. The last time he was seen he was in the company of another priest who vanished about the same time." He glanced at the paper in front of him. "Ronald Gallery."

"Are you serious?"

"Not sure why Brennan changed his name and Gallery did not. Gallery was easy to track… and according to our PI's government friends, both of them may have been involved in the startup of an intelligence agency designed to supplement the FBI and the CIA. He couldn't get anything more than that without trying to get his hands on classified information. Our best guess – he became Grant Davis to put Brennan behind him and to protect his wife and son from whatever work he was doing with this agency."

My head was pounding.

Grant and Ron had helped *start* the agency?

"Chip might be interested to know he has living relatives," Brad said. "His paternal grandparents are still alive and in their late nineties, and he has two uncles and an aunt. Tons of cousins. They're all in the Chicago area."

The phone rang and he picked it up without looking up from the information he was sorting through. He mumbled and I wasn't listening, still pondering Grant and Ron.

"That was Chip," he said, getting my attention. "Your daughter-in-law went into labor during a history test."

"Good grief, it's not due for two more weeks."

"Tell that to the baby." He followed me out to my desk. "I'll put everything together in a file and have a courier bring it to Chip in a day or so."

"I appreciate it, Brad," I said, trying to remember where I'd put my purse.

"Bottom drawer," he laughed. "Take tomorrow off, Grandma. Somehow I suspect you'd be useless if you came in."

Chip

The nurses in the OB ward seemed surprised that child-birth could be a family event. The waiting room was barely big enough for all of us; Paul wandered back and forth between the waiting room and birthing room, giving us updates on Monica and how much she alternately hated him and couldn't live without him, while Terry and I sat together and whispered our regrets on allowing the rest of the kids to wait at the hospital with us.

"There will be nothing to do," I warned them. "It will be boring. With a capital B."

They didn't care; they wanted to be in the same building when their first niece or nephew arrived.

Nick slouched in a chair, staring at the TV.

"Dude," Kevin said, "you're memorizing the freaking Weather Channel."

Nick didn't look at him or even acknowledge he'd spoken.

"A cold front is moving through North Bay Medical Center," Kevin announced playfully. "Expect frigid temperatures followed by extreme frost. Details at eleven."

Eileen pretended to not know either of them – though she was trying hard not to smile – while she occupied her time studying.

Nick's silence and Kevin's intermittent teasing lasted three hours, until Kevin pointed out a commercial for Midol and asked, of no one in particular, if that would clear up Nick's sixty two days of PMS.

Nick finally looked up. "I wish to hell one of the voices in your head would tell you to shut the fuck up."

Not that I was keeping score, but Kevin won that one.

I was about to tell them all to just shut up when Paul stumbled into the waiting room, excitedly motioning for us to follow him.

Monica was propped up in the bed, sheer joy etched into the fatigue that washed over her, her baby cuddled close.

I found myself staring into the sweetest, most wrinkled red face that I had seen since Kevin and Eileen were born. Wide blue eyes, head as bald as an egg, and mouth wide open in sustained protest of the sudden commotion.

Paul brushed a finger against his baby's cheek, so much like I had done with Nick almost eighteen years before, that same touch that spoke of wonder and bemusement at such a tiny bundle of heaven, the closest to heaven I was sure I would ever get.

"Her name is Nicole," he said softly. "Nicole Eileen. Kev, I'm sorry, but there was just no way to fit your name in there anywhere."

Kevin was standing behind Terry, his chin resting on the top of her head. "I don't care. She's fucking awesome, Paul."

That wasn't the way I would have put it, but the boy hit the nail on the head. Nicole Eileen Davis was one quarter Irish, half Catholic and half Presbyterian – a minor flaw I could overlook – and in her young uncle's apt words, fucking awesome.

Doug

I expected the house to be dark and for everyone else to be asleep when I got home at three in the morning, but Spider was sitting in the living room, his nose buried in a book, oblivious to the TV blaring for too loudly in the corner.

When he didn't look up I tapped the page he was looking at and then sat next to him.

"It's a girl," I said slowly, almost too tired to move my hands. "She's six pounds and six ounces, twenty inches long, and in perfect health."

"Name?"

"Nicole Eileen," I spelled slowly. "She came out crying and hasn't stopped since."

He smiled. "Is Monica all right?"

"She's fine. She'll leave the hospital tomorrow and go home with Uncle Chip and Aunt Terry for a few days so she can rest. You can probably go over and see them then."

"Will you call them first and make sure I don't show up at a bad time?"

"Sure."

He fingered the book in his lap, digging his thumbnail into the cover.

"Something else?" I asked.

"Would I be out of line if I asked Uncle Chip to get a TTY terminal? Sometimes I'd like to call Nick or even Aunt Terry and I'd like to do it without your help."

"The worst that can happen is that he'd say no," I said. "But I don't think it's out of line. I'm surprised you've never asked before."

"It never seemed important before."

I wanted to press for more, but he tossed the book aside and said it was time for bed.

He was seventeen.

I'm not sure I really wanted to know.

Nick

"Eat shit and die, Colonel Forrester. I'll call your daughter anytime of the goddamned day or night that I want."

All right, so I didn't actually say that, but I did think it when he balked at waking Katie up at what was six in the morning for him. No, I didn't want him to deliver a message, I wanted the news to come from me.

I was slowly learning, even over long distance, that the best way to deal with the Colonel was to take a stand and not budge.

He respected fortitude, even if it might be misplaced.

I hoped Katie kept that in mind.

By the time I got off the phone the adrenaline rush had caught up with me and all I wanted to do was crawl into bed. Paul was sound asleep on the living room couch – he was too tired to even make it up the stairs – Kevin was in the dining room with Mom and Dad, trying to explain that the school principal wanted to see them but not because he was in any kind of trouble. It was the same conversation I'd had when the school wanted to push me out and into higher education, only for Kevin it was coming a year earlier, and in his case, a year too late.

Eileen was waiting to bound into my room the moment my clothes were in a heap on the floor.

"What do you want?" I snapped, grabbing for a pair of shorts at the foot of my bed.

"Nick, what's Spider? Relative-wise, I mean."

I flopped down on the bed and sat against the headboard, trying to remember how distant a cousin Mom was to Aunt

Kris. "Second cousin once or twice removed, I guess."

"That's okay then," she mumbled to herself and not to me. For the moment, I didn't exist.

I bit. Tired or not and grumpy or not, she nipped at my curiosity. She was too serious for it to be a rhetorical question. "Why?"

She hesitated, but then stepped all the way into the room and sat next to me on the bed. "He broke up with Janet," she started, lamely. Everyone was well aware of that slice of trivia and it stopped being important two hours after the accomplished fact.

Except, I supposed, to her.

"Look, Nicky, I've been spending a lot of time with him at school, you know, just at lunch and in the library. Just talking and keeping him company. He looked kind of bored after they broke up and I didn't want him to feel lonely…"

I couldn't help grinning.

"You got a thing for Spider, Eileen?"

"I think so," she admitted in a quiet, uncertain voice. "God, don't tell anyone! I'd die!"

"Now that sounds pretty serious," I teased. "What's he say about it?"

She was horrified. "I haven't told him, and don't you dare!"

I sighed, striving for the most guilting sigh I could muster. Mom at her best, berating a spoiled little boy for doing something he shouldn't have. "Look, if you like him, tell him. He won't laugh or flick boogers on you."

Dubious glare.

"Come on. If he doesn't feel the same way he'll be nice about it. You might feel awkward for a couple days, and that'll be it. He won't make fun of you, if that's what you're worried about."

"Dad will explode."

"Dad's not going to like the idea of you dating anyone," I said, "but I'm willing to bet he'll make the most out of having Spider to tease. The night he comes to pick you up for the junior prom Dad will be on the front porch with a shot-gun, asking him what time he intends to bring you home."

She giggled. "If Spider tells him 'tomorrow' Dad will probably shoot him."

"Eh, could be."

"If I tell him and he makes me cry, will you come to my rescue and beat him up?"

"Sure," I laughed.

She got up and headed for the door. "I missed seeing you smile, Nick."

I watched the door close and listened for the sound of her door closing, too. I hadn't realized how long it had been since I had really laughed.

It felt good.

Chip

When each of our kids was born, I would have sworn the sound of their crying in the middle of the night was music to my ears. The seven times my granddaughter began to cry in the middle of the night I decided it was still music, but instead of the sweet classical sounds her father had oozed, it was more like death metal.

Nicole had lungs that extended to the tips of her toes, and she used every square inch of them to be heard. I woke for an eighth time around eleven in the morning, and Terry was still asleep, one arm strewn across my chest and a trim leg jammed possessively between mine.

I wondered if Nick was as magnanimous about the night

time racket as he had been when we brought Kevin and Eileen home. He'd been taken with the idea of babies then, curious about their tiny fingers and toes and how we brought home two of them.

I pulled him onto my lap so that he could get a better look into their bassinettes. Paul had taken one look at them, and run from the room, pretending not to care. Nick was fascinated and couldn't resist the urge to reach out and touch his baby sister's toes.

"Little shit isn't she, Daddy? So is he."

"It's going to be pretty noisy around here for a while," I said, ignoring his choice of words. His first words had been "oh shit" and nothing we did had been able to curb the habit.

"Baby noise is okay," he assured me. He turned in my lap to look at me, eyes serious and determined. "Paulie's not a baby anymore. Is that why Mommy had two more?"

In his young mind Mommy was expected to bring home a baby or two every year.

And he didn't mind the noise, at least not then.

The early spring brought with it a warm snap that insisted the cover be taken off the pool; I had turned the heater on the week before, relenting to the demands of the kids who swore they *needed* to be able to swim soon.

I disentangled myself from my wife and stretched, intending to make use of the pool, swimming a few laps to wake myself up.

I should have known someone would beat me to it.

The sound of Eileen shrieking could be heard from the living room; it was definite female indignation sprinkled with laughter. I wandered into the kitchen and looked outside; Spider had her trapped at the end of the diving board, and I was sure he was about to push her in.

Go for it.

"'Morning, Irish."

Terry stumbled into the kitchen and hugged me, following my gaze to the back yard. "What are those two up to?"

"I think Eileen is about to get baptized."

"And you're rooting for Spider, aren't you?"

"Damn right."

Eileen's hands were moving so fast that I couldn't make out what she was saying. Begging for mercy? Threatening him with the wedgy from hell? Spider stood there with his arms crossed, listening intently.

When she set her hands on her hips, I expected him to take the opportunity to shove her off the end of the diving board. But my godson, standing head and shoulders above her, instead reached a tentative hand to her face and touched her cheek.

Then he kissed her.

"I'll be damned."

Terry tightened her arms around my waist. "Don't you dare go out there and terrorize him."

"Shouldn't we worry about this?"

"I'd worry more if it was some boy we didn't know."

I frowned. "My baby is out there kissing my godson!"

"My baby," she snickered, "has very good taste in men."

I kept grumbling, but knew better than to blast through the door and say something that would mortify them both and cause Eileen to need therapy for the next five years. Instead, I swatted Terry on her rear end and said, "Come on, woman. Let's give them their privacy. We're going to get dressed, and then go out and enjoy a day without kidlet noise."

Nick

In four days I learned a few things.

New fathers don't want to let anyone else hold their baby. Mom gets first priority, but after that no one gets to hold her except for him. While Mom naps, Dad dotes.

Baby girls eat their weight in formula every day.

Grandma knows all. Every squeak, every funky sounding burp, every sleepy sigh that causes New Mom and New Dad to freak out is easily smoothed over by Grandma assuring them it's all perfectly normal.

New fathers *are* willing to let someone else change diapers.

Kevin throws up at the sight of a dirty diaper. That one is one to remember.

Terry

The first thing on Chip's agenda was to drive to Sacramento to go to the zoo. "We have to start investigating the places we're going to take Nicole," he reasoned. We walked around, holding hands, laughing at the toddlers who were seeing it for the first time, the peals of laughter and noses crinkled at the smell.

He leaned against the cement retaining wall that kept the zebras safe from the curious public. "You know, when Kevin and Eileen were about five years old I brought them out here and Kevin stood right here and convinced Eileen that he had seen a TV show about zebras, and in it there was a scientist who had made zebras with the stripes going sideways instead of up and down. He was so serious he damn near had me convinced... Eileen got excited she started begging to go see them – then Kevin was laughing so hard he had tears running down his cheeks. Eileen started screaming that if I ever made her go anywhere with him again she would never talk to me, not until she was really old. Like twelve."

"Oh no." I laughed right along with him. "I'm surprised she didn't kick him."

Eileen at five had a fondness for winning fights with Kevin by driving her knee straight into his groin. She kept it up until Kevin, tired of the abuse, cocked his arm back and punched her in the mouth. She lost two teeth and was surprised when she was the one who got into trouble, not Kevin.

It was the only time Chip threatened to lay a hand on any of the kids. "If you ever kick him like that again," he told her, "I *will* spank you. Do you understand?"

"She got over it within ten minutes," Chip said, reaching for my hand and moving on. "Sometimes I'm surprised those two survived past ten years old. I expected them to do each other in by then."

They learned to deal with each other. I wished I could remember how.

Along the way home he decided to drive past the exit we normally took and headed for Scandia to play a round of miniature golf.

"You're the only one I can beat," he said.

He was wrong.

Instead of going home for dinner we stopped at the restaurant and got food to go; he wanted to picnic in the park we used to go to when we dated. We'd spent hours walking around the pond, fending off the ducks, and sometimes sitting in the swings when there weren't kids waiting to play.

It was quiet when we got there, no children playing nearby and only a few adults walking the pond track. Age had caught up with us; we used to sit on the ground under a tree, now we looked for the closest bench.

"This place hasn't changed much in twenty years," he mused, leaning back.

"The trees are taller."

"More ducks, too. I kind of miss coming here with you, you know. We talked about a lot walking around that pond."

"Maybe that's what we need now," I ventured. "A few laps around the pond."

"Could be."

"Why is it so hard now, Chip?"

He slipped his arm around me and stared out at the water while I waited. After a while, he took a deep breath and then said, "I don't want to talk it out because I'm afraid that what I have to say would mean the death of our relationship, and I don't want to be the one who pounds that final nail into the coffin."

Kevin

Enigma. (*eh nig ma*). Noun. A perplexing , baffling, or seemingly inexplicable matter, person, etc.

I think I wanted to be an enigma from the day the word showed up on one of those vocabulary expansion worksheets teachers shove under students' noses when they think they've been dipped in the stupid pool one time too many. I knew the meaning of the word but that time it popped off the page at me. *Enigma.*

If I could spend most of my time trying to get people to figure me out, then I wouldn't have to work so hard at figuring out everything that was going on. I was twelve years old and life was imploding all around me. No one bothered to give me a good explanation of why it was happening; they just let it happen and expected me to deal with it on my own.

At twelve, you shouldn't have to ask. Things that aren't

your business become your business when it makes you crazy, when you can't even begin to understand how your parents can just walk away from each other. Kids are owed an explanation when it feels like it happened overnight. My parents never had a fight that I know of. The last time I saw them together, before Dad left, they were crawling all over each other. They were happy. They had to be. You just can't fake that.

So I decided to be an enigma and work hard at making them at least acknowledge my existence. The only problem with being an enigma is that in my family it meant no more than being a flake.

There were a couple of times I almost backed out of the idea. Mom once said I was acting like a complete jerk. That hurt. I mean, I was acting like a jerk because I blamed her for most of my misery, but no matter how pissed off you are at your mother, you still want her to love you. I wanted to confound her, not make her hate me.

After they got back together I still didn't know why they had broken up to begin with. Nick kept telling me that it was none of our business, to just get over it, but I couldn't. They screwed up my life, not just theirs. It was hard enough to be twelve, but to add familial implosion on top of it with no explanation was just unfair. I had to look for answers myself. I talked to Father Parker a lot and I read the Bible to the point where Eileen decided I was going to be a priest – I thought she might be right, but that wasn't why I was picking through my religion so much – and I even tried to talk to the school counselor.

Father Parker tried to help, but he couldn't tell me anything they were talking to him about. The school counselor bluntly said it was none of my business.

Everyone wanted me to get over it but no one was giving me any good reason to.

For sure, no one was telling me how.

I did what I shouldn't have even thought about doing; I violated my dad's trust and privacy, and while the house was quiet or when I was home alone, I picked through the papers Dad had been steadily collecting, and I read my grandfather's journal, complete with side notes that Dad had made.

Our family had been swinging on all of the branches of the stupid tree before it even started.

As the family flake, I couldn't keep what I had read to myself, and my brothers and sister deserved to know everything. At least I thought they did.

Nick and Paul were in the dining room. Nick was feeding his namesake and Paul had his feet up on the table, leaning back in his chair. Neither one of them looked like teenagers anymore. Paul had this new 'I'm a father now so I get to be in charge' look, and Nick just looked worn out.

"Have you read this?" I asked, setting the journal on the table.

They answered together. "Nope."

I opened the book to the first place I had marked. "Listen to this," I said. "It was written in sixty-eight. 'There is no forgiveness for the way I treated Jeremy when his mother died. There is no forgiveness for the truths I withhold from him. He believes me to be evil personified, and there is nothing I can say or do to change that. The only truth he knows is that the night his mother died I struck out at him with a butcher knife and could have killed him. There is no doubt in my mind that this is what he believed my intent to be.

'I love this boy as if he were my own flesh, and there are days when I think he might be. I sometimes see a glimmer in his eyes that reminds me of my own father, and his laughter is often a familiar sound from my own childhood. In my heart he is my son; how could I, for one moment, even clouded by the deepest grief, lash out at him when my intent was to harm only myself?

'Jeremy has no idea that he saved my life that night. In that moment when his eyes clouded with rage and fear and his hands were held tightly to his chest with blood seeping through his fingers, I understood my reasons for living. All he can believe is that I tried to kill him.

'I should release him to his biological father, but God help me, I don't have that kind of grace.'"

Nick shook his head in wonder, and Paul whistled softly.

"I knew Dad had a hard time growing up," Nick said, "but I never would have guessed his own father gave him that scar."

"Dad made a lot of notes, too," I said. "He wishes that his dad would have told him later. They started talking to each other just before he died but they never talked about anything important."

"Sounds familiar," Nick grunted.

"Well, at least he met mom and had a better life," Paul said. "Or it was until they split up."

"I don't think it was always so great, Paul."

He took his feet off the table and leaned forward, for once paying real attention to what I was saying. "How so, squirt?"

"Mom had an affair."

He rolled his eyes. "Oh, bullshit. There's no frickin' way Mom ever screwed around on Dad."

"It's in here," I said, tapping the cover of the journal. "Read it for yourself. She really did it."

"Is this another one of your freaky little practical jokes, Kevin? Because it's not funny."

"He's not lying," Nick handed the baby to Paul. "I was around three and you were just a baby. It wasn't some huge affair, it only happened once."

"Like you would know."

"She told me," Nick said.

"So then what the hell was his high moral ground when he was living alone all about?" Paul grumbled. "She's boffing her boss and Dad is turning down every available female that blinks at him. You know damn well that he could have had something going with Red."

"Mom wasn't doing Brad," Nick said.

"Yeah, right."

"She wasn't. And since you don't know the whole story, you don't really have the right to be passing judgment. You have no idea what was going on back then and I would think that if Dad can get over it, it shouldn't bother you at all."

"Bullshit."

"*Don't* hint to Mom that you know, Paul. It's none of our business."

Paul rolled his eyes again and got up, carrying Nicole into the living room.

"I guess I shouldn't tell him who she did it with," I said.

"Would not be your brightest moment, no. Why were you reading that, anyway? Dad would hang you up by your nuts if he found out."

"I was just trying to figure out why they broke up, that's all."

"Kev, I don't think they're exactly sure, either."

At least he didn't tell me to get over it or let it go.

"Can you tell me one thing?" I asked, getting up to take

the journal back into the study.

"Sure."

"Why is my sister sucking face with my freaking cousin?"

Chip

"If I told you everything I've been trying to make sense of over the last couple of years," I said, getting up from the bench and reaching for her hand, "it would only hurt you, and that's the last thing I want to do."

We weren't looking at each other; we either stared out at the water or down at our feet, so it made more sense to me to get up and start walking, circle the pond and make an attempt to face what she wanted without having to face each other. I could feel dread tingling in my fingertips, deadened only by the weight of her hand in mine.

"It doesn't have to be the last thing that you do, though," she said, leaning into me.

"I don't know what could come after, Terry."

"I don't either but I'm not letting you wiggle out of it this time. We have to figure this out, Chip."

"No," I sighed, "we don't. There's nothing that says we have to hurt each other to start healing. We can just let things go and we *will* get back on track. Give it enough time and it'll be like it was before."

"No." She stopped, still holding my hand, her fingers tightening slightly. "I won't let it go, Chip. Look, when you told me you were chasing after Alex Barstow, and eluded to having stayed with the agency, it ripped through me. I felt like I was losing you to the other woman, only worse. The hold that agency has on you is almost incestuous – it's like a mother wooing her son for her personal pleasure, and I had no chance to win that fight. There wasn't some flesh and blood female I could bare my teeth and claws at and attack... it's this huge *thing* that I can't even see, and you can't stay away from. I couldn't compete. I think I was so angry I decided to not even try. By the time I wasn't so angry, it was too late."

"Ask."

"What?"

I tugged at her hand to get her walking again. "Ask the questions that you've wanted to all along."

"I don't understand."

"Why didn't I fight to come home sooner? Why didn't I kick the door down, push Doug out of the way, and stake my claim to my home and my family?"

"It doesn't matter."

"But that's what all this about, isn't it? This is the point we have to work around. Why Chip didn't even try to come home. Why Chip rolled over and played dead like a trained dog. Why Chip displayed absolutely no backbone, and left with Doug without so much as a footprint on the door."

We came up on another bench and she muttered, "I need to sit down."

"Are you sure you want to do this?"

I didn't need an answer; as much as she probably did want to stop, turn around and go home, forget that she'd pushed to have this discussion, it was happening and wasn't about to stop.

"At first," I said, sitting next to her but not too close; I leaned forward with my elbows on my knees, staring at the ground near my feet, "I was stunned. I stumbled out of a taxi expecting to face you, even as pissed off as I was sure you'd be, but instead I get Doug coming out the front door to take me home with him. I was exhausted from days of debriefing, all the flying I'd done…and what I'd done to Alex.

"I had Doug take me to a motel instead, and that night while I tried to fall asleep my brain kept coming back to you, wanting to know what was happening… Terry, I even hit my knees and prayed about it. Somewhere around four in the morning I decided it was God's way of telling me I didn't deserve the comfort of a family and home and I had to pay for leaving in the first place, and I had to pay for breaking Barstow's neck. I didn't fight for you because I didn't deserve to."

"Chip…"

"Wait, there's more. After I'd had enough sleep and some time to digest the fact that I was going to have to find a place to live, I realized that I was doing a major disservice to God. Our mistakes were our own, and the consequences are our own. God was not going to sweep out of heaven and take away my favorite toys for doing what I had to do. I was using God to avoid blaming who I really thought was at fault."

"And that would be me," she prompted, her voice barely above a whisper.

"When I was on the plane headed for Brazil I sat with these kids, they couldn't have been more than twenty years old, probably younger. They'd just gotten married and were so damned excited about it. One of them asked me the secret to staying married and I told them that as long as I remembered that you're always right, things ran smoothly."

"You really told them that?"

"I'm always backing down on things, Terry, or I just give in without even saying what I think. You make unilateral decisions and tell me what we're doing, and I go along with it because it's easier.

"When I came home and found Doug there instead of you and the kids, it was the proverbial final straw. I knew you expected me to come pounding on the door to beg forgiveness. I decided not to this time. I decided to sit it out and wait for you to cave and apologize to me first, only you never did."

"Do I really do that to you?" she asked, voice beginning to break.

"Almost always. From little things like the clothes the kids wore when they were younger to their entire educational future. I wanted the kids in parochial schools, you wanted them in public, so you went ahead and enrolled them. And there's the big things, like Doug."

"Chip, that was fifteen years ago."

"And it still hurts. I forgave you because it was better than living in misery. I forgave Doug because you wanted me to. Our friendship has never been the same. We don't hang out like we used to. We go to the gym and work out together, but anything else we do involves you or the kids. I still love the man like he's my brother, but it's just not the same. I still get angry when I think about it… but I blame you more than I blame Doug."

Quietly, trying not to cry and failing miserably, she asked, "Why?"

"Because Doug never promised to be faithful to me. Doug never promised to love me or respect me. All you had to do was tell him no, but you didn't. You made that choice, and you hid behind the excuses of drunkenness and loneliness, and a vague feeling that I was dead. I know you were beyond sorry about it, but you've never really owned up to it."

I could hear her fighting the tears, her breath coming in

tight, shallow gasps, but I did nothing to comfort her.

"Terry, I didn't come home because I was tired."

She wiped away tears with the back of her hand. "Chip, I _am_ sorry…"

"I don't doubt that."

"Why did you come home, then?"

"Because I love you, and I missed you, and I'm not tired anymore." I scooted closer to her, making her look at me instead of staring off into the distance, trying to keep me from seeing the tears pouring down her cheeks. I brushed a thumb against her cheek and said, "This is one reason I wanted to just drop it."

"There are others?"

"Just one. You said you wanted to talk, but I know you, woman, you wanted to fight. That's why I cave in all the time – you want to fight. I don't."

"Some things are worth fighting for," she whispered.

"Nothing is worth putting you through the hell of me when I'm truly pissed off. I swore to myself years ago that I would never cut my temper loose on you again."

"Well, we're not fighting now, are we?"

"No, this time instead of hurting you with my temper, I'm ripping you up by making you think I believe that you're immature."

"Obviously, you do."

"No. I think you don't always stop to consider the fact that we don't share a brain, and that sometimes I don't want the same things you do. I think that keeps you from asking my opinion, or giving it serious consideration when I do bother to give it, but I don't think you're immature. Besides – " I ran my finger along the gold chain around her neck, and lifted the crucifix from under her shirt – "when you sent a replacement for mine with Nick, I figured you were at least considering how I felt."

"I thought I was trying to get you to hear me say that I love you."

"I heard that, too. And whether you realize it or not, since then you *have* listened to my opinions, and you've gone along with most of them, even when you probably didn't want to. I know you weren't at all sure that we should have let Paul get married."

She took in a deep breath, let it out with a shudder, and asked, very softly, "How do I own up to Doug, Chip? I don't know how to do anything more than apologize to you, and I've done that. Or haven't I said it enough?"

"I'm not the only one you need to apologize to."

She considered it.

"It's not too late," I said. "And as forgiving as Kris is, no matter how easily she brushed it off, you never admitted it to her, and you never told her you were sorry."

"I don't know if I can."

"You can," I said, slipping my arm around her and kissing the top of her head. "She won't bite, she won't hate you for it, and when it's over, we can all have one big happy, sloppy group hug, and be done with it."

"And then what?"

"And then we try to get back to our boring everyday lives."

"You want things to be like they were before Doug, don't you?"

"No. I want *us*, Terry. It's as simple as that."

She managed to stop crying on the ride home. Neither of us said anything; she stared out the window, occasionally sniffing, and I kept my eyes on the road, hands tight on the wheel. Every time something popped in my head that I wanted to tell her – that I didn't mean things the way they sounded, that I didn't really blame her for everything – she sniffed and I bit it back. I could bring it up later, when we were home, in the relative safety of a space where we wouldn't argue in tones so loud that the kids could hear.

I opened the front door to the house and stepped aside to let her in first. Nicole was crying and the dull sound of Monica's footsteps going back and forth seeped through the ceiling. Music was blaring in the study, but not loud enough to cause me to throw the door open and demand it be turned down. The TV was on in the living room, laugh track tittering riding over the hiss of someone's amusement.

Terry started up the stairs while I locked the door; I had one foot on the bottom stair when Kevin came out of the study, text book in hand.

"Dad. What do you know about calculus?"

"Nothing," I grunted, hoping he would go away. "Why?"

"I'm stuck and I need help."

Terry was halfway up the stairs, but she stopped and turned towards us. "Go ahead and try to help him figure it out," she said, sniffing.

Kevin looked up at her. Her eyes were still red and eyelashes still wet. He closed the book and said, "It's okay. I can ask Nick. He's not biting heads off today."

"He would know more than I would," I said dully.

"Help your son," Terry told me, climbing the rest of the stairs. I watched her until the bedroom door closed, torn between running up the stairs two at a time or giving her some time alone.

"I'll get Nick."

The TV clicked off and Nick came out of the living room. "Get me for what?"

"Mathematical torture." Kevin held the book up. "I'm stuck."

"And you asked Dad for help?" Nick laughed.

"I have time, Kevin," I said.

"I don't think you do." He looked back at the bedroom door, and I followed his gaze. When I looked back, I realized that I wasn't looking down at my youngest son; I was almost looking up at him. Sometime when I wasn't paying attention Kevin shot up and was at least an inch taller than me. I glanced at Nick; he barely reached Kevin's nose.

Nick had taken the book and was flipping through it; Kevin looked back at me, suddenly too serious to be the same boy who hid dirty magazines under his bed and teased his mother about gray hair and grandmotherhood.

I started to tell him not to worry, that it was all right, when he cut me off.

"You married *her*, not us."

He took the math book from his brother and headed back into the study. Nick shrugged and followed him in, closing the door with a quiet click.

My youngest child was telling me to get my priorities straight.

She already had water running and was trying to get a lighter to do more than hiss so that she could light candles. I reached into the drawer and pulled out the spare, then lit the candles for her while she poured bubble bath powder into the water.

"Do you want company," I asked, "or do you want to be alone?"

She didn't look up. "I wouldn't mind the company. Don't

expect me to be the best bathtub buddy, though."

I kicked off my shoes and stripped, then slid into the water behind her. She leaned back, resting her head on my shoulder, pulling my arms around her tightly.

"Do you just want to soak, or do you still want to talk? I said my piece, but you really haven't said yours."

"I don't have anything else." Almost a whisper, her voice still catching. "I'm still chewing on my own immaturity."

"I never said that, Terry. I don't want you to think that."

"I need to think it right now. All the way home I wanted to be mad as hell at you but I couldn't. I can think of too many times when I acted like a teenager with no impulse control."

"You've never been like that."

"Chip, I've been like that within the last six months." She ran a wet hand over my arms, leaving a trail of tiny bubbles, turning to look up at me. "When you had the flu, I did something so incredibly stupid."

"Aside from peeking under the blankets? I already knew about that. Doug told me."

She almost smiled.

"It's okay," I said. "You're allowed to peek."

"I told Nick everything. I dumped all of that onto my seventeen year old son with no good reason. I had no right to do that to him, and the only possible reason I did it was pure selfishness. You don't make your kid your confidant, not when it changes how they see the important people in their lives."

"What did you tell him?"

"I told him where you were when I kicked you out, and what you did for a living."

"Sooner or later I would have told the kids anyway. I should tell them all, really. They need to know before someone from the agency pops up trying to recruit them."

She slid in the water, head on my chest, and in one long breath said, "I told him about Doug."

She waited for a tirade, but I couldn't say anything.

"The second it was out of my mouth I knew I'd made a mistake," she said after a while. "I thought I told him because I wanted him to understand what had been going on and I thought he deserved the whole truth... Now I worry that it will cloud his relationship with Doug."

"He seems all right," I said, wondering if he really was. "I never would have guessed that he knew."

"Irish, you married a teenager but I'm sure you never expected to still be married to one at forty."

"Can we not rub the age thing in?"

"How angry are you that I told him so much?"

"Nick is old enough to keep the secrets that he needs to," I said. "And if he doesn't, we'll deal with it. If the other kids have problems with it, we'll talk to them together."

"Are you being nice to me just to get me into bed?"

"Probably."

She turned all the way around, sliding her legs over mine, and placed a wet hand on my chest. "Can you deal with it if the only thing I want to do is crawl into bed and cuddle?"

"I'll survive the disappointment."

"You're a good man, Irish."

"Sometimes," I allowed. "I'm sorry that what I said hurt so much."

"The truth tends to do that."

"You don't hate me for it?"

"I asked for it. I wanted to know, and now I do."

"Will we be okay?"

"Will you stick up for yourself when I have my head up my ass?"

"Only if I get to take pictures."

"Chip…"

"I'll stick up for myself," I assured her, "but before we call a complete truce, I have to tell you something. I'll cave in on it if it's something you really want, but I need you to hear me."

"Okay."

"I don't want any more kids, Terry. All I really want is to be Nicole's grandpa, and to be able to send her home to her parents when we're done playing."

She leaned in and kissed me.

"It was just another one of my whims, Irish. Knowing I was about to become a grandmother had me feeling a little old."

"You are old."

"You're older," she pointed out.

"You're mean, woman."

"Sometimes."

"I'll agree on another cat. Or a dog. Or a hamster. Whatever you want."

"Would you agree to me taking a leave of absence from my job?"

"Why?"

She was tracing her finger over the scar across my chest, an old habit I doubted she was even aware of. Soap bubbles ran in tiny streaks down my chest, the warm water turning cold as her finger moved on.

"Someone has to watch the baby when Monica and Paul are in school," she said. "Given the choice between putting up with Brad's pissed off clients or spending my days with my granddaughter…"

"You do whatever you want," I said, half hoping she'd

stop dribbling water down my chest and half hoping she wouldn't. "It's not like you worked because you had to. If you want to quit and take up underwater basket weaving instead, that's fine with me."

She pulled my head down to hers and kissed me, bubbles popping in my hair and water dribbling into my ears.

"Are you sure you don't want to nibble on my sense of humor?"

She smiled, gave me another quick kiss and said, "Just hold me tonight, okay?"

"Anything you want."

She slept with her head on my chest and a leg thrown over mine; it was comfortable, the sameness of sleeping together night after night, a habit begun when everything was new and we couldn't stand to not be touching. I held her, listening to Kevin playing his guitar, working on the same song he'd been tinkering with for weeks.

> *I see the stars in your eyes*
> *We whisper words, songs of sweet surprise*
> *The moon on your face*
> *Out of time, feeling out of place*
> *They're calling out your name, calling out your name*
>
> *The twinkling stars there await*
> *They hold the key to open Heaven's Gate*
> *You say you have to go*
> *And deep inside, deep inside I know*
> *They're calling out your name, calling out your name*
>
> *I look, I hope, and I see*
> *Everything you want the world to be*

You say you have to go
And through my tears, through the tears I know
They're calling out your name, calling out your name

I see the stars, clear blue skies
I whisper prayer, psalms of sweet surprise
I see that shining star
I see it blink, and wonder where you are
I'm calling out your name, calling out your name

I pulled Terry a little closer, and the last thing I thought of before drifting off was that I would always call out her name.

SEVEN

1995

Chip

    I wanted to go with him to the airport.

    There wasn't a snowball's chance in hell.

    Nick wanted to greet his fiancée without witnesses; the rest of us would have time to see her later. He agreed to a family dinner at the restaurant, but only, he said, because he intended to keep his hands off her for the coming two weeks, and he would need a host of chaperones to assure himself of that.

    While my son was pacing a hole into the airport's carpet, I sat in the gym's steam room, wondering why I was sweating on purpose when I knew that once I went outside I'd be whining about the June heat.

    "Your daughter," Doug informed me, "gave my son one hell of a hickey."

    I sometimes thought I should worry about that relationship, but in the end I knew I wouldn't be given a choice about it. Eileen was as serious about him as Nick had been about Katie at fourteen. Almost fifteen. Like it or not, Spider was there to stay.

"Your son," I assured him, "treats her like a lady."

"Sure," Doug grunted. "He knows what you'd do to him if he didn't."

I checked my watch.

Katie was probably wrapped up in Nick's arms, and it would be ten minutes before either one of them would be willing to let go. The first place she wanted to go was to see Nicole, who had just learned to roll over and had only recently discovered that the feet she constantly gnawed on were her own.

Jeff Russell had shown up at the restaurant two weeks before, lingering in my office doorway, waiting for an invitation before venturing in.

"I won't even ask you where she is," he said, staring down at my desk, fighting to look up at me, fighting to keep his temper. "I don't have my shit together yet and I don't know if I ever will, but I just want to know if she's all right."

"She's fine," I told him. "She graduated in May and seems happy enough."

"What about the baby?"

I reached into my back pocket for my wallet, and pulled out her picture, handing it to him. "Her name is Nicole. She's three months old, healthy, hellaciously loud and just as happy as her parents are. The kids are okay, Jeff."

He stared at the picture for a long time, and then reluctantly tried to hand it back to me.

"Keep it," I said. "She's your granddaughter, too."

He mumbled his thanks and turned to leave.

"How's Elizabeth?" I asked.

Jeff stopped at the door, but he didn't turn around. "I don't know. I haven't seen her since the day after you came and took our daughter."

"Time to check out of the hothouse," I mumbled, wiping a towel across my face. "I have to pick up Terry and then swing by to get Will before dinner. You will be there, right?"

"We'll be there."

The locker room felt cold, air conditioner blasting hard enough that I could feel the current against my skin. "If you're inclined to stay late, my father in law is taking the kids home after dinner, and the rest of us are invading the dance floor and the bar, and if I'm lucky, I might get felt up during a slow number."

I expected him to laugh, to at least make some sophomoric wisecrack about Terry's misfortune being stuck with me, with her trying to find something to feel. Instead he was quiet as I shoved a t-shirt over my head, and was looking at me curiously.

"Back in the game then?"

Thanks to Doug, I hated football. But he was right, the damn ball bounced halfway across the field and the quarterback was horrified at having let it go before the team was ready.

But I had never really walked off the field.

We let the play die and took a penalty, and when she was ready I was there, running down the field as fast as I could, hands stretched out to catch her pass.

"I'm in the game, Doug."

The fans had held their breath long enough, watching with hope as we moved in confusing slow motion. They huddled in the bleachers and waited with hope clenched in tight fists against their chests, wanting to see us finish the game before time ran out.

I had no choice.

I scored a touchdown.

As simple as that.

About the Author

K.A. Thompson is a freelance writer and former editor of *Martial Artists Wired*. She currently resides in Ohio with her husband of over 20 years, a United States Air Force Nurse Anesthetist; they have an adult son.

To peek inside the author's head, visit her weblog, *Thumper Thinks Out Loud*, at http://kathompson.blogspot.com

As Simple As That is the sequel to *Charybdis*; the final book in the series, *Finding Father Rabbit*, will be published August 2003.